# My
# Favorite
# Fangs

# My Favorite Fangs

## The Story of the von Trapp Family Vampires

ALAN GOLDSHER

THOMAS DUNNE BOOKS
ST. MARTIN'S GRIFFIN
NEW YORK

THOMAS DUNNE BOOKS.
An imprint of St. Martin's Press.

www.thomasdunnebooks.com
www.stmartins.com

Library of Congress Cataloging-in-Publication Data

Goldsher, Alan, 1966-
  My favorite fangs : the story of the Von Trapp family vampires / Alan Goldsher. — 1st ed.
      p. cm.
ISBN 978-0-312-64020-0 (trade paperback)
ISBN 978-1-250-01153-4 (e-book)

  1. Vampires—Fiction.    I. Title.
 PS3607.O48M9 2012
 813'.6—dc23

                                                2012014656

10   9   8   7   6   5   4   3   2

To Natalie, easily my favorite thing

# ACKNOWLEDGMENTS

Thanks to everybody at St. Martin's Press/Thomas Dunne Books, especially Peter Joseph, one of the editor-types who *get it*. Heartfelt shout-outs to Tom Dunne and Margaret Sutherland Brown.

Thanks to Jason Allen Ashlock of Movable Type Management, a righteous dude and an excellent agent.

Thanks to Lisa Wheatley, for offering her thoughts on the first draft, a draft that's now a mere twinkle in my eye.

And, as always, thanks and love to my wife, Natalie Rosenberg, for, well, for *everything*.

# INTRODUCTION

*Salzburg, Austria: The Last Revolting Days of the Thirties*

THE BAT WAS DIFFERENT, not at all like your common, everyday *Desmodus Rotundus.*

For one, it flew with a purpose, which was an oddity unto itself. Unless they were seeking out their evening feast, the majority of the bats who populated the Alps—and there was an enormous bat population in the Alps, which had been the case for as long as the locals could remember—drifted this way or that, no patterns, no destinations, no purpose. They simply flew for the sake of flying. This particular bat, however, glided as majestically as an eagle, sometimes moving in tight concentric circles and sometimes in magnificent up-and-down swoops. Sometimes it punched through the air like a bullet, and sometimes it floated like a dandelion puff. The rodent's movements were so precise that if one didn't know better, one might suspect that it was playing to an audience. Or a movie camera.

Yet another oddity: Your typical Austrian bat was ugly. Vile. Repulsive. Repellent. It wasn't uncommon for one of these

1

odious creatures to sport jagged rips in their wings, or oozing sores on their midsection, or an empty eye socket or two . . . or three. Our bat, on the other hand, was . . . was . . . was *radiant*. She—and it was fair to assume that our bat was a she, so daintily did she move—had lustrous coloring; her eyes were a clear brown—brown eyes are rare among rodents, of course—and her teeth were whiter than white. If one were so inclined, one might consider inviting that sort of bat into their home to keep as a pet.

If one were so inclined.

Our bat paused in the air, hovering motionlessly as if she were frozen in time, her black, spiky frame silhouetted against the preternaturally blue sky. After a moment of stillness in which she gazed over the grassy hills with an inscrutable expression on her squashed, triangular face, our divine bat spread her wings as widely as she could, and executed a perfect barrel roll, and then another, and then another. The speed of her twirls doubled, trebled, and quadrupled until she was a thick black smudge against the otherwise pristine tableau.

And then she came to a screeching halt, her cessation so abrupt and jolting that one might surmise she had crashed into an invisible wall . . . but one would be wrong. Firstly, it's common knowledge that there are no invisible walls in the Alps—there are plenty in the Pyrenees, of course, but none in the Alps—and secondly, our bat was just that skilled. She could stop on a shilling, and give you change.

Our bat had another rare, intriguing characteristic: She could sing.

She couldn't sing in the traditional sense, of course—bats have tiny lungs, tinier tongues, and even tinier vocal chords, making it impossible for them to form actual lyrics—but our bat could emit specific tones with intonation that could only be described as astounding. She let loose with a high E-flat that was three octaves above middle C, a note she held for a good 120 seconds. That was followed by an A440 three octaves below middle C, after which she modulated up a half step to a D-flat, then back down to a B-flat, after which she ran through an impressive series of Dorian minor scales. And then, as she flew, no, as she *rocketed* straight toward the sun, our bat launched into an aria from the second act of Joseph Haydn's "Il Mondo Della Luna." Perfect vibrato, perfect pitch, perfect everything. Had she been able to voice the words, the Vienna State Opera would have hired her on the spot . . . even if she was a bat.

Once she reached the edge of the atmosphere, she did an about-face and plummeted face first toward the grass-covered mountain. As she picked up speed, her wings grew hot, so hot that they smoked, and the smoke was crimson, and then gold, and then violet, and then azure, and then black. Several centimeters before she hit the Earth, our bat came to yet another jarring halt, after which she floated delicately to the ground. The second her claws touched land, the smoke doubled, trebled, and quadrupled until she was a rainbow against the otherwise pristine tableau. When the smoke dissipated, our bat was gone. Gone. Simply gone.

In her place stood a woman, an exquisite woman with short,

glossy brown hair, piercing brown eyes, and alabaster skin. The woman was naked, and not the least bit ashamed . . . but why should she have been? For you see, her body was perfect: Muscular arms, a graceful neck, firm breasts, a flat stomach, and strong thighs, the kind of flawless form that many a mortal would kill for.

Let's not forget her equally flawless fangs.

Our bat-woman spread out her arms and spun in circle after circle after circle, her face turned toward the sun, her short hair ruffling in the light breeze, a radiant smile plastered onto her countenance. She continued on with the Haydn aria, but now she added the words to the melody:

> *Oh che ninfe gentili! Oh che fortuna!*
> (Oh, the kind nymphs! Oh, what luck!)
> *Oh benedetto il mondo della luna!*
> (Oh, blessed the world of the moon!)

Before she could launch into the next line, her upper front fangs began to drip, no, *gush* blood. The stream of blood shot several meters straight up into the air, then rained down upon her hair, her face, and her shoulders. The blood—which was far more watery than one would have expected—dribbled down her entire body, leaving red streaks all over her almost-translucent skin, streaks that wouldn't have been out of place on an Oskar Kokoschka painting. She knelt down, then lay flat on her back and turned her face to the side, apparently hoping that the bloodstream would either spurt onto the grass, or cease altogether. A geyser of blood exploded from her ear, further soiling both the breathtaking landscape and her equally breathtaking body. When a single drop dripped onto her lady-parts, the woman at once shivered and screamed; it was difficult to discern whether the shriek was one of pain or ecstasy.

As she attempted to wipe the red mess from her eyes, she angrily grumbled, "I take to the skies when my heart is lonely, as my heart wants to scream every song it hears. My heart wants to beat like the wings of a flying rodent who leaps from the trees in the dark of night. My heart wants to sigh like the green stench of undeath that flies from a coffin in a breeze. I want to sing songs that have been sung since before the dawn of time, yet the constant liquid that leaks from the various orifices in my skull makes this well nigh impossible. I pray that my heart and ears will be blessed by the sound of something other than the sound of secretions spouting from my incisors."

This sort of thing—the singing, followed by the bleeding, followed by the rambling soliloquies that oftentimes sounded like bastardized song lyrics—happened to our bat-woman on a semi-regular basis.

Because, you see, our bat-woman was a Vampire.

A Vampire named Maria.

# PART ONE

# CHAPTER 1

Housed on what the majority of Austrians agreed was the most rancid corner in Salzburg, the nameless Abbey was an eyesore, so painful to look at that nobody looked at it. Its asymmetrically constructed grayish-brown and brownish-gray stones, its cracked windows, its spiked wrought-iron front gate, and its rotting vegetable garden were a blight upon the city's otherwise gorgeous architecture. And then there was the Abbey's stench, an almost-living-and-breathing odor that some likened to that of a leprosy-sufferer, while others said it was reminiscent of a decomposing stag. Thus the general public avoided and/or ignored the Abbey, which was just how the Abbey's Sisters of the Undead wanted it.

As was always the case, the moment the sun ducked under the horizon, the Abbey's Mother Zombie let out a nausea-inducing moan that rattled the bottles in the underground "wine" collection. (Why is "wine" in quotation marks, one might ask? Well, one would have to figure it out for one's self, but one shouldn't have to think too hard, considering the presence of a Vampire in our story.) The remainder of the Abbey's inhabitants followed suit, and the combined cacophony of their groans caused every dog within ten kilometers to howl as if their tails were being tied into knots . . . as was also always the case.

The 173 Zombies who made up the Abbey's population dressed identically—black robes, black shawls, black sandals, and black head-coverings—and as the Abbey was badly lit— and as all the inhabitants were unable to stand up straight—it was difficult for the untrained eye to tell the Zombie Sisters apart. The only way to discern one of the beings from another was by her shuffle: Zombie Sister Brandi, for instance, had her mortal life terminated in a terrible female deer accident—after she fell off of her gigantic doe, Golden Sun, the beast stepped on her left leg five, six, seven times, crushing Brandi's poor bones into powder—so she moved with a disjointed, distinct limp that could belong to nobody but her. As a human, Zombie Sister Cinnamon, on the other hand, died during childbirth, thus when Mother Zombie sucked her brains from her skull, Cinnamon's body was in pristine shape, so she was able to glide across the cobblestone floors with ease. (It should be noted that "glide" and "ease" are relative terms when it comes to Zombies, as an undead glide was far slower than that of a mortal glide, and in terms of ease, nothing comes easy for the brain-damaged undead.) And then there was Zombie Sister Chesty LaBumm, who was so emaciated at the time of her expiration—her family was impoverished, and she had passed

away from starvation—that even with Mother Zombie's reani-
mating kiss, the periodic infusion of mortal brain slime, and
the weekly silicone injections in her bosom, she did not possess the strength to move faster than the slowest tortoise.

While darkness enfolded the rancid Abbey, all 173 of the
Zombie Sisters made their way toward the Auditorium of
Worship. The Auditorium was, relatively speaking, an attractive room, replete with stained glass windows that were not *all*
broken, rows of splinter-filled wooden benches that could
more-or-less support the dead weight of the undead, and a
workable altar that housed a mold-covered, nine-meter-high
shale statue of The Being Whose Name Shall Not Be Uttered.
With its palpable odor of burnt garlic, rotting raccoon carcass,
and semi-fresh human feces, it was the ideal setting for a Zombie prayer gathering.

As they approached the Auditorium, the Zombies picked up
a unison chant: *Mortales spumae, et ne ius nostrum spirare au-
ram, mors est satis, mors est satis*, the loose translation of which
is, "Mortals are scum, they should not be allowed to breathe
our air, death is not enough, death is not enough." Once the
Zombies were seated, the Mother Zombie took to the altar, and
wordlessly approached the statue. With surprising reverence,
she slowly caressed The Being Whose Name Shall Not Be Uttered with her right hand, beginning at his feet, working her
way up to his nose. She then stood on her tiptoes and ran her
acne-covered tongue over the top of The Being Whose Name
Shall Not Be Uttered's head, after which she licked every milli-
meter of the statue, from top to bottom, and every bit in

between. Following Mother Zombie's tongue bath, each Zombie approached the altar one at a time and licked only the statue's feet. (For centuries, each Zombie licked the entire statue, but once the Abbey's populace grew to 81 inhabitants fifteen years before, Mother Zombie decided it was prohibitively time-consuming to have each and every one slobber over the entire T.B.W.N.S.N.B.U. sculpture. Zombies had many tasks, and as they moved sluggishly from duty to duty, it wasn't logical to spend five hours in the Auditorium of Worship, and Mother Zombie was nothing if not logical.)

After the final Zombie Sister delivered the final Zombie lick, Mother Zombie gave her nightly benediction: *Abite cretins terrae abi foetidus creaturis, abite sceleratos deformis, bathe secretion spiritalis entis cui nomen non dixisti, complectere foeditas, complectere foeditas, complectere foeditas*, the loose translation of which is, "Be gone, cretins of the Earth, be gone, fetid creatures, be gone, hideous miscreants, bathe in the spiritual secretion of The Being Whose Name Shall Not Be Uttered, embrace the foulness, embrace the foulness, embrace the foulness."

In the fifth row, Zombie Sister Cinnamon turned to Zombie Sister Brandi and whispered, "When will Mother Zombie learn that not a single one of us understands Latin?"

Unfortunately for Cinnamon, her whisper wasn't whispery enough. "*Do you have something to say, Zombie Sister?!*" Mother Zombie roared.

Cinnamon stammered, "I . . . I . . . I . . . I . . ."

Mother Zombie said, "You . . . you . . . you . . . you must . . . you must . . . you must *suffer*." And then she took a golden cleaver from under her robe and threw it at Zombie Sister Cinnamon's neck.

The Mother had brilliant aim.

But Cinnamon ducked.

And thus ended the life—or, more accurately, the undeath— of Zombie Sister Blaze Starr, the unfortunate creature seated in the sixth row.

The Sister Zombies stared at Mother Zombie, and Mother Zombie stared right on back. As Blaze Starr's decapitated head rolled down the aisle, one of the Zombies in the back of the room mumbled, "This again?"

Mother roared, "*Silence, you odious death mongers!* One of you, feed Blaze Starr to the goats."

In unison, the Zombies chanted, "Lady, oh the lady, oh the lay hee hoo."

Mother Zombie nodded, the tiniest of smiles playing about her lips. "That's correct, my beloved ones. Lady, oh the lady, oh the lay hee hoo."

After the goats were fed, and after the service was completed, Mother Zombie motioned Zombie Sister Brandi and Zombie Sister Cinnamon to join her in the courtyard. Brandi and Cinnamon both turned pale—or, more accurately, paler; most undead are already quite pale to begin with, especially those who spend nine-tenths of their lives in a dark, dank dump like the Abbey—because nothing good ever came of those meetings. For instance, earlier in the month, Zombie Sister Foxxxy was summoned to the courtyard to discuss her cleanliness, or lack thereof. "Foxxxy," Mother Zombie had said with a quiet, albeit fearsome whisper, "we have discussed your fluid situation. Numerous times."

Foxxxy stared at the floor. "Yes, Mother," she mumbled.

"Your nightly discharge is completely covering the floor of the water closet."

"Yes, Mother."

"To clarify: I mean the *nightly* discharge."

"Yes, Mother."

"That's the *yellow* discharge."

"Yes, Mother."

"Contrary to your *daily* discharge."

"Yes, Mother."

"That being the *brown* discharge."

"Yes, Mother."

"We must also discuss your brown discharge, however."

"Why is that, Mother?"

"Because it's covering the entire floor of your sleeping chambers."

Foxxxy mustered the strength to meet Mother Zombie's eyes. "That brown discharge didn't come from me, Mother."

"No? Who, then? Who did it come from? Who left brown discharge by your bed? Who in this Abbey would do such a thing?"

"I, um, I believe it was Vampire Sister Maria, Mother."

Mother Zombie moaned, then spit a gob of green goo on the wall; the wall steamed where the goo stuck. "Foxxxy, I'm aware that we tend to blame most of our problems on Maria. And that's certainly understandable, because Maria *is* a problem, and an unsolvable one at that. But the discharge by your bed isn't Maria's discharge. You see, it's common knowledge that any and all discharge coming from Maria is red. *Any* discharge."

"What do you mean, *any* discharge, Mother? I thought the different types of discharge were limited," Foxxxy asked.

"When you're a woman, there's *plenty* of discharge, Foxxxy."

"What kind of discharge, Mother?"

"You don't know?"

"I might have known at one time, but most of my mortal memories are a blur."

"It doesn't matter."

"But I want to know!"

"It doesn't matter!"

*"But I want . . ."*

Interrupting, Mother Zombie roared, "Never contradict me, Foxxxy! *Never!*"

"But I . . . but I . . . but I . . ."

"But you . . . but you . . . but you . . . but *nothing!*" She pulled her trusty golden cleaver from under her robe and said, "Now put out your hand. The left one shall do."

"But I . . . but I . . . but I . . ."

"But you . . . but you . . . but you . . . but *shut up!* Which finger do you wish to sacrifice?"

Foxxxy held out her hand and looked at the floor. "My pinky, Mother Zombie."

"Your pinky it shall be." And then Mother Zombie chopped

off Zombie Sister Foxxxy's entire hand. After Foxxxy stopped moaning some six minutes later, Mother Zombie smiled and said, "Oh, dear me. My aim isn't what it used to be."

This was why nobody liked being called to the courtyard.

Presently, Zombie Sisters Brandi and Cinnamon knew better than to dawdle, so they hustled after Mother Zombie as if they were squirrels chasing nuts . . . that is, if the squirrels happened to be undead squirrels slogging through the Seventh Ring of Hell with Sisyphean rocks strapped to their backs. In other words, Brandi and Cinnamon didn't move at a great rate of speed, as was the case with all zombies, a point that has now been hammered to death.

Once they caught up with Mother Zombie, Cinnamon curtsied, took a knee, and said, "To what do we owe the honor of a private audience, Mother?"

Brandi also curtsied, then kneeled down beside Cinnamon. "Yes, Mother, it's always a thrill to be invited to your office, because . . ."

Without warning—and with surprising quickness—Mother Zombie kicked Cinnamon in the chest, then punched Brandi in the jaw. "Both of you, *shut it*. Your grating voices and your lies about being pleased to meet with me make my undead soul cry out in pain, and I've neither the time nor the patience for this sort of blather. Be honest with me, Zombie Sisters: you're *not* honored to be in my presence."

Brandi and Cinnamon said nothing.

Mother Zombie nodded. "Silence means consent. But this comes as little surprise, as you both despise me. I'm perfectly content with that, though, because I, too, despise you. Let's finish this discussion so you can get out of my sight, and I, yours."

In unison, Cinnamon and Brandi said, "Yes, Mother."

"*Silence!* Not another word from either of you." And then, for the sake of symmetry, Mother Zombie punched Cinnamon in the jaw, then kicked Brandi in the chest. "Now. You two are Vampire Sister Maria's closest, no, *only* friends on the premises; am I correct?"

Brandi and Cinnamon said nothing.

Mother Zombie gave the Zombie Sisters simultaneous backhands. "Answer me, idiots!"

Near tears, Brandi whispered, "You said you didn't want another word from either of us, Mother."

"I say a lot of things, Brandi. You're intelligent enough to figure out which of the things you should take to heart. You two are intelligent beings. Correct?" (Incorrect. Brandi and Cinnamon were far from intelligent beings. For that matter, Brandi and Cinnamon were subhuman morons who were considered to be among the stupidest Zombies in the Abbey, and being that the Abbey was a haven of idiocy, that's saying something.) When neither responded, Mother Zombie repeated, "You two are Vampire Sister Maria's only friends on the premises, correct?" After a moment of silence, Mother Zombie said, "You may answer me now."

Cinnamon said, "In this instance, friend is a relative term."

Brandi said, "If you're being technical, Maria isn't a friend, so much as a somewhat tolerated associate."

Cinnamon said, "We've tried to be friends for realsies, but she's proven to be, well, a problem."

Brandi said, "A big problem."

Cinnamon said, "You see, Vampire Sister Maria is a bit of a flibbertijibbet."

Mother Zombie said, "What in the Devil's name is a flibbertijibbet?"

Brandi explained, "A whore."

"Ah," Mother Zombie said. "Flibbertijibbet. Whore. Makes sense to me. I'm not sure how Hammerstein would feel about it, but, you know, *fick* him."

"Who's Hammerstein?" Brandi asked.

Mother Zombie said, "None of your business. Getting back to Maria . . ."

Cinnamon said, "Now that I think about it, Maria might be more than a bit of a flibbertijibbet."

Brandi said, "You mean Maria is a *huge* whore?"

"Yes, Brandi," Cinnamon said, "I mean Maria is a huge whore."

Mother Zombie said, "We need this huge whore business confirmed." She cupped her hands over her mouth and roared, "Zombie Sister Jazzmine! Zombie Sister Diamond! Zombie Sister Bubbles! Join us in the courtyard immediately!" Twenty-seven minutes later, Jazzmine, Diamond, and Bubbles knelt beside Brandi and Cinnamon. Smiling, Mother Zombie said, "You made it in record time. Now tell me, my darlings, how do you feel about Maria?"

Jazzmine said, "I think I speak for my fellow Sisters when I say that she's the worst Vampire we have ever met, but we suck it up and deal."

Bubbles snickered. "Vampire. Suck it up. Nice."

Mother Zombie screamed, *"Shut it, Bubbles!"* To Jazzmine, she said, "What's so awful about her?"

"What *isn't* awful about her?" Jazzmine asked. "She ignores every established Abbey rule, she's unattractive as all get-out, and that hair. I mean, would a little conditioner once in a while kill her?"

Zombie Sister Diamond added, "And can we talk about her behavior in the cafeteria? She puts piles and piles of food on her tray, and never takes a bite. It's always, *'I want blood'* this, and *'I want blood'* that. And yet she never leaves any dessert for the rest of us."

"So not only is she a whore," Brandi noted, "but she's a *selfish* whore."

Mother Zombie nodded. "A selfish whore indeed."

Cinnamon told Mother Zombie, "Though we all agree Maria is a selfish whore, I don't want you to throw her out onto the street."

Diamond said, "I concur. Despite her selfishness and her whorishness, we *need* somebody like that around here. The lot of you are truly disgusting, of course, and a day without true disgustingness is like a day without holding a moonbeam in your hand, but when Maria brings home a bloodied corpse, it's far from your run-of-the-mill repulsive. It's . . . it's . . . it's *magically* repulsive. Watching her suck those dead bodies dry is foul. Nothing is more vomit inducing than seeing a Vampire have lunch, and a day without throwing up is like . . ."

Bubbles interrupted, ". . . a day without holding a moonbeam in your hand. We all agree."

"Here here," Jazzmine said, "Quite the will o' the wisp, Maria is."

"Goodness, all these new phrases," Mother Zombie said. "I'm out of the loop. What's a will o' the wisp?"

Brandi explained, "A whore."

Jazzmine said, "No, Brandi, a flibbertijibbet is a whore. A will o' the wisp is a magical being who elevates everything around them with their mere presence."

Bubbles asked, "Can a flibbertijibbet be a will o' the wisp?"

Diamond said, "No, but a will o' the wisp can be a flibbertijibbet."

Bubbles reasoned, "But a flibbertijibbet can elevate everything around them with their mere presence . . . or at least they can elevate *one* thing around them with their mere presence, if you know what I mean." (They all knew what she meant. Even Brandi.)

Cinnamon asked, "So is Maria a flibbertijibbet, or a will o' the wisp, or some sort of combination of the two?"

Jazzmine said, "She might not be either. Maria is as unpredictable as the rain . . ."

At the same time, Bubbles, Cinnamon, Diamond, Jazzmine, and Brandi said, "*She's a whore!*"

"Oftentimes a pain."

*"A whore!"*

"No brain. Inane. A bane."

*"A whore, a whore, a whore!"*

Mother Zombie held up her hand and nodded. "I think I see what's happening here. One of the deadly sins has infiltrated our home. *Envy.*"

Brandi scowled. "What could Maria possibly have that would make us jealous?"

"Like every, how you say, flibbertijibbet," Mother Zombie said, "Maria possesses the ability to fornicate. And we Zombies, thanks to the frustrating lack of non-lubricative discharge from our lady-parts, don't."

"How do you solve a problem like dead lady-parts?" Diamond asked.

Mother Zombie pouted, "That's a problem that will never be solved. For Zombies, arousal is impossible, sort of like, well, like holding a moonbeam in your hand." She gave Diamond, Jazzmine, and Bubbles a disdainful glare. "The three of you, return to your chambers."

"Mother Zombie," Bubbles asked, "why would you demand to see us, then send us on our way without really accomplishing much of anything, plot-wise?"

"Because I thought you could lend this scene some tight three-part vocal harmonies . . ."

"What are tight three-part vocal harmonies?" Diamond asked.

". . . but I was obviously mistaken. So be gone. Brandi and Cinnamon, go find that flying flibbertijibbet o' the wisp and bring her to me."

Sixty-six-some-odd hours later, Brandi and Cinnamon shuffled dejectedly into Mother Zombie's office. "Mother Zombie?" Cinnamon asked nervously.

"Yes, Cinnamon?"

"Maria is gone."

Brandi said, "Perhaps we should have put a cowbell in between her legs." She paused, then added, "But the whore would probably enjoy that."

Mother Zombie asked, "Have you looked by the lake? You know how much she adores the Swamp Monsters."

"We searched everywhere," Cinnamon said, "even in some, um, er, *unusual* places."

Mother Zombie perked up. "Unusual? Details, child."

Cinnamon said, "We looked at Chez Cristin, and Coco NR1, and Donau Dreams, and Erotikbörse, and the Funpalast, and Helga's Kabinsex, and the Kontakof, and Prinse Eugen Stasse, and Zucker Puppen, and . . ."

"Stop, Cinnamon," Mother Zombie said. "I know not of any of these establishments. Are they Vampire meeting places?"

"Possibly."

"What do you mean, possibly?"

"Well, Vampires *could* meet there."

Brandi said, "But flibbertijibbets *definitely* meet there."

Mother Zombie lifted her desk above her head and threw it across the room, where it hit the wall, cracked into several dozen pieces, and fell onto a pile of previously thrown desks. "You mean to tell me that you spent almost four days going in and out of *brothels*?!" she roared.

In unison, Brandi and Cinnamon said, "Yes, Mother Zombie."

"You two do realize that Maria isn't literally a prostitute. When we call her a whore, we mean that she's of ill repute, not that she has intercourse in exchange for money."

"As far as you know," Cinnamon pointed out.

Nodding, Mother Zombie said, "I'll grant you that, Cinnamon—as far as we know, Vampire Sister Maria doesn't fornicate for pay . . ."

From a ways away, the three Zombies heard a door slam shut, followed in quick succession by a vase breaking, a bell ringing, a cat yowling, a Zombie moaning, a chair crumbling, a tympani boinging, and a Vampire cursing.

With her black cat suit in tatters—in the last revolting days of the thirties, cat suits were the favored uniform of Austrian Vampires—and her alabaster skin glowing in the dark, and crusted blood dotting her face, Maria stood in the doorway of Mother Zombie's office and grinned. What little light there was in the room was drawn to her fangs, which shimmered like pearls.

"Good eeeeeevening, ladies," she said, then clapped her hands together once and asked, "So what'd I miss?"

Mother Zombie shook her head sadly. "Maria. Maria. Maria. Say it loud, and there's music playing. Say it soft, and it's almost like praying."

Brandi said, "Wrong musical, whore."

Without breaking eye contact with Brandi, Mother Zombie reached behind her, picked up the nearest piece of office equipment—which happened to be a dot matrix printer—lifted it above her head, and said, "Brandi, Cinnamon, I'm sick of the sight of you. Be gone."

Ducking to avoid being clocked by Mother Zombie's printer, Brandi and Cinnamon said, "Yes, Mother," then left. On their way out of the office, Brandi and Cinnamon both accidentally-on-purpose elbowed Maria on either side of her head. Unfazed, Maria than purposely-on-purpose kicked them across the hallway, sending the Zombie Sisters into the wall at a speed of 42.618 kilometers per hour.

After Cinnamon stood up and readjusted her head, she told Maria, "You repulse me, darling."

Maria curtsied. "That's the kindest thing you have ever said to me, dear Cinnamon." She nodded at Brandi. "Do I repulse you, sweetie?"

Brandi projectile vomited up seven of the nine brains she'd eaten that afternoon right onto the front of Maria's cat suit. The regurgitate was brown, and loaded with living, wiggling worms.

Maria took a deep inhale, absorbed the scent, grinned, and said, "Oh, Brandi, I love you most of all!"

From her chamber, Mother Zombie roared, "Enough dilly-dallying, ladies! Brandi, Cinnamon, be gone! Maria, come closer."

The striking, hurl-covered Vampire approached the desk, dropped to her knees, and licked Mother Zombie's hand. Mother Zombie gagged, then backhanded Maria, first on the left cheek, and then on the right; it sounded as if she had hit a stone. Maria, who didn't flinch, said, "Thank you, Mother Zombie. May I have another?"

"No. Two slaps is even too good for the likes of you." Mother Zombie gestured to the chair in front of where her desk used to be and said, "Sit."

Maria followed her order, then said, "Oh, Mother Zombie, I'm so sorry for departing from the Abbey without permission, but when my muse muses, I have to follow it. The front entrance was open, and the hills were beckoning, and my fangs needed release, and the scent of fresh kill was so overpowering and seductive that before I knew it . . ." She again reached for Mother Zombie's hand; Mother Zombie pulled it away, then, for good measure, punched Maria in the chest. Again, it was like she had hit stone, and again, Maria didn't flinch. "Oh, please, Mother, might I beg for mercy?"

"Fine, Maria. Go ahead and beg. Beg like you have never begged. Beg like you're a dog. Which you are."

"Mother Zombie, I beg your mercy."

"You can't have it. Even though you have brought me five-score fresh kills over the past month, you shall not be forgiven for your transgressions, and your blatant disregard for Zombie Law."

"Then why did you allow me to *ask* you for mercy?"

Mother Zombie shrugged. "Who am I to refuse a request?"

"But I just requested your mercy, and you refused *that* request"

"I can refuse a request when I *choose* to refuse a request."

"But you just said, 'Who am I to refuse a request?'" Maria pointed out. "Thus, I refuse your refusal."

"This is my Abbey, and I make the decisions, so I refuse your refusal of my refusal."

"Then I refuse *your* refusal of *my* refusal of *your* refusal."

"And I refuse your . . . wait, what were we talking about again?"

Maria scratched her head. "I haven't the foggiest."

"Nor do I." She stood up, elbowed Maria in the temple, then said, "Just tell me why you left the Abbey without permission."

Utterly unaffected by the punch, Maria rose and smiled dreamily. "You see, Mother Zombie, the summer sky was so seductive, and the air smelled of both life and death, and my cortex was so engorged with singing white cells and dancing red cells that I just *had* to be a part of it. Also, the pressure in my head was great, and had I not let my blood flow onto the mountain grass, my brain might well have exploded."

Mother Zombie mumbled, "I wish."

Maria cupped her ear. "Excuse me?"

"Nothing. Continue."

"Very well. The Untersberg was calling for me . . . no, yelling for me . . . no, *screaming* for me! And when the Untersberg talks, people listen."

Mother Zombie squinched up her face. "The Untersberg? What's the Untersberg?"

"The Untersberg is a mountain massif of the Berchtesgaten Alps that straddles the borders of Berchtesgaten, Germany, and our very own town of Salzburg. The Berchtesgaten Alps are popular with tourists and Austrian Vampires alike because they're a mere sixteen kilometers to Salzburg. The first recorded ascent of the Berchtesgaten Alps was in the first half of the twelfth Century by Eberwein, a member of the Augustinian Hydra Monastery at Berchtesgaten. As you may recall, the mountain lent its name to an 1829 opera by Johann Nepomuk, Baron of Poissl."

Mother Zombie stared at Maria. "Could you have not just said the Alps?" she asked.

"No. Like all female Vampires, I'm quite precise."

Mother Zombie mumbled, "Like all female Vampires, you're quite a know-it-all bitch."

Maria cupped her ear. "Excuse me?"

"Nothing. Continue."

"The point is, that's my land. I was transformed with an eternal bite on it. I was brought up on it. I've killed on it. I've feasted on it. I've bled upon it." She paused, inched her hand slowly toward her waist, then said, "I've fornicated on it."

Mother Zombie took a ruler from under her cloak—a ruler fashioned from the corpses of ten King Brown snakes—and slapped Maria's hand just before it moved below her beltline. "Do that on your own time, please."

Maria gave her lady-parts a rueful flick, then said, "That's what compelled me to come to the Abbey, Mother Zombie."

Rolling her eyes, Mother Zombie said, "For the love of all that's evil in the world, do I have to listen to this story again? How many times must you . . ."

Maria launched into her tale. "The year was 1331. I was a young woman just getting in touch with her sensuality . . ."

"For the love of Jesus Christ burning in *Hölle*, yes, I know . . ."

". . . and I'd come down from the mountain and fly to the top of a building and look over into your courtyard. I'd see the Zombie Sisters eating their luscious brains, and I'd hear their mournful moans as they made their way to vespers . . ."

"You have mentioned this several hundred . . ."

". . . then one afternoon, while skipping gaily atop the Berchtesgaten, I was attacked by a bat. A beautiful, beautiful bat . . ."

"I recall . . ."

". . . and this bat changed my life! The bite! The blood! The fever! The . . . the . . . the *transformation*! The magic! The boys! The men! The release! The *multiple* releases!"

Mother Zombie yawned, then slapped her own face. "Apologies, Maria, I almost nodded off. Are you still talking?"

Maria again dreamily moved her fingers down to her lady-parts, but she caught a glimpse of Mother Zombie's snake ruler, then abruptly stopped her hand and changed the subject. "Which brings me to another transgression, Reverend Mother. I discharged my teeth today without permission."

Shrugging, Mother Zombie said, "Honestly, Vampire, I could care less."

"But there are rules, Mother. Everybody knows that in Zombie Law, there are edicts against unauthorized blood-letting."

"I've told you dozens of times, that only applies to the blood-letting of *postulants*. You can let out your *own* blood as often as you wish."

Maria ignored Mother Zombie and bulled ahead. "And what's even worse, I've developed a tendency to burst into song."

With that, Mother Zombie perked up. "Songs? What sort of songs? I like songs. Especially ones with tight three-part vocal harmonies."

"Songs with nice melodies and interesting chord changes, but corny lyrics."

"Would you care to sing one right now?"

"I'd love to, but there might be issues with royalties."

"Royalties as in King von Habsburg of Austria?"

"Er, no. Royalties as in usage-based payments made by a licensor to a licensee for use of an ongoing asset—the asset, in this instance, being a song lyric—sometimes, for instance, an intellectual property that . . ."

Under her breath, Mother Zombie said, "Know-it-all bitch."

Maria cupped her ear. "Excuse me?"

"Nothing. Go on about this singing."

"There isn't anything more to go on about. I sing corny songs that have very little to do with what's going on around me. Also, they do very little to advance the plot."

"What's this *plot* business that everybody's talking about?"

Maria disregarded her, and again changed the subject. "And

I've been having many a disagreement with Zombie Sister Brandi, who has taken to calling me a whore."

"So I've heard."

"But I've taken to yanking off her arm before our disagreement has even started, because I know I'll eventually get to that anyhow."

Mother Zombie turned around and banged her head against the wall. And then she did it again. And again. Then, with her back still turned to the Vampire, she said, "Maria, when you saw us over the Abbey wall and longed to be one of us, did you not realize we were zombies?"

"Of course I realized it. But you're undead, and I'm undead, and I believed the undead can live together in harmony, regardless of how they were killed then reanimated. I was mistaken, of course—Zombies are scum and Vampires are beautiful, and the two genera can't cohabitate without the disdain boiling over into outright hatred—but I believe that after six centuries, I'm finally learning how to co-exist with you vile creatures."

"We find you equally vile, Maria." She spun around. "And while vileness is an essential part of our lives here at the Abbey, and while we have come to tolerate your presence, enough is enough. It is time for you to be gone."

"Oh, no, Mother Zombie! I beg you, don't do that! Don't cast me away! I belong here in my feces-smelling home. You're my ghastly family. It's my entire life, er, my entire undeath."

"Life is unfair, Maria, and undeath, even more so. Perhaps if you go out into the mortal world for a time, you'll have a chance to find out if you're worthy of being in the eternal company of Zombiekind, to see if you have the capacity to *truly* live your life under Zombie Law. There's a brood near Salzburg in need of a Governess. You'll be taking care of seven mortal children. How do you feel about kids, Maria?"

"They have stringy necks, but they generally taste sweeter than adults. The combination of innocence and premature death makes for a well-nigh irresistible dessert."

"For us, for Zombies, children's brains, while tasty, are useless. The sourness of their taste mitigates any worth they might have. But that's neither here nor there. I'll alert Captain Georg von Trapp that you'll be at his doorstep posthaste. The Captain is a widower, and his children are, well, let's just say that the von Trapps have had trouble keeping their Governesses. It's a problem."

"That's good to hear, Mother Zombie, because nobody fixes problems like Maria."

Mother Zombie shoved her out of the office. "That isn't what I heard." As Maria skittered away, Mother Zombie yelled, "One piece of advice, Vampire Sister: When you enter mortal society, don't go Edelweissing anybody!"

Maria called back, "Never, Mother Zombie! *Never.* I must get dressed. I made myself some new cat suits! Red ones, and blue ones, and yellow ones, and purple ones!"

"Fan*tas*tic," Mother Zombie mumbled, rubbing her temples as if this scene would never end.

After returning to her chambers, Maria tried on cat suit after cat suit after cat suit, each more ill-fitting, badly-sewn and horribly-colored than the last. Finally—believing that an ill-fitting, badly sewn, and horribly colored cat suit would make a bad first impression on Captain von Trapp and his brood—she tore the new outfits to shreds and donned one of her reliable black numbers, as well as a floppy hat that she had sewn in 1832, but had not seen the light of day since. The chapeau was musty, dusty, and odiferous, and thusly, Maria believed, a piece of clothing that would make the von Trapps realize she was a force to be reckoned with. (Most Vampires have a wonderful feel for style, and would realize that a musty, dusty, odiferous hat would repel any human being within smelling distance, but after decades of living with Zombies, Maria's fashion sense had evaporated.)

The Vampire then packed up her suitcase and her tenor saxophone—that's correct, dear reader, our Maria was the only sax-toting Vampire in all of Europe—then trudged toward the Abbey's exit, irked that nary a soul was waiting to bid her adieu. Maria snarled, "Those petty Zombies don't even have the courtesy to say goodbye. They shall feel my wrath when I return home. And I'll return. After I prove myself to be the best Governess I can be, Mother Zombie will have no choice but to invite me back." She then touched the wrought iron gate and whispered, "When the Devil closes a door, somewhere he opens a window, and shoves somebody right on out of it, and into the fires of *Hölle*. Am I worthy of being shoved? Shall I be burnt to a crisp in said righteous fire? What does a burning Vampire smell like? Ah, questions, questions, questions. But the main question is, how the *fick* am I supposed to get to this guy's house?"

She stepped through the Abbey's gate, and into the real world, homeless for the first time in centuries . . . and, much to her surprise and chagrin, the tiniest bit frightened. So Maria did what she did when she needed comforting and there were no human necks around to suck on: She unsheathed her sax.

After Maria attached the mouthpiece, she cleared her throat and blew a loud F-sharp that broke every window within a three-block radius. She mumbled an inaudible apology to the neighbors—which, had it been audible, would be called insincere at best, and a pile of Zombie excrement at worst—after which she blew a series of arpeggios that would have knocked saxophone inventor Adolphe Sax onto his Belgian backside. She held another F-sharp that grew louder, and louder, and louder, then, right as she ran out of breath, several tendrils of smoke escaped from the instrument's bell. The tendrils then weaved themselves into a braid, and the braid began to take shape. As it grew taller and wider, its shape became that of a human being, a male, to be precise, a black male, a stocky black male with close-cropped hair, wide eyes, and thick, sensual lips.

Maria dropped her saxophone and gave the man a through once-over, taking in his regal chest, his large fingers, and his impeccably pressed tan suit. Her stomach fluttered, and it took all of her restraint to keep from fondling her lady-parts. She reverentially whispered, "Come to mama, Chocolate Thunder."

As the man floated to the Earth, he said, "Excuse me, young Vampiress?"

Clearing her throat, Maria said, "Nothing. Dare I ask, what are you?"

The man favored Maria with a warm smile. "Not *what*, young Vampiress—*who*." He tipped an imaginary hat. "John Coltrane, at your service."

She gave this John Coltrane character a closer examination, then leered, "I hope you *can* be at my service, my thick ebony saxophone spirit. No, let me rephrase that: I hope you can service me. If you get what I'm saying."

"I know exactly what you are saying, young Vampiress; I'm a spirit, not a eunuch. But as a spirit, I don't have the means to, um, service humans."

Maria sighed. "That's unfortunate." She picked up her saxophone from the ground and licked her mouthpiece. "Since you can't be of service, I must ask you to take your leave. I have no time to dilly-dally. I'm off to see the wizard."

"The wizard?"

"Oh, apologies, wrong musical. I'm off to begin my new job . . . no, my new life . . . no, my new undeath."

John Coltrane frowned. "That's truly unfortunate, because we need to talk. I believe you have some questions, and I might be able to offer you some answers." He ran his index finger up and down Maria's saxophone—causing her to again shiver—and said, "How about you pack that thing up and we'll go on a walk. Or even a skip."

"A skip?"

"Yes, Maria. A skip."

Saxophone safe in its case, John Coltrane took Maria's hand

and the two skipped down the street, nary a word spoken between them. They skipped for miles and miles, Maria's foul hat flopping in the breeze, its otherworldly stench leaving dozens of birds dead in its wake.

Maria said, "This skipping business is ridiculous, John Coltrane. I look like a fool. I can transform into a bat and fly, you know."

"Be quiet, little girl. I want to skip, so we're going to skip, and you're going to like it." His voice took on a menacing tone. "Now clam up unless you want me to stick that saxophone where the sun never shines."

She licked her lips and said, "Don't make promises you don't intend to keep."

Finally, after thirty-plus kilometers of silence, Maria spoke up: "What will my future be, oh dashing spectre? I'm about to enter a new and exciting phase of my undeath. I should be excited to go out into the world, to be free, to have my choice of beings to feed upon. My fangs should be gushing with excitement, yet they remain dry. What's wrong with me?"

"You're an Austrian Vampire, Maria. The list of things wrong with you is long."

Ignoring John Coltrane, Maria said, "From the moment I became what I've become, I've dreamed of having adventures—adventures such as killing the Pope during a Sunday mass, or having intimate relations with a large-breasted sixteen-going-on-seventeen-year-old girl—but I've never brought these dreams to reality."

"That's probably for the best, Vampiress."

"That's your opinion. But the point is, if I consider these dreams, then my soul—my inner-self—has the courage to consider anything, and if I have the courage to consider anything, I could . . ."

John Coltrane interrupted, "Apparently what you lack, Maria, is confidence."

"Confidence?"

"You have plenty of courage—you couldn't have survived in that hellacious Abbey for as long as you did without it—but here you're in the outside world, all alone, all by yourself, and you're scared. You have doubts . . ."

"Do not."

". . . and worries . . ."

"Nuh unh."

". . . and you must seek for what you lack."

"I lack nothing!" She paused thoughtfully, then said, "No, John Coltrane, you're correct. I lack the fortitude to serve them with assurance."

"Vampiress, the truth is that servitude is a two-way street. The responsibility isn't entirely yours."

"It's my responsibility to own up to my mistakes without argument."

John Coltrane frowned. "Your only responsibilities are to keep those von Trapp brats out of prison, and to learn to play your tenor sax in tune. And to maybe take up soprano sax, while you're at it."

Maria ignored him. "It's my responsibility to show them I'm worthy."

"Worthy of what?" John Coltrane asked.

"Worthy of their respect."

"Maria, you have murdered 19,216,145 people . . ."

"19,216,146," she corrected.

"Right, 19,216,146. No mortal will respect you, and justifiably so. You don't deserve respect. Just fear. And, some would say, a stake in the heart . . ."

"That stake in the heart business is a laughable myth."

"Fine. Then a stake in your lady-parts."

Maria said, "Leave my lady-parts out of this, Chocolate Thunder . . ." She flicked her left nipple. ". . . unless you intend to, um, *peruse* them."

"No perusal," John Coltrane said. "We must continue examining the confidence issue."

Full of false bravado, Maria puffed up her chest and bared her fangs. "I ooze confidence, John Coltrane . . ."

He gestured to the reddish liquid dribbling from her teeth. "You sure are oozing *something*."

Clapping her hands, Maria said, "Oh, hoorah, my fangs gush anew." She gave John Coltrane yet another lascivious look. "Looks like you got me wet, spectre."

John Coltrane shook his head sadly. "Can we get back to this confidence business? My time here grows short."

"Okay, fine, so like I was saying, let them bring on all their problems," she said. "I'll do better than my best . . ."

He gestured at her bloodstains on her chin. "Looks like you're already doing better than your best."

". . . and I have confidence they'll put me to the test!"

"If you have confidence, if you *really* have confidence, then I've done my job here. Now if you'll excuse me, I have to rein-habit my mortal, living body. I'm late for a recording session with . . ."

"But I'll make them see I have confidence in me."

"Wonderful, Maria, just wonderful. Now that it's well estab-lished that you have confidence . . ."

"Somehow I'll astonish them. *Somehow.*"

Resigned, John Coltrane sighed, "Okay, Maria. I'll bite. How will you astonish them?"

"Well, um, I'll be . . . I'll be . . . I'll be . . ." She grinned and nodded. ". . . firm but kind!"

"From what I've heard, you have never been kind in your entire life. *Never.*"

"Have so."

"When?"

"Well, um, okay, there was the time when I ripped off the head of a peasant farmer, then stitched it back on with a string made from hay."

After a pause, John Coltrane asked, "And that's your defini-tion of kindness?"

"Well, it was kinder than the alternative."

"Which was? . . ."

"Throwing his head into the pig pen. Which is what I usu-ally do when I'm at a farm."

John Coltrane shook his head. "So what you're saying to me is that because one time—*one single time*—you managed to restrain yourself from feeding one of your victims to a gaggle of swine, you have the temperament to be a proper Governess?"

"You know what, Chocolate Thunder . . ."

"I wish you would stop calling me that."

". . . this isn't about me, but rather the children. Ah, those kids, *Hölle* bless them, they *will* adore me!"

"They'll run from you, Maria."

"They'll follow my instructions!"

"They'll attempt to drive a stake into your heart. *And* your lady-parts."

"Everything will turn out fine, John Coltrane. I have confidence."

John Coltrane shook his head and mumbled to himself, "Man, this confidence thing was a bad idea. If she says *confidence* one more time, I swear . . ."

"I have confidence!" Maria cried. "Confidence the world can all be mine! Confidence in clouds! Confidence in tornados! Confidence in eternal winter! Confidence in *Hölle*!" She gave John Coltrane a penetrating look in his eyes. "And it's clear, Chocolate Thunder, that you're now able to see I have confidence in me."

"You mean confidence in *myself*."

"What?"

"Grammatically speaking, you should say I have confidence in *myself* rather than I have confidence in *me*."

"Tell that to that jerk Hammerstein," Maria mumbled.

"Why bother?" Coltrane said. "There's no talking to that guy."

"Tell me about it. In any event, the point I'm making here is that I have confidence in confidence alone."

"Then, to repeat, I've done my job." Under his breath, he added, "Thank *Gott*. I can't wait to get away from this neurotic whore." Then, in full voice, said, "Well, Vampiress, it looks like we have arrived."

What with all of her incessant babbling about confidence, Maria didn't notice how far she and the spectre had skipped. "Already?"

"Already," John Coltrane agreed, gesturing at the beautiful white mansion in front of which they stood.

Maria peered through the wrought-iron gate, then, after taking in the perfectly manicured front lawn, the pristine brick, and the flawless architecture of the von Trapp residence, she whispered, "Goodness, this sure as *scheisse* is an improvement over the Abbey."

John Coltrane's body began to evaporate. "Goodbye, Maria. You may see me again in a couple of chapters. Or maybe not. I may be too obscure of a reference to be invited back into the story. I understand I will make it into the epilogue, but beyond that, one never knows."

"Wait, John Coltrane, wait! Before you go back into my saxophone, answer me this: Why is it you who have come to me in the night, and skipped with me in the day, and given me confidence, and set my loins on fire. Why you?"

John Coltrane smiled an inscrutable smile. "Atlantic Records, catalog number 1361."

Maria gave him a quizzical look. "I'm afraid I don't under-stand."

"In March of 1961, Atlantic Records will release an album called *My Favorite Things* by yours truly."

"What's Atlantic Records?"

"Don't worry about it."

"What's *My Favorite Things*?"

"Don't worry about it."

"What does this all have to do with me?"

"I'll answer that with a question, Vampiress: What are *your* favorite things?"

"That's easy: Blood drops on roses and bloody-nosed kit-tens, and . . ."

John Coltrane raised his index finger and said, "Shh, shh, shh. Save that bit for later. It's a showstopper. And I'll perform it on soprano saxophone, and it will be a watershed moment in my career."

"This is gibberish."

As John Coltrane faded into nothingness, he said, "If there's anybody in this story who knows gibberish, Maria, it's you."

# CHAPTER 2

AFTER GAWKING AT THE MANSION for a good ten minutes, Maria finally tugged at the gate.

Locked.

She tugged a little harder.

It barely moved.

She tugged a *lot* harder . . . ripped the door clean off its hinge. Chuckling, she casually tossed the door over her shoulder; it flew several hundred yards, narrowly missing a stray dog, a lost child, and a confused Sea Monster.

Maria took a few steps into the yard, cleared her throat, and whispered, "Help." No response. A little louder: "Help!" Nothing. Louder yet: "*Help!*" Bupkis. Even louder yet: "HEEEEELLLLLLLLLPPPPPP!"

She heard a cranky, Cockney-accented voice call from the house, "*What in the name of the Lord is the problem out there?*"

Maria called back, "I have confidence in confidence alone! Besides which you see I have confidence in me!"

*"What in the name of the Lord are you talking about?"*

"I left home yesterday evening, and soon after I began the long journey, I pulled my trusty tenor saxophone from its case, and after I played several arpeggios—arpeggios which, I should note, killed a flock of geese, thank you very much—I was visited by a Negro spirit who went by the name of John Coltrane. This John Coltrane and I skipped for miles and miles, all while talking about confidence, and responsibility, and Atlantic Records. And now, here I am."

After a lengthy pause, the voice called, "You must be the freak from the Abbey!"

"You can call me all the names you want, sir, but it won't bother me. Because I have confidence."

"Of course you do. Approach the front door, please."

Maria clutched her saxophone and her suitcase to her chest, then skipped across the lawn. Halfway to the door, she caught a reflection of herself in the fountain—yes, we're aware that according to the familiar lore, Vampires don't cast reflections, but this particular Vampire did, and that's the way it is because that's the way we *say* it is, so don't complain about this on your blog—and, realizing how silly it looks for a centuries-old Vampire to skip without the accompaniment of an innovative neo-bop/avant garde saxophonist, she slowed to a walk.

Once on the porch, she took a deep breath and rang the doorbell. Right after the *ding*, and right before the *dong*, the door opened, and there stood a man who had the posture of a weeping willow, the complexion of an overcooked marmoset stew, the hairline of King Mongkut of Siam, and the hangdog expression of Michael Caine.

The butler—whose name, according to his "HELLO MY NAME IS ALFRED" nametag, was Alfred—gave Maria a dismissive look. "So," he said, "you're the freak from the Abbey."

She smiled broadly and waved. "Hello! Here I am! I'm the new Governess!"

Alfred took in her shiny cat suit and her rancid hat. "Nice outfit."

With a *p'shaw* of her hand, she said, "Oh, this old thing? You're too kind. I'm Maria. What's your name?"

Glowering, he pointed at his nametag.

"Oh. Right. Alfred." She proffered her hand. "Lovely to meet you, Alfred."

He stared at her hand, grunted, then headed into the house.

As Maria followed the old butler, she thought, *I shall kill him tonight; perhaps I'll suck him dry as he sleeps.* Before she finished hatching her plan to murder the elderly servant, her jaw dropped and her cases crashed to the floor. She spun around, and around, and around, so taken was she by the opulence of the von Trapp's entryway: The gilded furniture, the glittering crystal chandeliers, the pristine white tile floors, and the opulent staircase that led to the divine balcony all added up to a sight unlike any Maria had ever seen. The Vampire had called the Abbey home for so long that she had no idea people lived like this.

And it repulsed her. Maria couldn't wait to cover the entire floor with Alfred's blood . . . especially that pristine white tile. *That will show these rich* arschlochs *to disrespect . . .*

Alfred interrupted her reverie: "You'll wait here, Maria," he Cockney'd. "I shall fetch Master Wayne."

"Who?"

"I mean, I shall fetch Captain von Trapp."

Offering him a sugary smile, she simpered, "Wonderful!" As he strolled away, she bared her fangs and hissed.

Maria glided across the room—when she wanted to, she could glide with the best of them, unlike her Zombie Sisters— stopping only to knock over what she assumed to be a priceless heirloom of a vase. After she hid the evidence by eating the shards, she walked toward a closed set of double doors. Touch- ing the knobs, she peeked furtively over her left shoulder, then her right, and then, comfortable she was alone, pushed open the doors. It was a ballroom, and it was magnificent: More crystal chandeliers, tremendous picture windows covered with beautiful curtains, an ornate bar, and mirrors everywhere. (Yes, she could still see herself in the mirrors. Now please do shut up about the reflection issue already.)

She tiptoed to the middle of the floor, then, holding an imaginary partner, began to dance. Badly. Very badly. Like a toddler on absinthe.

And then she turned into a *Desmodus Rotundus.*

(Let's explain: Once in a while, when Maria went into her artistic place—e.g., when she sang and/or danced—she shifted into her rodent form. Why? One doesn't know. Why does one not know? Because one doesn't care, as isn't important to our story. So why does one even mention it in the first place? Because sticklers about Vampire legend and mythos will complain even more than they're already complaining, and one wants to nip at least a few of these complaints in the bud right now, as one knows that one will have either the word count or the inclination to deal with these complaints later on down the line.)

Unprepared for the transformation, our bat-girl flew about the room as if she were unprepared for the transformation. She crashed into a wall, then the bar on the far side of the room, then a window, then a mirror, then another mirror, then another wall, and then, finally, a chandelier, before coming to an awkward landing right by the door. After she regained her footing—or her winging, as the case was—she began the bat-to-Vampire transformation, a process too complex to describe here. Suffice it to say that the explanation contains words that don't have a language, a dictionary definition, or something that can be turned into a pun.

When she retook her human form, she found herself face-to-face with a tall, dapper, lantern-jawed gent who reeked of gin. She coughed, then, unable to stop herself, blurted, "Aaugh, you stink."

The gin-scented gentleman said, "I *stink*? No, I don't stink. *You* stink! *You* stink!"

Self-conscious about her body odor, Maria blushed. "It isn't my fault. If you lived in close proximity to Zombies for centuries, you would stink, too."

Somewhat regaining his composure, the man slurred, "I assume you're Fraulein Marjorie . . ."

"Maria, sir."

The Captain burped. "Right. Maria. I'm Captain Georg von Trapp. In the foo-sure . . ." He cleared his throat, then said, "In the *future*, you will not enter a new room unless you're invited into . . ."

And then he vomited onto his shoes.

Maria's stomach was already a tad on edge due to both nerves and the gentleman's prevalent juniper berry scent. Trying her best to hold down her gorge, she gurgled, "Yes, Captain. Sir."

And then she coughed.

And then she gagged.

And then she upchucked.

All over the Captain's crisp nicely-pressed, impeccably-tailored jacket.

The Captain stared at the chunky Technicolor mess on his chest. Unfazed, he turned around and closed the doors to the ballroom, then spun back around to face Maria. "I guess you can take the girl out of the Abbey, but you can't take the Abbey out of the girl." He took a deep breath, scrunched up his face, looked at his chest, then regurgitated on Maria's regurgitate.

Maria's stomach did another somersault as she watched the piles of vomit intermingle. She said, "Captain, I apologize for my . . ." Before anybody could find out what Maria was going to say sorry for, a stream of red-flecked bile shot from her mouth, and into the Captain's face. A second serving then flew from Maria's maw, splatting on the floor in front of the ballroom doors.

Pawing at his eyes, the Captain roared, "It stings! For the love of *Gott*, it stings!"

The doors flew open and Alfred said, "Is everything alright, master?" He took two steps into the room, then slipped on Maria's spew, falling rump-first into the mess. He attempted to lift himself from the floor, managing only to slip again; this time, however, he landed face first. Alfred then sat up, gulped, then discharged last night's dinner, this morning's breakfast, and this afternoon's lunch all over his lap.

The Captain knelt down and touched his loyal servant's shoulder. "Alfred, I apologize for . . ." Before anybody could find out what von Trapp was going to say sorry for, a stream of green-flecked bile shot from his mouth, hitting Alfred squarely in the face.

Near tears, Alfred crawled toward the door, stopping twice to hurl. By the time he made it through the doorway, he had nothing left in his stomach, so he dry-heaved his way toward the living room.

The Captain crawled through the puddle of sick and closed the ballroom doors. He grabbed the doorknob, lifted himself up, took off his foul jacket, and leaned against the wall. Noticing that Maria was staring at him, he said, "See something green?"

With the sleeve of her cat suit, Maria wiped some chunks from the side of her mouth, then said, "Well, yes. But my question is, what kind of Captain are you? Because I don't picture you as a seafarer."

"Oh? And why do you say that?"

She gestured at the myriad piles of vomit and said, "I'd

suspect that seafarers could hold down their gorge . . . even in the presence of other gorge."

The Captain pulled at her sleeve; Maria winced as the stretchy material snapped back. "Well," he said, "you don't look like the kind of person who can take care of a family."

Maria mumbled, "Racist."

"What?"

"Nothing."

"Exactly. Nothing. Now turn around, please."

Maria blinked. "What? Why?"

"Do as I say, Maggie May."

"Maria, sir."

The Captain burped. "Right. Maria. Now turn around. Let me see your hindquarters."

As she showed the Captain her rump, she felt his eyes running up and down her back . . . and she liked it. She moaned softly and was seconds away from showing the Captain her bosom, when he roared, "That's the most foul hat I've ever seen or smelled! Lose it!"

She faced von Trapp, then seductively took off the rancid hat and rubbed it in between her legs. The Captain looked on, unimpressed.

"You'll have to put on different clothes before you meet the brats, er, the children. I don't think Friedrich could handle . . ." He gestured drunkenly at the cat suit, ". . . this."

She said, "But I don't have any other clothes!" That was a fib. She had dozens of other outfits. The problem is, they were all cat suits.

"Why?"

Thinking on the fly, Maria lied, "When we leave the Abbey, our clothes are donated to charity."

Again, the Captain pulled at her sleeve, and again, Maria winced as the stretchy material snapped back. "What about this . . . this . . . this *thing*? Why didn't this get donated?"

"Oh, I tried. No charities were interested."

"Is that right? So if I understand correctly, had the poor accepted this . . . this . . . this *thing*, you would have left the Abbey without clothes."

Maria beamed. "Correct!"

"So the head of the Abbey is comfortable sending her minions out into the world naked?"

"Is that something you would like, Captain von Trapp? Me out into the world naked?" She pursed her lips and jutted out her right hip.

"I could use a big stiff one," he grumbled.

Screwing up her face, Maria said, "What with all your children, I wouldn't have guessed you swung that way, sir."

The Captain shook his head. "I'm referring to a drink, young lady. Now can we do something about this outfit? I kid you not, Friedrich will burst out of his pants if he sees you in this."

"Hmm, is that right? Tell me about this Friedrich. He sounds fun."

The Captain ignored her. "Now, Mariska . . ."

"Maria, sir."

"Right. Maria. I don't know how much your Mother Zombie told you about the family von Trapp."

"Not a thing, sir." Pursing her lips, she added, "But I intend to find out everything about everybody, both above and below the waist."

He opened the ballroom door and called, "Alfred!"

"Yes, sir!" Alfred called back.

"A big stiff one!"

"Right away, sir!"

Moments later, Alfred tiptoed into the room—mindful to avoid the drying pools of sick—and handed the Captain a drink so large that it could have inebriated the entire Bazillus Bar-Betriebsgesellschaft on a Friday night, and those of you who have spent a Friday at the Bazillus Bar-Betriebsgesellschaft know that that's saying something.

Von Trapp took a substantial hit of his gin, made the contorted gin-face that all longtime gin drinkers have made at one time or another, then said, "You're the seventy-eighth Governess who has come to look after my brood since their mother died. Your predecessor left after six or seven seconds, which is why I've reached out to Mother Zombie. I told her that only a Zombie could keep those brats in line, but she disagreed. Apparently she felt that you had a better chance."

"I can tell you exactly why she sent me instead of a Zombie. She wanted me *gone*. She *exiled* me." Maria sniffled, then a single tear of blood rolled down her cheek. "She exiled me to a beautiful mansion in a lovely part of the country. Mother Zombie is *awful*."

"Right. Now back to the brats."

"Brats?"

"A term of affection."

"Ah. Brats. What's wrong with them?"

"*There isn't a thing wrong with my children!*" he roared. "*They're innocent, and warm, and caring, and they mean nobody any harm, and they had nothing to do with the fire and subsequent robbery at the* Bank Vontobel Osterreich! *They were nowhere near downtown that evening! They were with me! The entire day! They never left my sight! And anybody who tells you differently is full of* scheisse!" He cleared his throat, polished off his drink, flicked a dried chunk of vomit from his sleeve, then said, "What I meant to say was, there's nothing wrong with the children, only the Governesses."

Nonplussed, Maria said, "If you say so."

"I do say so, Morticia . . ."

"Maria, sir."

"Right. Maria. The fact is, the other Governesses were weak. Those brats need somebody with physical strength, because if they're not ruled with an iron fist, this house can't be properly run. Mother Zombie said you're strong."

In the blink of an eye, Maria was on the other side of the room. She ripped one of the three wet bars from the floor, lifted it over her head, then tossed it into the air. As it crashed to the floor, she said, "I indeed possess physical strength, sir."

The Captain rubbed his temples, opened the door, and yelled, "*Alfred!*"

"Another beverage on the way, sir!"

"You read my mind!" To Maria, he said, "Every morning you'll aid the children with their schooling, lead them in marching lessons, and give them an hour of etiquette lessons, because those brats need to learn how to mind their P's and Q's. And you'll work them, and work them *hard*. I won't permit them to dream away their summer holidays, nor will I permit them to rob another bank . . ."

"I thought you said they were nowhere near the bank, sir."

*"Of course they were nowhere near the bank!"* he snapped. Regaining his composure, he said, "Bedtime is to be strictly observed, no exceptions. They'll fight you on that, Morgana . . ."

"Maria, sir."

"Right. Maria. They'll fight you hard about bedtime. But you tuck those brats into bed on schedule, or else there will be *Hölle* to pay. And do you know what *Hölle* to pay means?"

"Better than anybody, sir. One other thing: Are they allowed to, well, um, let's see, how should I phrase this, *have fun*?"

"Have fun? *Fun*?! Fraulein, you don't want my children to have fun. Last time they had fun, they caused 50,000 shillings worth of damage to the guesthouse. I shudder to think about it." And then, as if to prove his point, he shuddered. "You're in command. Do with them what you will."

"Anything?"

"Anything."

Saluting him, she said, "Yes, Captain!"

"Very good, Monogram." He left the ballroom, and gestured to Maria that she should follow; both neatly avoided the yet-to-have-fully-dried lake of sick. Once in the hallway, Captain von Trapp pulled a whistle from his pocket and said, "Here we go."

Vampires are sensitive to shrill, high-pitched tones, so when

Captain von Trapp blew his whistle, a glop of blood dripped from Maria's left ear and fell onto the white tile floor with an audible splat. The Captain stared at the gob and said, "You repulse me, Fraulein."

"Thank you, sir. I repulse you because I am who I am, and I have confidence in me."

"Don't you mean, 'I have confidence in *myself*'?"

"Listen—for some reason, Hammerstein's word is law in this story, even if his word is grammatically incorrect. The man seems to have some strange hold over . . ."

Before she could finish the thought, von Trapp tooted "Shave and a Haircut" on his whistle. A second later, Maria heard unison footsteps from above that sounded somehow creepy. As the footsteps became louder and louder, Maria grew more and more excited. *This has to be the brood,* she thought. *These are the brats.*

Thirty seconds later, there they were, in all their glory, standing in a row—tallest to shortest, left to right—glaring at their new Governess: The von Trapp kids.

Maria's first thought: *The Captain has issues with the way I dress? Really?* She couldn't be blamed for being taken aback with the children's identical blue sailor suits; the best that could be said about those pantywaist outfits was that they matched.

Maria's second thought: *No wonder the Captain showed no interest in bedding me. The man is too potent for his own good.*

The Captain again blew that infernal whistle, which Maria promptly slapped from his hand. It flew high into the air and broke several light bulbs on the largest of the large chandeliers, before falling onto the floor and shattering into sixteen-going-on-seventeen pieces. The tallest boy locked his eyes onto Maria's chest and whispered, *"Nice."*

As she watched a lump grow right below the boy's waistline, she smiled a secret smile and thought, *Ah, that must be Friedrich.* Maria took an involuntary step toward the boy, but stopped herself when the Captain roared, *"Ten hut!"*

He marched slowly up and down the line, glaring the entire way, stopping only to straighten the chubbiest boy's collar. "The way you wear your suit, Kurt," the Captain said, "simply disgusts me."

Friedrich said, "Me, too."

Von Trapp turned on his heel and roared, "Shut it, Gretl!"

"I'm not Gretl, Father," the boy said.

The Captain wiped a bit of sweat from his brow, squinted at his oldest son, and said, "I know that, son. I . . . I . . . I wanted to see if you were paying attention."

As the brats rolled their eyes, the boy pointed at his father's stained shirt. "What's that mess on your chest?"

The Captain pawed at the now dry vomit. "Never you mind." He cuffed Friedrich on the ear. "Now straighten up, boy."

Staring right at Friedrich's crotch, Maria mumbled, "He looks pretty straight to me."

One of the short sailor-suit-clad girls stepped out of line, wandered over to the tall, pretty girl who stood on the far left, and sneezed onto her stomach. The tall girl gave her little sister a shove, but the shorter girl neatly avoided falling—Maria guessed that they had played this game before—then gave her sister a wet, wet raspberry, so wet that the smaller von Trapp spent sixteen-going-on-seventeen seconds wiping the spittle from her face with her sleeve. After she returned to her proper place in line, the Captain glared at his offspring and asked, "Are you brats very much finished?"

In unison, they said, "Yes, Father."

"Thank you." He then lifted his hand to his mouth and blew into . . . nothing. As the chubby von Trapp boy snorted, the Captain asked, "Which one of you took my whistle?"

Friedrich said, "If you'll recall, not more than a minute ago, your attractive friend over here knocked it from your hand." Then, under his breath, he added, "Have another drink, why don't you?"

"I know that, boy. I . . . I . . . I wanted to see if you were paying attention." (At that, even Maria rolled her eyes.) "Now then, this is your new Governess, Magdalene."

"Maria, sir."

"Right. Maria. Now introduce yourselves!"

The tallest girl—who Maria realized upon closer inspection was one of the prettiest mortals she had ever seen—stepped forward and said, "Liesl! I hate you, Governess!"

And then, Friedrich. "You know who I am. And unlike my sister, I love you, Governess. A *lot*."

Then came a cute girl with braids: "Louisa! You resemble a troll, Governess!"

Next, a chubby boy: "Kurt! You're fat, Governess!"

Kurt was followed by the girl who had sneezed on Liesl: "Brigitta! You reek like cattle, Governess!"

And then came another girl: "Marta! You reek like cattle, Governess!"

Brigitta stomped her foot. "I just said that. You always steal my things."

Finally, a five-ish-year-old girl who Maria thought looked good enough to eat: "Gretl! I don't have enough vulgar words in my vocabulary to insult you in the manner to which you deserve to be insulted, Governess!"

The Captain nodded approvingly. "Wonderful, children. You have represented the von Trapp name well." He then asked Maria, "You remember all that?"

"You mean do I remember that your offspring told me that they hate me, they love me, I look like a troll, I'm fat, I smell like cattle, and I'm awful beyond words? Yes, Captain, that's the kind of thing that sticks in your head."

The Captain chuckled. "Oh, no, I meant do you remember their names?"

"Of course I do. How could I forget! Such lovely names they are! *Kurt*. Rolls right off the tongue. *Gretl*. Evokes spring flowers. And *Brigitta*. Brr . . . Gee . . . *Tuh*. All those hard consonants are so very, very attractive." She paused, then added, "I'm not sure about Marta—that presents a problem we'll address later in the chapter—but otherwise, we're talking some serious perfection."

Von Trapp beamed proudly. "Why thank you. They were all my choices, Maria . . ."

"Sir, you got my name right!"

The Captain burped. "Did I ever have it wrong?" Before the

Vampire could answer, he said, "Where's that whistle of mine?"

Staring at the blop of blood on the floor, Maria asked, "Is the whistle really necessary?"

"In my regime, the children answer only to a whistle."

With blinding speed, Maria picked up all sixteen-going-on-seventeen pieces of the broken whistle and said, "Well, sir, it's now my regime, and they'll answer to those mellifluous Germanic names of theirs."

The Captain shook his head. "The whistle."

Maria said, "The Germanic names."

"Whistle!"

"Germanic names!"

"*Whistle!*"

"*Germanic names!*"

"WHISTLE, WHISTLE, WHISTLE!"

"GERMANIC NAMES, GERMANIC NAMES, GERMANIC NAMES!"

"ALFRED! A DRINK! *NOW!*"

From off in the Batcave . . . er, from off in the distance, the butler called, "Right away, sir!"

Von Trapp took a deep breath, then told Maria, "Were you this much of a pain in the hindquarters at the Abbey, Fraulein?"

Remembering the joys of flying through the Alps, and disemboweling townspeople on the way back home, she said, "You don't know the half of it, sir."

"Nor do I *want* to know the half of it." He turned to go. "Have fun with the brats."

After the Captain was out of earshot, Maria—aware she had to gain control of these brats right away—snarled, "Alright, children, there's a new sheriff in town, and her name is Maria."

Louisa asked, "What's a sheriff, Governess?"

"Crack a dictionary, blondie. Now here is the deal: My word is law. When I say frog, you jump. If I tell you to eat mud, you'll ask for seconds. Is that clear?"

The brats belted her with a barrage of *schiesses* and *ficks*.

Maria said, "I'll choose to ignore that. Now there are a whole lot of you von Trapps, so to keep things straight for our readers, let's hear those mellifluous Germanic names again."

The tallest girl stepped forward and said, "I'm Liesl. I'm sixteen-years-old, and I believe all Governesses are scum."

"Of course you do. Next!"

Friedrich stepped forward. "You know who I am, beautiful."

Maria sauntered over to the boy, stood a few millimeters in front of him, gave him the tiniest glimpse of fang, and said, "I certainly do."

He gulped, then said, "I'm fourteen. And I'm throbbing."

She whispered in his ear, "I am sure you are," then gave his neck the gentlest of nibbles.

At that, Friedrich shivered, quietly moaned, then stumbled back into the line.

Maria gave a sexy chuckle, then cleared her throat and said, "Next."

Louisa took a step forward and said, "I'm Brigitta."

Maria—who already remembered each of the children's

names—lifted Louisa by her right braid, twirled her three times in the air, then gently placed her back on the ground. "Would you like to try that again, blondie?"

Barely fazed, Louisa said, "I'm Louisa."

"And how old are you?"

"Five million," Louisa said, then stomped back into the line.

Without being asked, Brigitta stepped forward and said, "She isn't five million, Governess. She's thirteen. I'm ten."

Liesl said, "Oh, do shut it, you goody-goody twat."

"Who are you calling a twat, twat?"

"I'm calling you a twat, you little . . ."

The chubby boy interrupted, "My turn, my turn! I'm Kurt! I'm eleven! I'm incorrigible!"

Maria asked, "Do you even know what the word incorrigible means?"

Liesl said, "It means he's a twat."

Sighing, Maria pointed at the second-to-last girl in line. "You. Speak."

"I'm Marta, and I'm going to be seven next week, and for my present, I'd like a squirrel."

"A living squirrel or a dead squirrel?" Maria asked.

"Dead would be fine, Governess."

Maria beamed, then knelt down and gave the little girl a hug. "Oh, Marta, I love you most of all!" She rubbed her chin for a moment, then said, "But there's one problem: The names *Marta* and *Maria* look practically the same in print, and there are so many of you brats that things are confusing enough without having two names that are only one letter apart. So to eliminate any necessary uncertainty, can we change your name to, oh, say Barta? Or Tarta? Or Charta?"

Friedrich said, "How about Farta?"

As her beam grew even more beamy Maria said, "Farta! Perfection."

The von Trapp formerly known as Marta said, "But I don't want to be . . ."

Interrupting the newly christened Farta, Maria tapped the girl at the end of the line—the littlest von Trapp—on the forehead and said, "You. What's your story?"

The little girl shook her head.

"Cat got your tongue?" The little girl hawked on the floor; her sputum got some good distance, and landed right next to the glop of Maria's ear blood. "That's some wonderful aiming! My, you're practically a lady!"

Liesl said, "She's practically a twat."

Maria surveyed the children and thought, *I could kill each of them and be in Romania before anybody notices . . . except Mother Zombie. She would most certainly notice.* Not wanting to hurt her chances of being invited back into the Abbey, she sighed and said, "Okay, children, I have two secrets to tell you: First, before I came to this house, I was living in a house filled with undead women . . ."

In unison, the children roared, *"Stierscheisse!"*

". . . and second, I've never been a Governess before."

Each child's face broke into a predatory grin. "Is that right?" Louisa asked.

"That's right."

Kurt said, "We can offer you some suggestions."

"I need all the advice I can get, children."

Louisa said, "If you want to earn points with my Father, I'd recommend hiding all of his gin."

"Sound thinking, blondie," Maria said.

Brigitta said, "I find that excreting on the seat of the toilet bowl in the ballroom's bathroom is a wonderful way to brighten up the house."

"I'll be staying out of the ballroom for a while, but consider it done!" Maria said.

Friedrich said, "It's crucial that the Governess tuck me in at night. A good, long tuck."

Maria ran the tip of her tongue across her lips. "It will be my pleasure."

Kurt piped up, "And during dessert, always chew your food, then spit it back onto your plate!"

Gretl said, "Don't believe a word they say, Fraulein Maria."

"Wonderful," Liesl groaned, "the goody-goody twat has spoken."

A woman clad in a light blue short-sleeved dress and a white apron goosestepped into the room, clapping her hands sharply. "Alright, Bradys, er, von Trapps, outside," she roared. "Now! Hurry up! Move, move, move, move, move!"

While the children trudged toward the back of the house—

cursing the entire way, naturally—the female Alfred said, "I'm Frau Alice. I singlehandedly run this dump."

Maria said, "I apologize in advance for the state of the ballroom. But it wasn't entirely my fault."

"What's this about the ballroom, now?" Frau Alice asked.

"Nothing. It's wonderful to meet you, Frau. Everybody here at the von Trapp mansion has been simply *lovely* to me."

Frau gave Maria a skeptical look. "Really? Do you even know what the word 'lovely' means?" Before Maria could answer, Frau said, "Let me show you to your room," then collected the Vampire's suitcase and saxophone.

As the housekeeper headed up the stairs, Maria felt a piercing sting in her backside. She put her hand on her rump, and came across a dart. After removing the pointy thing, Maria looked across the living room; the seven children were staring icily back at her . . . and Liesl held a blow-gun in her left hand. They all remained motionless, except for Friedrich, who stuck out his tongue at Maria, mouthed the word, "Sorry," then cupped his testicles through his pants with his left hand, made a pretend telephone with his right, and mouthed, "Call me."

As they headed upstairs, Frau Alice said, "You're very lucky. They lit the last Governess on fire. Now *that's* a story. Of a girl named Brady."

"A girl named who?"

"I can't discuss it. You'll have to talk to Sam the Butcher."

"Is Sam the Butcher like Jack the Ripper? Because he was a friend. Quite a lovely man. As misunderstood as the day was long."

Shaking her head, Alice repeated, "They lit the last Governess on fire." She paused, then added, "Maybe it'll happen again."

Maria looked over her shoulder and gave the von Trapp brood a patently evil grin. Then, in a cold tone that made the housekeeper shiver, said, "Trust me, Frau, that won't happen. *Ever.*"

Maria then revealed her fangs.

At that, Farta burst into tears.

The Captain, clutching a bottle of gin, sprinted into the room and belched, "What? Who? Who's that? Is that the sound of a little girl crying? Must be Kurt." And then he leaned to the left, leaned to the right, belched again, and fell face first onto the floor.

At that, Louisa burst into tears, after which each child, save for Liesl and Friedrich, followed suit.

Maria nodded. "That's right, children. Cry. *Cry!* Feel my *wrath*, er, my *authority!*"

Liesl stepped toward her new Governess and said, "Fraulein, I'd like to speak to you in private, please. Would you do me the favor of joining me in the backyard?"

"It would be my pleasure." Maria glared at the remaining von Trapp children, then snapped her fingers four times, after which the brats froze solid.

Nonplussed, Liesl stared icily at her unmoving brothers and sisters, then nodded. "As I suspected. Come."

Gazing longingly at Liesl's bosomy bosom, Maria told Frau Alice, "Catch you on the flipside," then skipped over to the eldest von Trapp child.

Once they were outside, Liesl said, "I can tell what you are,

Governess. I've read about your kind. You're a Vampire, are you not?"

Maria said, "Indeed," and then she opened her mouth and clicked her fangs together three times.

Liesl knelt down, held her hands together in supplication, and said, "I know what you can do, and I want to do that, and then some. So I beg you, please, please, *please* give me the bite of transformation. Please give me eternal life. My life here is boring and empty. Look around you. I live in a gilded cage, beauty all around, but absolutely no freedom. My siblings are horrible . . ."

"No *scheisse*," Maria said.

". . . and I want to be different from them. I want to be like you." She repeated, "Please, please, *please* give me the bite of transformation," after which she closed her eyes and bowed her head.

Having never been *asked* to suck somebody's hemoglobin—she had always been the decision-maker in the blood-sucking arena—Maria was more than a little taken aback. Her initial inclination was to pick Liesl up by her hair, twirl her around several times, and throw her into the lake, but Mother Zombie would probably catch wind of that, and Maria knew that there was no way she would be invited back into the Abbey if she had a random murder on her hands. *But a transformation,* she thought, *is in my nature. A Vampire gets hungry, and can't help but chew on the neck of a lovely young woman. I most certainly won't be punished for that.*

Maria leaned over and cupped Liesl's chin, then gently lifted her face until their eyes met. "Are you sure this is what you want, child?"

Liesl whispered, "Yes. I want to live in the night. I want to feed on the innocent. And I want one of those cat suits."

"We'll see about the cat suit. But as for the rest of it, well, lay down."

Liesl flopped onto her back. "Like this, Fraulein?"

Maria lay down beside her. "Yes, my dear. Just like that." And then she rolled onto her side, grabbed Liesl's face, turned her neck sharply in the opposite direction, and sank her four front fangs into the girl's sweet, sweet neck. As Maria sucked the luscious blood from Liesl's jugular, the eldest von Trapp child's body stiffened and paled. Maria began panting through her nose, and her nipples hardened. She released Liesl's neck, screamed at the sky in ecstasy. She then bit her own wrist until a strong stream of blue blood oozed from the wound, then opened Liesl's mouth and let the viscous liquid spurt onto the girl's tongue. With each drop, Liesl became more animated; after two-or-so minutes of feasting, Liesl sat straight up, her face landing in between Maria's breasts.

She buried her face in the Governess's chest, took a deep inhale, then released a shuddery breath. "*Mein Gott,* Maria," she moaned, "that was . . . that was . . . that was . . ."

Maria nodded. "I know, darling. I know *exactly* what that was." Again, she took the child by the chin and kissed her on the mouth. Liesl's new fangs clacked against Maria's ancient ones, their tongues intertwined, and their saliva mixed into a tasty stew. Maria then grabbed Liesl's hands and pinned her wrists over her head. After she ended the kiss, she asked, "Did you like that, Miss von Trapp?"

Liesl nodded eagerly.

"Do you want more?"

Another eager nod.

"Then more you shall have."

For the next forty-nine minutes, more she did get.

When the two Vampires returned to the dining room, Maria unfroze the children. If anybody noticed Liesl's newly acquired pale complexion, they kept their mouth shut about it.

Which Maria believed was best for everybody. At least for the time being.

# INTERLUDE #1

**D**RACULA PEERED AROUND *his living room, a disappointed look plastered on his pale mug. "I see three. There should be four. Where's Big B.?"*

*The short, felt-faced man with the black cape gazed at his friends, and counted, "One, two, three! I count three people!" He paused, then added, "I love to count things."*

*A handsome young man who bore a striking resemblance to the English thespian Robert Pattinson said, "We know, mate. You've mentioned that at every book club meeting we've had since 2002." He then turned to Dracula and asked, "You didn't hear?"*

*"Hear what?"*

*"The Blademeister's being investigated for tax evasion."*

*"If he didn't buy so many damn pairs of sunglasses, he'd have enough money for Uncle Sam," said a cartoony man with a brown cape.*

*"Look who's talking," Dracula said. "If you didn't buy so many damn boxes of cereal, you'd be able to get your car fixed, and I*

*wouldn't have to cart you all over the damn city. This is the kind of crap that makes book club a chore. I have to buy all the munchies, then pick you up, then lead the discussion, then drive you home, then come back here and clean up everybody's mess. And you guys don't even read the damn books."*

*Handsome Boy said, "Hey, I've read every single book, bloke."*

*"I've read two," said Felt Face. "One, two. Two books."*

*Dracula asked, "Did any of you chumps read this one?"*

*Brown Cape picked up the paperback, scanned the title, and said, "Who are the von Trapp Family Vampires?"*

*"I guess that's a no," Dracula sighed.*

*"I read it," Handsome Boy said.*

*"One," Felt Face said. "I count one brown-noser."*

*Holding up his hands, Dracula said, "Okay, for those of you who didn't read the damn thing, here's the deal." Dracula gave his fellow Vampires a synopsis of the first two chapters of* My Favorite Fangs, *then said, "At that point, I was on the fence. This melding of Vampire mythos, Broadway musical cheese, and gross-out humor is . . . I don't know, it's clever I guess, but I feel like the author could have come up with his own story."*

*"Drac, those first two chapters are insanely original," Handsome Boy said. "It's not like he took some public domain novel then slapped in a bunch of paranormal entities and called it a day. He clearly thought it through. Zombie nuns? Cat suits and Coltrane? That stuff is bloody genius, if you ask me. In my mind, he's giving that Bram Stoker a run for his money."*

*Dracula bared his fangs and growled, "No dissing Stoker, haircut."*

Handsome Boy held up his hands and said, "No diss, no diss. Just saying that based on two chapters, this is a solid book."

"It sounds like it has potential," Brown Cape said, pulling a handful of brown cereal from his brown pocket. "Maybe I'll actually give it a peek."

Sighing, Dracula said, "Dude, you say that every week, and every week, nothing. Okay, screw it, I'll just give you idiots the Cliff's Notes version. So it's the next evening, and Liesl's a Vampire, and the Captain's hungover . . ."

# CHAPTER 3

THE SHARP KNOCK at the front door roused the Captain from on the sofa. "*Alfred*," he called, pulling himself up to standing, "*door! Now!*"

"Yes, sir."

Snottily, Friedrich called from the back of the living room, "That's right, Alfred! Get the door. Immediately!"

The butler said, "That's enough from you, Master Friedrich. I can make one phone call and have the Joker, the Penguin, and King Tut on you like brown on schnitzel."

Captain von Trapp grinned, said, "Ah, banter. Good one, Alfred," and then plopped down onto his hindquarters.

"Quite," Alfred said, then opened the door and sneered at the teenage boy on the stoop. "Ah. Rolfe. Good evening. Wonderful to see you. As always." His voice dripped with disdain.

With his perfectly coiffed blond hair, his piercing blue eyes, and his strapping body, Rolfe was the Aryan ideal, a perfect candidate to join the Master Race. Alfred despised him. The

Captain tolerated him. All the children found him to be a nuisance . . . except for Liesl, who wanted to do things to him.

"Good evening, Alfred. Wonderful to see you, too. As always." When Rolfe spoke, he tended to jut out his chin and clench his teeth together, which made him sound like a German version of Jay Gatsby, so much so that one expected him to end every other sentence with "old boy." He continued, "Everything is copacetic, yes?"

Alfred screwed up his face. "Copacetic?"

"Yes, copacetic, old boy." (There it is! He said it! Told you so!)

"What's supposed to be copacetic?"

Rolfe looked nervously over his right shoulder, and then his left. "The *thing*," he said.

Alfred knew full well what *the thing* was, but what with having to deal with yesterday's vomitous mess in the ballroom, he felt like messing with Rolfe's head. "I have no clue what you're talking about, young man."

Rolfe sighed. "The *thing*, Alfred, the *thing*." He pointed at his pocket. "*This* thing."

Affecting a disgusted expression, Alfred said, "Young man, I'll respectfully ask you to stop pointing at . . . your *thing*."

Rolfe's pale cheeks reddened. "I'm not pointing at *my* thing. I'm pointing at *the* thing. Is the Captain available?"

"Maybe."

"Is he, er, lucid?"

"Doubtfully."

"May I come in?"

"Absolutely . . ."

"Thank you."

". . . not."

Somewhat of a thin-skinned nancy-boy, Rolfe appeared as if he were about to cry. He reached into his pocket and said, "Can you at least give him the thing?"

"I'm not touching your thing, Rolfe."

Rolfe stomped his foot like a little girl—as thin-skinned nancy-boys are wont to do—and said, "Not *my* thing." He showed Alfred a telegram. "*This* thing. Tell him it's about *the* thing."

Alfred took the paper and said, "Very good, young man. Good night." Then he slammed the door in Rolfe's face, squashing both his Aryan nose and his tender feelings.

As any self-respecting nancy-boy would do, Rolfe screamed like a little girl.

Alfred walked over to the sofa and showed Captain von Trapp the paper. "This came for you, sir."

"What is it?"

"Look for yourself, sir." He dropped it on the Captain's lap. As the Captain peered at the communiqué, Alfred caught Maria's eye, then mimed he was drinking, then squinched up his face in an approximation of drunken buffoonery.

Maria winked at the butler, then ran her tongue over her lips, then blew him a kiss. Alfred hustled out of the room as if he had seen a ghost.

Liesl ran after the old man; when she caught up with him, she tapped him rudely on the shoulder and asked, "Alfred, who delivered the telegram?"

"The blond nancy-boy."

"You mean Rolfe?"

"Do you know any other blond nancy-boys who deliver telegrams, Mistress Liesl?"

Liesl said, "Do shut up, Alfred," then stomped back to the living room.

By the time she returned, the Captain was just finished up reading the note. He called, "Brats, fall in!" After the brood converged in a straight line, the Captain said, "Tomorrow morning, I will be leaving for Vienna. On a, um, business trip."

All at once, the children broke into heartfelt applause.

Gretl said, "How long will you be gone, Father? I ask because at this time of year, the weather in Vienna can change at the drop of a hat. You see, the fluctuating temperature leads to an unstable barometric environment, which makes the atmosphere ripe for a weather event of some sort . . ."

Louisa butted in: "Do shut up, Gretl." She then asked her father, "Be honest with us for a change. These are not business trips, are they? You're going to see the Baroness."

"Okay, fine, yes, Louisa, I'm going to see the Baroness, you've found me out, you're so smart, blah blah blah, whatever." He mopped his brow, then mumbled, "Brat."

"I heard that," Louisa said.

Farta asked, "Why doesn't the Baroness come visit us? It'd be nice to meet the woman who'll be replacing our dead, dead mother."

"She won't be replacing . . ."

Kurt said, "Father won't bring her here because your ugly face would make her puke all over the ballroom."

Maria put a hand to her stomach and said, "Please, can we not talk about puking in the ballroom?"

Ignoring the Governess, von Trapp said, "Shut it, Kurt. Okay, fine, I'm so confident that Farta's ugly face will not cause the Baroness gastrointestinal distress that I'll bring her home tomorrow." He paused. "And speaking of gastrointestinal distress, I think Uncle Max will be joining us."

Friedrich roared, *"Scheisse,"* then ran into the kitchen, grabbed a plate, and threw it at his father's head. Kurt followed suit . . . and then Louisa . . . and then Farta . . . and then whichever of those bratty von Trapp kids were left. Shards of plate were everywhere, and all the Captain could do was keep ducking and wait it out.

In the ensuing commotion, Liesl slipped out the back door and headed to her favorite place in all of the world, the gazebo.

Those who knew the von Trapp family always wondered why Georg's children were so ill-behaved. Sure, one could point a finger at the drunk Father and the dead Mother. And sure, one could point a finger at the sense of entitlement that seemed so inborn to the offspring of the wealthy. But if one got a look at the entirety of the von Trapp's property, one might tell the kids to get over it, because millions of children all over the world had it far, far worse.

The garden, for instance, was a marvel: Trees that reached the sky; a contemporary-looking, glass-walled, well-lit gazebo;

and the most lustrous flowers in all of Austria. (The secret to the flowers' beauty? The garden was Kurt's favorite place to urinate.)

Before reaching the gazebo, Liesl decided to practice her human-to-bat transformation. She came to a stop under a big tree, then, after making certain she was unobserved, took a deep breath, closed her eyes, held her nose, and puffed up her cheeks as if she were trying to pop her ears.

Nothing.

She then bent forward and did a headstand, and recited the "Hail Mary" backwards.

Nothing.

She then did twenty push-ups . . . and they were "boy" push-ups, mind you.

Nothing.

She then rolled over on her back and let loose with a word-less scream.

And there it was.

As her female form morphed into that of an androgynous bat's, Liesl's human roar morphed into a rodent squeak, and next thing she knew, she was a hundred meters above the ground, flying as if she had been doing so her entire life. She spread her wings as far as she could, and executed a perfect barrel roll, and then another, and then another. The speed of her twirls dou-bled, trebled, and quadrupled until she was all but invisible against the black nighttime tableau.

As she floated down toward the gazebo, she heard a rustle in the bushes, so, wanting to avoid detection, she touched down near a tree, and turned herself human again, a simple and speedy, yet disgusting process that's far too vile to be described here. Suffice it to say it involves guano.

Once rehumanized, Liesl peeked out from behind the tree, hoping to catch a glimpse of whoever it was that had the temerity to trespass upon the von Trapp property this late at night. *Maybe this could be my first kill,* she thought.

She heard another rustle, then a crash, then a vaguely effeminate voice whisper, "Watch where you're going, old boy. You're going to kill yourself."

Liesl called, "Rolfe?"

"Liesl? Is that you?"

She revealed herself. "It's me, Rolfe. I was hoping you would be here."

"And I just knew you would be here. I just *knew* it. I've been dreaming about your touch for days."

Liesl threw her arms around Rolfe's neck and breathed, "Then touch me, you hot piece of Aryan beef. Touch me where you have always wanted to touch me. Touch me where you have never touched me before."

They kissed, but after a few seconds, Rolfe pulled away. "You feel different," he said. "You . . . you . . . you *taste* different."

"Do I taste good?"

"I suppose."

"And you like tasting me?"

"I suppose."

"And you came here to taste me."

"I suppose."

"If you were to send me a telegram saying how much you want to taste me, what would it say?"

Rolfe pulled himself from Liesl's embrace. "Hmm. That's putting me on the spot. Wow. Um. I have no idea where to even begin."

"You can begin by telling me how beautiful I am, dunderhead."

"Right. Okay. Dear Liesl. Stop. You're beautiful. Stop." And then he stopped.

She stared at the nervous young man. "And that's the best you can do?"

"Um, I guess not."

"Good. Tell me what you think my most attractive feature is."

"Okay. Starting again from the top. Dear Liesl. Stop. You're beautiful. Stop. Especially your eyes. Stop. They're especially beautiful. Stop."

"That's a little bit better. What do you think about my mouth?"

"It's the most kissable mouth in all of Austria. Stop."

"And my ears?"

"They're the prettiest little ears I've ever seen. Stop."

"And my breasts?"

Rolfe gulped. "I have not seen your breasts, Liesl. You know that."

"Do you want to?" she purred.

Again, he gulped. "Of course."

Liesl took Rolfe's hand and pulled him toward the gazebo. "I want you to see me in the light," she said.

All Rolfe could do was gurgle.

After they stepped into the glass enclosure, Liesl gave Rolfe a strong shove—Rolfe seemed surprised at just how strong it was—and he tumbled onto the bench. She said, "Don't take your eyes off of me."

All Rolfe could do was gurgle.

She undid one button of her sailor suit, then the next, then the next, and so on, until it slid off of her body and she was only covered by her bra and panties. She stepped toward Rolfe and said, "Go ahead. Touch me. Wherever you want."

He said, "Anywhere?"

Liesl removed her bra. "Anywhere." (It must be noted here that in Austria, in the last revolting days of the thirties, it was legal for sixteen-year-olds who were going on seventeen to engage in sexual congress. Not only was it legal—it was encouraged.) Rolfe stood up, put his arms around her waist, then buried his face in her neck. She said, "I'm surprised you didn't go for my breasts, but this is still a good start."

Rolfe said something that she couldn't understand, then he began licking her neck. His tongue was thick and strong, and she couldn't help but grab his throbbing man-part. After she gave it a less-than-gentle tug, he pulled away from her and asked, "What's that?"

Exasperated, Liesl said, "That's me squeezing you where I thought you might want to be squeezed, dunderhead."

"No. What's that on your neck?"

She touched the spot where Maria had given her the transformative Vampire kiss. "What, this? It's nothing. Probably some acne."

Rolfe nodded, then grabbed her by the waist, jerked her body into his, and sniffed the tiny red mark. "That isn't some acne, Liesl." He pushed her away. "Do me a favor. Smile."

Liesl blinked. "Smile? Okay, if you insist." She turned up the corners of her mouth in the approximation of a grin, careful not to reveal her fangs.

With a never-before-heard sense of manliness in his voice, Rolfe said, "Show me your teeth, Liesl." His eyes thinned, his erection softened, and his voice dropped to a menacing whisper. "Show me your teeth *now*."

In an attempt to distract him she said, "Did you know that in Austria, it's legal for a sixteen-year-old to fornicate? Being that I'm sixteen going on seventeen, I'm legal. If we get caught making love, we wouldn't be in serious trouble; for that matter, we would be celebrated, so we don't have to wait. I want you to . . . to . . . to write on my page with your pearl ink, because I'm on the brink, Rolfe, the *brink,* and *I* know that *you* know what I mean by *on the brink*. Despite what you or others may think, I'm *not* unprepared to face a world of men. Some would have you believe that I'm as innocent as a rose, but that's far from the truth. I know things about bachelor dandies and drinkers of brandies that you wouldn't believe. Some might say that I need somebody older and wiser, but trust me, Rolfe, I'm as wise as any of you. So I say bring on the eager young cads!

Bring on the roués and the cads! I'm canny, and I'm wise . . . and I know how to make you feel *good*. Really, really good." She peeked at his crotch to see if she had gotten through to him.

Nothing.

He fixed her with an impassive stare, then whispered, "When did you become a Vampire, Liesl?"

Liesl made a split-second decision: She would play dumb. "Whaaaat? A *Vampire*? Me? That's crazy talk, Rolfe. I mean, gosh, I barely even know what a Vampire is. As a matter of fact, I have *no idea* what a Vampire is! Is it some sort of elected official? Or a servant? Or, well, I don't have a clue, boy oh boy, I'm lost, Rolfe, just lost."

Rolfe repeated, "When did you become a Vampire?" He touched the spot on her neck. "I know the Vampire kiss. I know the Vampire scent." He stepped to her and tried to pry open her lips, then added, "I know the Vampire teeth."

She slapped his hand away. "Is that so, Rolfe? How do you know all this?"

He tore off his shirt—buttons flew everywhere—pointed at the swastika tattooed above his left nipple, and roared, "Private Rolfe Mueller, Nazi Undeath Squad!" He puffed up his chest, and sucked in his stomach; suddenly the nancy-boy telegram deliveryman was a force to be reckoned with. He took a deep breath, then roared, "Liesl von Trapp, I condemn you to, er, no, I *welcome* you in the name of Adolf Hitler." He held out his hand. "Please come with me. You'll be taken to an area where you can mingle with others of your kind, and you have my personal guarantee that you'll be safe there."

"The only others of my kind I want to mingle with are my family. Now let's put on our clothes and go on our respective ways."

"I don't think you understand, Fraulein von Trapp. This isn't a request. This is a command. I'm prepared to do what needs to be done to get you to Germany."

Liesl looked around the gazebo for some kind of weapon; seeing nothing, she backed toward the exit. "This is craziness, Rolfe. Go home. Now."

He leapt around her with blinding speed and blocked the door, then yelled, "Don't take another step, Fraulein! If you do, I won't hesitate to use force!"

Liesl von Trapp felt a surge of something in her stomach—maybe bile, maybe adrenaline, maybe the remnants of the horrible *tafelspitz* from last night—and her body began to move of its own accord. She spun on her heel and swiped at Rolfe's face, and he leaned away, but not quickly enough; the scratches immediately dripped blood, covering his cheek and chin. As Rolfe screamed, Liesl did a drop roll into his legs, hoping Rolfe would fall onto his face, and then she could make herself scarce. Rolfe seemed to know what was coming, however; he leapt straight into the air, causing Liesl to roll out of the gazebo and onto the cold ground. Mud caked her naked breasts, her bare stomach, and her strong thighs.

With a deadly calm, Rolfe said, "I've trained with the Undeath Squads for two years, Liesl, and I'm one of their finest students. You can't escape. I can tell you're a new Vampire, and you don't have the strength to win a battle with *anybody* from the Squads. For both of our sakes, come with me. As I said, I promise your safety."

She sat up, pulled a clump of mud from her hair, and said, "Maybe you're right, Rolfe. Maybe I should be with others of my kind. I could learn the ways of the undead. I could be happy."

Rolfe smiled. "That's the spirit, Liesl."

"I suppose it is." She held out both of her arms. "Can you help me up, please? I hurt my leg."

"Of course, Liesl." He took her hands in his, and pulled her to her feet.

"Thank you, Rolfe."

"But of course. Now if you'll . . ."

He didn't finish the sentence, but you probably wouldn't have been able to do so either if an angry, spurned female Vampire kicked you in the stomach with all her might. While Rolfe was doubled over, Liesl zipped over to the gazebo and punched its side. The structure shattered, and glass flew everywhere. She picked up the biggest shard she could find and held it by Rolfe's neck. "I don't want to kill you, Rolfe," she said, "but I will. If you leave, you'll leave unharmed, but if you stay, you'll die. I have not yet killed, but I know I can."

Through gritted teeth, he said, "I think not." And then, he stood up as if he had never been injured in the first place, knocked the glass out of Liesl's hand, and put her in a headlock.

Without thinking, Liesl roared, "*I have confidence in me!*" then stomped Rolfe's foot as hard as she could, which, now that she had otherworldly Vampire strength, was pretty darn hard.

Rolfe growled, then lost his grip on Liesl's neck. She grabbed another piece of glass off of the ground and raked it along Rolfe's bare chest—right through his odd tattoo—somehow managing to restrain herself from licking up every last drop of the Nazi's sweet, sweet blood. He staggered backward and crashed headfirst into a tree, then emitted a tiny grunt and fell facedown, unconscious.

Liesl sat down on the edge of the gazebo, not even feeling the broken glass digging into her backside. She gulped and panted, her naked, mud-coated breasts heaving rhythmically. As she stared sadly at Rolfe's unmoving body, she whispered, "That's right, Rolfe, I have confidence in me."

And then the rains came.

Precipitation was problematic for Liesl, as it was difficult for a new Vampire to pick tiny shards of glass from her backside in the midst of a downpour. For Maria, on the other hand, the hellacious rain was exactly what she needed, as it offered a taste of home. The constant lightning flashes, the deafening booms of thunder, and the roaring winds made the pristine von Trapp mansion feel sinister, and after centuries of living in the Abbey, sinister was just the way she liked it.

Maria's new bedroom was well-lit and spacious, which, for somebody who spent the majority of her nights nestled safely in a coffin, was disconcerting. She wanted to smash the overhead lights and paint the windows black so the room would be eternally bathed in darkness, but suspected that if she purposefully destroyed the von Trapp's property, Mother Zombie would never let her return to the Abbey. So she dealt with it.

Just like that, the past two days caught up with her, and all she wanted to do was crawl into her horribly soft bed with its disgustingly clean sheets, and fall asleep to the sound of the wonderful storm. Right after she pushed aside the hideous green-and-yellow striped curtains, opened the window, and stripped off her cat suit, there was a knock at the door. It took all of her restraint not to tell the door-knocker to take a flying leap off of the Lavant Viaduct; instead, she took a deep breath, closed her eyes, went to her happy place, then said, "Come in."

It was Frau Alice. Logically enough, Maria said, "Frau Alice."

If the housekeeper was taken aback by Maria's lack of clothing, she did a magnificent job of hiding it. Alice dropped an armful of material onto the floor, then said, "The Captain told me to tell you to make yourself some new dresses."

Maria stared at the material. There were dozens of designs and colors to choose from: Reds, blues, yellows, greens, stripes, dots, plaids, paisleys, the works. The fabric was clearly the finest money could buy, soft and shimmering. And Maria despised every square centimeter of it. "I'd gladly do so, but I can't sew," she told Alice.

"The Captain figured that would be the case, so he told me to tell you, Tough *scheisse.*"

"Oh, Frau Alice, I love you most of all!" In order to keep the peace, Maria took the material and said, "These will make the prettiest clothes I've ever had! They'll make me feel pretty. Pretty, and witty, and gay. And you know what, Frau Alice? Do you know what? I pity any girl who isn't me today."

From outside came a scream of, "*Wrong musical, whore!*"

Frau Alice blinked. "Did you hear something?"

Maria shook her head. "Nope." She walked to the other side of the room and shut the window. "So tell me," she said, "might the Captain get me some more material if I asked him?"

"How many outfits do you really need?" Frau Alice asked.

"Okay, let's be honest here: There's no way in *Hölle* that I'm letting that fabric near my body. It's lovely to the touch, and appealing to the eye, and I want nothing to do with it. No, it isn't for me. It's for the kids."

The housekeeper squinched up her face. "But the kids have plenty of clothes. Sailor suits in every color you can imagine. According to the Captain, that's what they've worn every day of their lives, that's what they're currently wearing every day of their lives, and that's what they'll wear every day for the rest of their lives."

"That's fantastic, Frau," Maria said, "but do you agree with me that the suits are a bit . . . a bit . . . a bit . . . oh, dear me, how do I put this?"

Frau Alice said, "Might the word you're searching for be *gay*?"

Maria said, "That *might* be the word. But I want it to be known that I don't mean gay in a homosexual sense. You see, Frau, the last thing I want to do is upset the gay community. I embrace homosexuality in all forms, shapes, and sizes—I've dabbled in the world of Sappho many a time myself—and I mean no offense. It's just that gay is the *perfect* word to describe those fruity little sailor suits." She paused, looked away from Frau Alice and into an imaginary film camera, then added, "And I mean no offense with the word *fruit*, either."

Frau Alice said, "What's homo . . . homo . . . homo . . ."

"Homosexuality?" Maria finished.

"Yes. Homosexuality."

Maria sat on her bed, unconsciously spread her bare legs apart a couple of millimeters, and said, "Well, Frau Alice, when a girl and a girl love each other very, very much, there are certain ways they can express their love on a physical level. Soon enough, physiological changes occur that can lead to what's known as *arousal* . . ."

"You can stop right there, Maria. I have no idea what you're going on about. In my world, the only thing *gay* means is *colorful*. The children's sailor suits are *colorful*. That's all I'm saying. No more, no less."

"Oh," Maria said. "That's unfortunate."

"What is?"

She spread her legs a bit further apart. "I thought you might want to learn about Sappho."

Frau Alice was silent.

"All right, then," Maria said, "give me the material. I'll try to make some play clothes for them. They could do with a bit of fun."

Frau Alice walked across the room and opened the window. "It suddenly smells odd in here," she said, fanning the air in front of her face. "Like day-old fish."

Maria slammed her thighs shut, then took the top sheet

from the bed and wrapped it around her waist. "I know not of what you're talking about."

The housekeeper said, "In any event, the von Trapp children don't have fun. They hatch and scheme."

"Hatch and scheme what?" Maria asked.

"*Plans,*" Frau Alice hissed. "Evil plans. Evil plans that involve destruction and pain. Evil plans that would land most in jail. Evil plans that end up with me cleaning up indescribable messes. Evil plans that have me wondering, *Why are Friedrich's bed sheets always stiff and crusty*?"

"Can you offer me any specifics?"

"I shudder to discuss it, Maria." And then, as if to prove her point, she shuddered. "You'll find out soon enough. My only piece of advice would be, *When you least expect it, expect it.* On that note, good night."

Before Frau Alice made it to the door, Maria called, "Don't forget to ask the Captain for more material!"

"Oh. Right. Replacing the kids' gay sailor suits."

To the invisible camera, Maria said, "Remember, folks, that's *gay* as in *colorful.*"

The housekeeper stopped, then said, "I should mention that the Captain is departing for Vienna tomorrow morning to see his *fick* buddy, Baroness Schrader."

"How long will he be gone?"

"Depends. The last time he visited the Baroness, he disappeared for three days."

"Disappeared?"

"Disappeared. He was found under a bridge, naked, drooling, reeking of juniper berries, and playing with six kittens."

"Oh."

"Right. Oh." Frau Alice paused, then said, "The Captain is thinking about making the Baroness an honest woman."

"Oh, that would be lovely. The kids will have a new female figure to look up to." *And they won't need me, and I can go back to the Abbey.*

"I don't know how wonderful that would be. There's something off about the Baroness. Something I can't put my finger on." Frau Alice gave Maria a long once-over. "You know what? You two have something in common."

"What's that?"

Frau Alice shook her head. "Again, it's something I can't put my finger on. Just . . . *something.*"

"On that note, goodnight, Alice."

"Good night, Governess. And please remember: Mom always said, don't play ball in the house."

After the housekeeper took her leave, Maria knelt down, made the sign of the inverted cross, and began to pray:

"Dear Lucifer, now I know why you have sent me here: To help these children prepare themselves for a new mother. I know you believe that before things get better, they must get much, much worse, and making things worse is something I'm quite good at, because nobody causes problems like Maria—am I right, or am I right? And I pray that this will become an even more awful family in thy sight. So. Go straight to *Hölle,* Captain. Go straight to *Hölle,* Liesl and Friedrich. Go straight to *Hölle,* Louisa, Brigitta, Farta, and that pretentious know-it-all twerp Gretl. And, oh, I forgot what the other boy is called, the chunky one, but he can go straight to *Hölle,* too."

Just then, Maria heard a commotion at her window. She ignored it.

"Go to *Hölle,* Mother Zombie," she continued, "and Cinnamon, and Brandi, and all the other sluts at the Abbey, and . . ." She felt a harsh tap on the crown of her head.

Maria looked over her shoulder. Soaking wet, covered in mud and scratches, and naked as the day she was born, there stood Liesl. Maria stood up and took the eldest von Trapp daughter into her arms and kissed her gently on the neck, their nude bodies melding together. "So," she said, "it appears that somebody has been out, shall we say, *experimenting.*" She held Liesl at shoulder's distance. "And quite badly, I might add."

With her wrist, Liesl wiped the rainwater from her eyes. "You won't tell Father, will you? It's well past curfew."

"What, tell my new employer that I turned his child into a Vampire, then, on her first full night with her new powers, she wandered the countryside for several hours—probably feasting on several humans and a few animals—before flying into my window wearing nothing but mud and blood? No, I think I'll keep that one quiet. Now let me clean you up."

Maria took the blanket from her bed, stood behind Liesl, and slowly, sensually dried her hair. She then wiped the dirt from the girl's shoulders, stopping to speak into her ear. (Unfortunately, whatever Maria said was indiscernible, but whatever it was, it caused Liesl to blush, then pinch her own nipples.) Maria then wiped down Liesl's breasts; she continued wiping them long after they were clean, and Liesl didn't complain.

And then the girl and the Governess visited the land of Sappho.

Afterward, as the two lay on the floor, spent, Liesl said, apropos of nothing, "Louisa has a collection of spiders in her bedroom. She likes to stash them around the house."

Maria jumped up as if she had been electrocuted. "*Spiders*?! I *despise* spiders. You tell that little blonde twat if I see a one of those eight-legged demons anywhere near me, she'll be blamed, and punished. *Severely.*"

Liesl sat up and rubbed Maria's backside. "Don't worry, baby," she whispered. "None of my idiot siblings will do anything to you on my watch." She rose, grabbed a nightgown from the armoire, covered herself, then said, "Before today, I didn't believe I needed a Governess. Well, I guess I was wrong."

Maria stood up and the two women engaged in a lingering, fang-clattering kiss, then Liesl took her leave. After Liesl gently shut the door, Maria walked over to the bed and tentatively picked up the pillow. No spiders. She then removed the remaining sheets. Still no spiders. She then lifted up the mattress.

Spiders. Lots and lots of spiders.

A hairy Brazilian Purple Tarantula, a slimy Starbellied

Orbweaver, a stringy Northern Black Widow, a bouncy Ant-mimic Jumper, a creepy-crawly Pirate Wolf, and several genera that Maria didn't recognize, which is saying something, because Maria was a member of the Know Thine Enemy school, so was well-versed in everything Arthropod.

Maria covered her mouth to stifle the scream. She backed into the wall, and—without meaning to or wanting to—she turned into a *Desmodus Rotundus.* Unprepared for the transformation, she flew straight up and crashed into the ceiling at a high enough speed that she was momentarily knocked unconscious. When she came to some ten seconds later, she found herself on the mattress, in the center of a spider gang.

The Northern Black Widow attacked first, shooting a web at Maria's right wing. Maria backed away . . . right into the eight arms of the Pirate Wolf. The Wolf was a mean one, but slow and weak, so Maria broke out of his hold and flicked him out of the open window, where he fell to a painful death.

Maria glared at the rest of the spiders, her eyes saying, *Which one of you is next?* Unfortunately, spiders can't read the eyes of a bat, so they all attacked at once. Now that she had her bearings, Maria swatted them with her wings, alternating left and right, left and right. Her aim was impeccable, and soon all the spiders had been knocked through the window.

Except for the Brazilian Purple. The fuzzy, fat, frightening Brazilian Purple.

He crawled toward her, moving slowly. When he was in shooting distance, Maria shot out her wing and waited to hear the telltale splat.

But there was no splat. Because she missed. She spun around, and there he was, directly behind her. Maria thought, *I had no idea Brazilian Purples are so fast.* So, not wanting to prolong the battle, Maria switched back into her human form and squashed the Brazilian Purple with her fist. Game over.

Just then, the sky was broken with the evening's brightest lightning bolt and loudest thunderclap. Maria's door flew open, and in flew Gretl. Maria wiped the spider spew off of her hand, picked the bed sheet from the floor, and covered herself. "Gretl," she said, "are you frightened?"

"Fright is an interesting thing, Maria," Gretl said. "There are countless ways to handle it. You can succumb to it, or you can embrace it, or you can stare it in the eye and say, *Fright, I own you, you don't own me.* And of course there are multiple levels of fright, and they all have different effects on the body, primarily because the level of the fright and the level of adrenal secretion . . ."

Then came an even brighter bolt and an even louder clap, at which Gretl ran into Maria's arms, knocking her onto the bed.

Maria patted her back. "There, there, there, you pretentious little know-it-all. Never you fear. Your level of fright is under your control. You can stay here."

"Thank you, Governess."

"Now answer me this, Gretl: Are your brothers and sisters this skittish? I ask because the last thing I'd expect from any of you brats is fear."

"You're correct to feel that way, Governess. We fear nothing except for inclement weather. Why, you might ask? Well, it's a long story." She took a deep breath and said, "It was June 19, 1937. A Tuesday, I believe. The day started out sunny, but soon after lunch, things began to change for the worse . . ."

"Do shut up, Gretl." And then, more thunder, and more lightning . . . and more von Trapps burst into Maria's bedroom, this time in the form of Louisa, Brigitta, and Farta. Maria mumbled, "Hail, hail, the gang's all here."

From outside came a faint scream of, "Wrong musical, whore!"

Maria yelled back, "*Pirates of Penzance* isn't a musical, it's an opera!" She looked at the other three girls and said, "Get over here."

All the girls huddled onto the bed and buried their faces into various parts of Maria's body. Maria held them tight, and said, "Now, all we have to do is to wait for the boys."

Louisa said, "They'll be here momentarily. Show them rain and they turn into a bunch of bedwetters."

Sure enough, after the next lightning/thunder combo— which, admittedly, was insanely bright and loud, and would cause even the sturdiest bladder to take stock of itself—in came Kurt and Friedrich. Their respective pajama bottoms were soaked, Kurt's from fright, and Friedrich's from . . . other things.

At the sight of Maria's barely covered body, Friedrich gasped. Maria smiled, showing the slightest bit of fang. "Were you scared, boys?" Staring Friedrich dead in the eye, she said, "Or did you want to pay me a visit?"

Kurt said, "Scared."

Friedrich said, "Pay you a visit."

"Get over here, both of you."

While Kurt jumped into the von Trapp pile, Friedrich snatched a pillow from the bed, sat on the floor, covered his crotch with said pillow, and said, "I think I'll stay down here."

Maria whispered, "Are you sure? You can join us up here, if you would like."

"Maybe another time?" he asked hopefully.

"Maybe, Friedrich. Maybe."

Another flash, another boom. Farta whined, "Why does it do that?"

Maria said, "Well, the lightning and the thunder are having a conversation about . . . about . . . about sailor suits!"

Gretl said, "That's one of the most ridiculous things I've ever heard in my life."

Louisa said, "You're only five, Gretl. You haven't heard much."

"Living with you idiots, I've heard more ridiculous things than your average five-year-old. For that matter, living with you idiots, I've heard more ridiculous things than your average *fifty*-five-year-old."

Brigitta cuffed Gretl on the ear and growled, "Can it, shrimp."

Maria held up her hands and said, "All of you, stop it. We're all unhappy, and we're all annoyed, and when anything annoys me and I'm feeling sad, I try and think of nice things."

At once, Louisa and Farta asked, "What kind of things?"

"Nice things. Like daffodils."

Kurt said, "What's so nice about daffodils? Yellow flowers? So what?"

"Alright," Maria said, "how about green meadows?"

Farta said, "I have allergies. Next."

"Um, okay, skies full of stars."

Brigitta said, "What's the point of that, Governess? You can't see the stars right now. Duh."

"Okay, how about raindrops on roses? Or whiskers on kittens?"

Farta said, "Allergic and allergic."

"Wow, tough room. Let me try this: Bright copper kettles!"

"Governess, I'll give you five shillings if you can make bright copper kettles even the tiniest bit interesting," Louisa said. "No, *ten* shillings."

Ignoring her, Maria said, "What about warm woolen mittens?"

Gretl said, "I have horrible circulation in my extremities, and my hands are always cold—they call it Peripheral Vascular Disease, I believe—so I admit to having a healthy appreciation for warm woolen mittens."

Friedrich said, "And I have a healthy appreciation for shoving warm woolen mittens down your throat. *Next.*"

Maria sighed. "Alright, how about brown paper packages?"

"Seriously?" Friedrich said. "Brown paper packages? That's the best you can come up with?"

"You didn't let me finish, Friedrich. Brown paper packages tied up with string!"

Kurt scoffed, "Ohhhh, that's *much* better, Maria. Because *nothing* is more fun than string."

Maria glared at the boy, then said, "How about horses? Do you brats like horses? Every kid likes horses."

After a moment of silence, Farta said, "I like horses."

"I knew it! What about cream-colored ponies? I bet you *love* cream-colored ponies!"

Farta winced. "Oh, no, I was bitten by a cream-colored pony last year."

"I remember that," Kurt said, "That was fan*tas*tic. She bled everywhere."

Maria looked at Kurt. "I have one for you, chubby: Crisp apple strudel. And schnitzel with noodles. All eaten to the sound of doorbells and sleigh bells. I bet that's your idea of heaven!"

Kurt's stomach audibly rumbled. "I'll admit, the food sounds lovely, Maria. But why in *Gott's* name . . ."

At once, Maria and Friedrich mumbled, "There's no *Gott*."

". . . would I want to have dinner with all that . . . that . . . that *incorrigible* doorbell and sleigh bell ringing going on? That's stupid. For that matter, *you're* stupid. And I hate you."

"And I, you." To Friedrich, she purred, "I know something you like."

He adjusted the pillow on his lap. "What's that?" he croaked.

"Girls in white dresses."

Nodding, he admitted, "I do like girls in white dresses. But you know what I like even more?"

"Blue satin sashes?"

"Oh, no, I was going to say breasts. But sashes are okay, I suppose."

"You know what else I like?" Maria asked.

Louisa said, "Something stupid, probably."

"You're right . . . if you think snowflakes are stupid. But I know you don't think snowflakes are stupid, because you know as well as I do that anybody who thinks snowflakes are stupid is stupid . . . especially if you're referring to snowflakes that stay on your nose and eyelashes."

Gretl said, "The human body is thirty-seven degrees Celsius, and water will only stay frozen at a temperature of zero degrees Celsius or below, so it's empirically impossible for snowflakes to *stay* on one's nose and eyelashes. They'll remain in their flake form for three seconds at the most. So in this instance, *stay* is a relative term."

Friedrich said, "You know what would make me feel better, Gretl?"

"No. What?"

"If you got bitten by a dog and stung by a bee. That would be two of my favorite things. That would make me feel considerably less bad. *Considerably.*"

Maria extricated herself from the clutches of the von Trapp brood and said, "Alright, people, you tell me: What makes you feel better?"

Farta said, "Pussy willows!"

Friedrich whispered, "Pussy."

Louisa said, "Christmas!"

Friedrich whispered, "What's the point of Christmas? There's no *Gott.*"

Gretl said, "Bunny rabbits?"

Friedrich whispered, "Dead bunny rabbits."

Kurt said, "Snakes!"

Friedrich said, "Snakes! Now *that* would make *anybody* feel better."

The door flew open, and in came Liesl. "I agree with Friedrich! Pussy!"

Maria made a shushing motion.

Liesl said, "Er, I mean telegrams!"

Kurt asked, "Why telegrams?"

"Because Hammerstein said so," Liesl said.

"Who's Hammerstein?" Farta asked.

Simultaneously, Maria and Liesl said, "No comment."

At that, the children began spitting out more than a few of their theoretical favorite things: Birthday presents, bugs, cats, rats, sneezes, spiders (naturally), and dart guns. After they ran out of steam, Brigitta asked, "None of this made me feel any better, Maria."

"For that matter," Louisa said, "I feel worse."

Staring at a figure loitering in the doorway, Maria said, "Well, blondie, you're about to feel even worse than that."

They all turned to check out who Maria was checking out: The Captain.

Maria threw the kids off of the bed, then grabbed the pillow from Friedrich and used it to cover her breasts. The lump in his pants visible for all to see, Friedrich yelped, then lay on the ground, face down.

Giving him what she believed to be her most seductive look, Maria said, "Hi, Captain. What's a nice guy like you doing in a place like this?"

Gretl said, "He lives here."

At once, everybody in the room roared, *"Do shut up, Gretl!"*

The Captain cleared his throat, belched, and said, "Well, Fraulein Mandarin . . ."

"Maria."

"Right. Maria. Didn't I tell you that bedtime is set in stone in this house?"

"You said a lot of things, Captain. About half of which I understood."

Von Trapp nodded. "I get that a lot," he said. "So what in the name of *Gott* are all of you doing in here?"

Friedrich mumbled, "There's no *Gott.*"

Louisa said, "The storm scared us."

The Captain nodded. "Off to bed, wimps. Leave your Governess alone." As they scurried out, he said to Maria, "Fraulein, you are aware that I'm going on a business trip, yes?"

Friedrich mumbled, "A business trip with your *schvantz.*"

After Maria nodded, von Trapp said, "Good. Do you also recall that one of the edicts of the house is that the children be disciplined early and often?" After she nodded again, he said, "Good. Then I trust before I return, you'll do some disciplining?"

Recalling the lump that jutted from Friedrich's jammies, she said, "Nothing would make me happier." And then, seemingly out of nowhere, she added, "Just in case Alice forgets to mention this, I'd like to make the kids some more clothes, and for that, I need more fabric."

He glared at her. "That fabric was for you. The brats already have plenty of clothes. Thirty sailor suits each, one for every day of the month."

She thought, *You mean one for every gay of the month*. And then she pushed that thought away, because using the word gay to trivialize an inanimate object is rude, and Maria liked to think of herself as a polite Vampire.

"So no more fabric?"

"Correct. No more fabric."

She shook her head sadly. "Captain von Trapp, I'll ask you to leave. You're not one of my favorite things."

"You know what, Moronica?"

"Maria."

"I couldn't care less." And then he turned on his heel and stomped out of the room.

Dejected, Maria tore all the fabric to bits, then ate the remnants. Stomach filled, she trudged to the window, seeking solace from the rain, but, much to her chagrin, the downpour had come to a halt, and the sun was taking its rightful place in the sky. "The light was never this bright at the Abbey," she sighed. "I'll never enjoy such darkness again. I guess there isn't a thing to do but whistle a happy tune."

The bummed-out Vampire waited for the cry of, *Wrong musical, whore,* but it never came. This only increased her bummed-out-ed-ness, so she did what she always did when she was feeling blue: Unsheathed her reliable tenor saxophone.

Was Maria a good saxophonist, one might ask? Considering her Vampire-like powers, one would expect that answer to be a resounding yes, but the fact of the matter was, while she was technically proficient, she lacked the one thing that all saxophonists need to transcend: A soul. Sure, she could let loose with a series of arpeggios that would knock saxophone inventor Adolphe Sax onto his Belgian backside. And sure, she could hold an F-sharp that would send tendrils of smoke from her instrument's bell. But could she play the blues? Absolutely not. Not even when she was feeling blue. Like right at this very moment.

Maria tooted a few etudes to warm up her lips and fangs, and then, from the saxophone bell emerged another saxophone bell, followed by another saxophone, followed by another saxophonist: John Coltrane.

The Vampire dropped her horn and gasped, "Chocolate Thunder! I thought I wouldn't see you again until the epilogue."

"And yet, here I am."

She gulped, then reached out to touch the hem of his suit jacket and huskily whispered, "How about a jam session? First I blow. Then you blow. Then I blow. Then you blow. Then . . ."

Coltrane gave the Vampire an indulgent chuckle. "Oh, Maria, come talk to me when you can handle a diminished cycle."

Sighing, Maria said, "I'm still stuck on my cycle of fifths."

Coltrane nodded. "No surprise. Vampires and musical theory don't get along. But that's neither here nor there. According to the movie's timeline, you have some transformations to do, correct?"

"Movie? Timeline? Transformations?"

"It's time to turn those damn brats into Vampires."

"Oh. Right. Any thoughts on how I might do that?"

"Well, as you're well aware, Vampires don't transform humans if they're asleep, so . . ." And then tapped her saxophone.

Nodding knowingly, Maria took a deep breath, jammed the tenor's mouthpiece in between her lips, and blew a low and loud E-flat that killed the five innocent bluebirds who had been hovering outside the window.

Coltrane winced, said, "That ought to do it," then cocked his ear. "Ah, sure enough, I hear something from the other room. The sound of a boy. The sound of a chunky boy. The sound of a chunky boy awakening. The sound of a chunky boy awakening, then wiping the drool from his face. And the sound of another boy. The sound of a boy who's, as we say in the jazz world, tuning his clarinet."

"That would be Kurt and Friedrich."

"And they need transforming."

"Yes."

"Have you ever transformed young boys before?"

With a small smile, Maria said, "Only in my dreams, Chocolate Thunder. Only in my dreams."

"Well, you should probably know that when you bite a boy's neck, a yellow acidic bile will jet from his nose and burn a hole in his mattress."

"Ooooh," Maria squealed happily.

"And a chunky, odoriferous red discharge will flow from your lady-parts and stain the floor."

"Ooooooooooooh," Maria squealed even more happily, then skipped into the boys' bedroom.

A quarter of an hour later, after Maria had finished feeding, and after the boys had finished bleeding, Friedrich sat up and grimaced, his new fangs growing—and growing sharper—by the second. He touched his front teeth and asked, "Did you just do what I think you did?"

"What do you think I did?"

"I think you turned me into a Vampire."

"And I think you're correct."

He cried a single wordless syllable, then punched a hole in the wall.

Maria blanched. "Oh. My. Did I misread you, Friedrich? I thought this might be something you would enjoy. If that's the case, I apologize." She scratched her head. "The problem here is that, well, I am unable to undo what has been done."

Another wordless syllable. Another hole in the wall.

"Friedrich, I'm so sorry. Say something, please!"

Friedrich's grimace became a grin. "You have nothing to be sorry about, Governess. My screams are joyful! My punching is a celebration! I can now live forever, and feed in the night, and make passionate love to the Vampire of my dreams." He made a motion to touch her breasts. "Right?"

She swatted his hand away and stood up. "Well, Friedrich, now that I think about it, fourteen might be a tad young for me."

"But . . . but . . . but I shall now be fourteen forever!"

Maria said, "Riiiiiight. So. Um. What do you say we touch base on this one in a few decades?"

He pouted. "At least can you give me some hand relief?"

She glanced at the imaginary watch on her wrist. "Goodness, look at the time! We must start the day. What's the best way to awaken your sisters?"

Sullenly, Friedrich said, "Turn them into Vampires, for all I care."

Which is exactly what Maria did.

Later that morning, while Liesl sharpened her front fangs with a fingernail file, and while Friedrich transformed back and forth from bat to human, and while Kurt wandered around the kitchen looking for something to eat, Louisa, Farta, Brigitta, and Gretl lay on the lawn, staring blankly into outer space, the bite marks on their respective necks trickling a thin stream of blood. After a few minutes, their wounds closed, leaving a shilling-sized splotch, and several minutes after that, they each sat up, at once paler and more beautiful than they had ever been.

Maria gave the newly undead foursome a benevolent smile. "Welcome, children. Welcome to my family. You're now in a family that I believe you will find to be more nurturing and fulfilling to you than your own."

They said nothing.

"Now I understand you may be confused," Maria said, "but I'm here to help you. If you have any questions, I'll answer them. If you need some advice, it shall be given. Think of me as your Mother."

With a flat tone, Louisa said, "Our Mother is dead."

Maria nodded. "That she is, Louisa, that she is." She paused, then smiled. "But the good news is that you now have one *dead* mother, and one *undead* mother! Now how about you turn those frowns upside down, and let's go and have some fun."

"I don't like any of this one bit," Farta said, touching the gash on her neck. "I feel dreadful. So cold. So very, very cold."

The bat version of Friedrich touched down directly in front of Farta, then morphed back into the Friedrich version of Friedrich. "You get used to it pretty quickly," he said. "It's . . . *nice*."

Liesl said, "He's right, Farta. Quit complaining. Embrace it. It isn't like our life was so exciting before all this."

Kurt wandered out the front door, munching on a raw steak. "Liesl has a point. What's fun for us? Nothing. Father is a drunk. Frau Alice and Alfred are *arschlochs* . . ."

"Especially Frau Alice," Brigitta said. "Why does she keep calling me Marcia Marcia Marcia?"

". . . and all the shopkeepers in town have guns now," Kurt continued, "so we have no place left to rob or vandalize. Our clothes make us look like fools. And except for Liesl, none of us have any friends, and her only friend is a nancy-boy . . ."

"Rolfe is no longer my friend," Liesl said, looking in the direction of the destroyed gazebo.

". . . so we should make the most of it," Kurt continued. "Maria will show us what to do. Right?"

Maria beamed. "That's right, Kurt. I love you most of all! Now children, all of you gather 'round! We're going to show off your new state of being to the world! We shall frolic about the town! How does that sound?"

Liesl said, "Frolicking? *Frolicking?* That sounds simply horrible."

"I knew you would all love it, I just *knew* it!" Maria said. After she picked up her saxophone case, she said, "Follow me," then skipped toward the front gate.

None of the children moved a muscle. After ten skip-steps, Maria came to a screeching halt. "Are you coming, brats?" she asked.

Brigitta said, "That depends on where we're going."

"We're going out and about! Hither and yon! Here and there! And we're going to sing!"

Friedrich winced. "Ugh. Why?"

"Because," Maria explained, "singing soothes the soul."

Gretl raised her hand. "Governess?"

Maria rolled her eyes and thought, *Here we go again.* "Yes, Gretl?"

"I might be mistaken about this—and correct me if I'm wrong—but I believe that Vampires have no souls to soothe."

*Why did I make her undead when I could have killed her outright?* Maria wondered, then took a deep breath, went to her happy place, and said, "We can do things other than sing."

"Like what?" Kurt asked.

"Well, er, frolic."

"You mentioned frolicking," Louisa said, "and nobody was impressed."

Friedrich grinned, his fangs shining in the morning sun. "I think we should test out our new Vampire powers. We might need them someday."

"That's foreshadowing if I've ever heard it," Gretl mumbled. The tiny turd was ignored.

Maria said, "Okay, brats, you win. No singing. Just Vampire exercises."

Gretl clapped her hands. "Oh, goody! That's the best news I've ever . . ."

Before she could finish her sentence, Liesl shoved her to the ground and said, "Shut it, sunshine." To Maria, she said, "So which way do we go?"

"This way," Maria said, skipping speedily, her saxophone case banging against her legs. The children followed. None of them skipped. Eventually they ended up in the Salzburg business district, a bustling area filled with newfangled automobiles, horse-drawn carriages, and mortals who looked mighty tasty to the von Trapp Vampire brood.

Gazing hungrily at the masses, Louisa asked Maria, "Can we feast?"

Maria looked aghast. "Heavens no, Louisa. The repercussions of daytime mangling—especially in the middle of the busiest section in town—would be unspeakable . . ."

Liesl whispered under her breath, "The Nazi Undeath Squads might get us."

". . . so if you're hungry, we must eat human food."

Rubbing his jiggly belly, Kurt said, "Works for me."

Maria skipped and the children trudged to an outdoor market, where the town's farmers were hawking their wares. Maria nodded a greeting to one of the farmers, then snatched up three tomatoes from his wooden baskets. "Watch me, children," she said, then juggled the tomatoes . . . for six seconds . . . before she dropped them and they splattered all over the streets.

The farmer glared at Maria. "Are you planning to pay for those, Skippy?"

Maria pointed at her cat suit. "I'm afraid this outfit doesn't have any pockets in which to house coins. And I have not yet received my first paycheck, so I don't have any coins to put in there anyhow. Can I come back tomorrow and reimburse you?"

Sneering, the farmer said, "I'm not letting you out of my sight until you pay for those vegetables." He held out his hand, palm up. "Two shillings, please."

Maria said, "I don't have it."

"Then get it. I've got a family to feed." Maria thought she heard him say, *Whore*, but that might have been her ears playing tricks on her.

"If you don't behave yourself," Maria hissed, "I'll do some feeding myself." And then she showed the farmer her fangs. The farmer backed up a few steps, knocking over baskets of tomatoes, zucchini, eggplant, and strawberries. Maria said to the farmer, "So are we good here?"

Nodding eagerly, the farmer said, "We're wonderful here." He picked up a tomato. "Take this as a token of my apology."

Maria beamed. "Why thank you, sir! What a lovely gesture." She handed the tomato to Louisa. "If I'm not mistaken, you mentioned that you were hungry, darling?"

"Not for this," Louisa said, before hurling the tomato into the farmer's face.

Breathing heavily, the farmer reached into the waistband of his pants and pulled out a gun. "Get out of my sight, all of you," he whispered.

Maria laughed. "We'll get out of your sight, sir, because we're a polite group, but for future reference, guns basically have no effect on our kind." Again, she bared her teeth and hissed, then added, "You have a lovely day!"

As the clan walked away, Gretl turned around and growled at the farmer. For the first time in his life, Friedrich simultaneously put his arm around his little sister and smiled.

Once they were away from the masses, Maria said, "Please, children, please can we please skip? It would mean ever so much to me!"

Friedrich turned to his siblings and said, "For the love of *Gott*, let's skip just so she'll shut up about it already."

With the biggest (and falsest) of smiles, the kids joined hands and skipped, and skipped, and skipped until Farta screeched to a halt and said, "Does anybody else hear music, or is it just me?"

The brats all stopped skipping, after which Kurt asked, "What kind of music?"

Farta closed her eyes. "Horns, and strings, and drums. It's jaunty, almost happy. Perfect for a montage. And frankly, it's painful. It hurts my soul."

Gretl said, "You have no soul."

"Forget the awful montage music," Maria said, "for there's more skipping to be done!" She pointed to the north. "Look, brats, a flatbed truck! Let's jump on and let it take us where it will!"

The children groaned. "Can we go home?" Brigitta whined. "If we can't dine on human flesh, what's the point of being out?"

Friedrich said, "Vampire exercises, remember?"

"We can do Vampire exercises in our yard," Brigitta said. "The smell of flesh out here is dizzying, and if I can't indulge, I'll explode."

Maria said, "The truck will drive us away from these people. Skip with me!"

Sure enough, the truck did take them away from these people. After they jumped off of the moving vehicle, Maria and the brats skipped to a grassy meadow at the foot of Maria's favorite stomping (and singing) (and skipping) (and flying) (and self-pleasuring) grounds, the Alps. Once they found what Maria called, ". . . the grass I love most of all," she plopped down onto the grass and directed the kids through a series of acrobatics and feats of strength.

"Friedrich," she called, "bend over and stand on one finger!" He did. For five minutes.

"Gretl," she called, "jump as high as you can!" She did. To the tune of fifteen meters.

"Brigitta," she called, "scream at the top of your lungs!" She did. Five kilometers away, a window shattered.

"Kurt," she called, "rip that tree up from the ground!" He did. Without even breaking a sweat.

"Louisa," she called, "do ten cartwheels, one right after the other!" She did. And another ten after that.

"Farta," she called, "turn into a bat and fly to the sun." She did. She didn't, however, hit the sun . . . but she came darn close.

"Liesl," she called, "come to me!"

Liesl jogged over. "Yes, Governess?"

"Liesl, I want you to lick your own lady-parts."

"Pardon me?"

"Lick your lady-parts. Since you can now do it, I'd recommend doing it every chance you get. Once you figure out what's going on down there, you'll thank me. Profusely."

"If you say so," Liesl said, then, after making sure none of her siblings were paying attention—they were not—she lifted the hem of her sailor skirt, pushed aside her panties, then contorted herself so her tongue was directly in front of her hallowed ground. After a tentative lick, she coughed, taken aback by the metallic taste. But a few seconds later, she got used to it, and a few seconds after that, she grew to like it, and a few seconds after that, she knew Maria was right. Someday, she would thank the Governess. Profusely.

Just when it was getting hot and heavy down South, Louisa cartwheeled over and said, "Fraulein Maria?"

Maria, who was sitting on the grass and fondling her own lady-parts, tore her gaze away from Liesl and said, "Hmmmm?"

Noticing the guilty looks on both Liesl and Maria's faces, she asked, "What's going on here?"

Clearing her throat, Maria said, "Nothing, dear. What can I help you with?"

"Can we do Vampire exercises every day?" she asked.

Liesl wiped her lips. "Yes, Fraulein Maria. Can we?"

Kurt wandered over, still carrying the tree. "I haven't had this much fun since the day we rolled those drunk Frenchmen in the square last spring."

"I don't understand how kids as wonderful as you can play such mean tricks," Maria said.

Friedrich lay down on the grass, then rolled over so his face was in Maria's lap. "Who says we're wonderful?"

Maria pushed him away. "Back off, pal. Access is by invitation only."

Liesl said, "This sort of behavior is the only way we can get Father to pay attention to us."

Farta said, "But the truth is, that rarely works. *Nothing* works."

"Because he's always drunk on his wacky juice," Kurt said.

"Well, maybe he'll be more lucid when he returns with the Baroness," Maria said.

"Doubtful," Gretl said. "The man is a full-blown alcoholic. His blood is probably half juniper berries, one-quarter erythrocytes, and one-quarter leukocytes." Nobody asked what erythrocytes and leukocytes were, because nobody cared.

"Let's be optimistic, children," Maria said. "Maybe he'll be in good shape when he returns. Maybe we can do something to get him to notice you, something to make the Baroness love and respect you. Like . . . like . . . like *singing*!" Each of the kids ripped up a handful of grass and dirt from the ground and threw it at Maria. Wiping the mud from her eyes, the Governess said, "I guess singing is out. Any other suggestions?"

Brigitta said, "A puppet show! A von Trapp family puppet show!"

Liesl gawked at her little sister. "*Puppets?* In *Austria?* Are you *insane?*"

Friedrich said, "Brigitta, I *scheisse* on your puppets! No puppets!"

Brigitta nodded as if it had been decided. "Puppets."

(In the midst of all the puppet discussion, Maria heard a distant noise from the North. It sounded like Mother Zombie's nightly benediction: *Lady, oh the lady, oh the lay hee hoo.* And then once the talk of puppets ceased, so did the chant. *Odd,* Maria thought, *quite odd.*)

"We shall do Vampire exercises for them," Friedrich continued. "That's the only thing we should be doing. The *only* thing."

"Fine," Maria said, "but you have to start at the very beginning. Which, as you might guess, is a very good place to start."

"Beginning?" Gretl asked. "What do you mean beginning? Like the beginning of the alphabet? Like A, and B, and C?"

Friedrich said, "Why would she mean the beginning of the alphabet, shrimp?"

Maria held up a single finger. "It just so happens, Friedrich, that Gretl is sort of right . . ."

"She's *always* right," Louisa said, "the little twit."

". . . but not *entirely* right. We start at the beginning of the alphabet . . . but not the human alphabet. The Vampire alphabet."

Liesl gave her a skeptical look. "There's a Vampire alphabet?"

"There sure is," Maria said, unpacking her saxophone. After she put the reed in the mouthpiece, and the mouthpiece on the sax, she honked out an E Phrygian scale, then said, "The Vampire alphabet is only seven letters, and those letters are do, ray, me, fah, so, la, tee. Seven letters. No more, no less."

"That's ridiculous," Brigitta said. "What can you spell with seven letters?"

"Plenty," Maria said. "Like you can spell *meeraytee*."

"What's *meeraytee*?" Farta asked.

"A dead deer that's ready to be eaten."

All at once, the brats said, "*Meeraytee*."

"That's right," Maria said. "You can also spell *solafah*."

Liesl asked, "And what, Governess, pray tell, is *solafah*?"

"Why everybody knows that *solafah* is a drop of acid rain."

"And what, Governess, pray tell, is acid rain?"

"Never you mind. You can also spell *fahdoe*."

"Fine, I'll bite," Kurt said. "What's *fahdoe*?"

"A long, long way to fly, naturally. And we Vampires oftentimes have a long, long way to fly."

"Right, naturally," Liesl said, "what else would *fahdoe* be? Let me do one. Is, um, *dorayme* a word?"

"Of course it is," Maria said. "It means 'disjointed plot line.'"

"So you could use *dorayme* to describe the genesis of this book?"

Maria grinned. "You're correct, Liesl! I love you most of all!"

At that, the children simultaneously rolled their eyes.

Farta said, "My turn, my turn! *Lalateeray*!"

Maria clapped once. "Very good, dear. *Lalateeray* is what you do after you finish with your *dorayme*."

Gretl asked, "And what exactly does one do after *dorayme*?"

"You *lalateeray*."

"I understand," Gretl said, "but what specifically is *lalateeray*?"

"It's what you do after *dorayme*. Now shut it, so I can tell you the last word of the day, which is *teeteeteedoe*, which means dinner. A meager dinner, granted—we're talking jam and bread, and maybe some lukewarm tea to wash it down with—but dinner nonetheless." At that, Kurt's stomach rumbled.

"Governess?" Friedrich asked.

"Yes, Friedrich?"

"The Vampire alphabet is a stupid, stupid alphabet."

Maria said, "I didn't make it up. It was here when I was transformed, and it will be here long after I'm gone. Not that I'll ever be gone, but you know what I mean. But if you look at it the right way, it isn't that bad. Once you have those letters in your heads, you can spell a million different words by mixing them up. Like *sodola*."

"Or *fahmeedo*," Farta said.

"Or *sodofahfah*," Louisa said.

"Or *dolahdolatee*," Kurt said.

For the next hour, the children sang thousands of words in Vampire, some of which meant nothing, to which we say, *Doedoerayfah meemeemee*. And we mean it.

# INTERLUDE #2

*H*ANDSOME BOY POINTED *to Felt Face and said, "You must be loving all this bollocks about puppets, mate."*

*Giggling, Brown Cape said, "Oooh, watch it, limey, you don't want to make him mad. You wouldn't want to imply that he himself is a puppet. Because if he's a puppet, then he's not a living being, and he really, really, really thinks he's a living being."*

*Felt Face said, "One, two. I count two obnoxious jerks whose cars I'll be egging on Halloween."*

*Dracula glared at Handsome Boy and Brown Cape, and growled, "Lay off of him, you twinks." After a lengthy staring contest which the two younger Vampires lost by a mile, Dracula turned to Felt Face and said, "Listen, buddy, there's nothing wrong with not being a living being. Living's overrated. Maria von Trapp knows that. That's why she turned all the kids into Vampires. She was being nice."*

*"Give me a bloody break," Handsome Boy said. "She turned*

*them because she was hungry." Pointing an accusatory, pointy-nailed finger at Dracula, he said, "And if anybody would know about turning innocents due to hunger, it's you, you sloppy git." He grabbed some Fritos, then said, "You know what? The first two chapters were bloody good, but now I'm bloody tired of this bloody book. Can't we just discuss some bloody Franzen like every other bloody book club in the world? He's a boring fuck, but I always feel superior when I tell people I've read his stuff."*

*Ignoring him, Dracula told Felt Face, "Everybody knows that undeath has advantages galore. Like you get a true sense of the passing of world history . . ."*

*Handsome Boy blew a raspberry and said, "Booooooring!"*

*". . . and you get to see how humanity advances . . ."*

*Another raspberry. "Snooooooore!"*

*". . . and you get to experience the evolution of art . . ."*

*Another raspberry. "Zzzzzzzz! Besides, if the evolution of art means taking a perfectly boring movie musical and turning it into an even more boring book, I'd rather die for good." Handsome Boy stood up and walked over to the window, then, staring at the cloudy night sky, said, "I will say, though, that this Maria twat knew how to live her undeath to the fullest: Lots of sex and lots of blood. The best one-two punch imaginable."*

*Felt Face mumbled, "One, two. I'd like to give you a one-two punch right in your nutsack."*

*Without turning around, Handsome Boy said, "Zip it, wank job. I know where your coffin is."*

*"Yeah, while I know where your butthole is. One. I count one butthole that I'll fill with . . . with . . . with . . ."*

*"Chocolate cereal?" Brown Cape suggested.*

*"Right. With chocolate cereal."*

*Handsome Boy said, "Or copies of this book."*

*"Speaking of which," Dracula said, "can we get back to it?"*

*"Sure, but can we get a move on?" Handsome Boy said. "I'm meeting this pale, skinny bird at midnight, and she's simply gagging for it."*

*"Still sniffing around the high school chicks, eh, Prince Charles?" Dracula asked.*

*"Two words, Drac: Tom Cruise. Two more words: Kirsten Dunst." He shook his head sadly and said, "The crap that that psycho Anne Rice comes up with makes me look like a right gentleman." He pointed at the paperback book on the coffee table. "And speaking of crap literature, let's finish with this mess."*

*Dracula sighed and said, "Thank you," then read, "Captain Georg von Trapp had two vices . . ."*

# CHAPTER 4

Captain Georg von Trapp had two vices: Alcohol and expensive cars.

Drink-wise, he was neither discerning nor brand-loyal, simply content to guzzle gin of every size, shape, and strength, be it Steinhager, or Bruichladdich, or Fleischmann's, or Sipsmith's. When his liquor cabinet was empty, the cloudy-looking slop that his neighbor Klaus Hass made down in his basement was sufficient. If there was no gin, lager sufficed.

Automobiles were a different story. Cars, he was choosy about.

Only the best of the best would do for the Captain, and his fleet was the envy of Salzburg's car buffs. The flashiest was a giant red 1921 Steyr with a white stripe along the side, so arresting that every time he took it out for a spin, it elicited envious hoots and whistles amongst the Austrian populace. His 1931 Austro-Tata was sky blue, and could tear up the roads to the tune of forty kilometers per hour. But his pride and joy was the 1901 Leesdorfer, a huge black convertible that was the very last one the short-lived manufacturer ever produced. (The car's lack of success both in terms of sales and mechanics stems from the fact that it was a convertible built to seat twelve.) It broke down at least once a month, and a sharp turn would cause it to stall, and it was bumpy to the point that if one rode in it for more than twenty minutes, one would exit the car with black and blue buttocks, but the Captain adored it, in part because he could use it to transport the entire family.

The Leesdorfer, as was its wont, hiccupped its way down the highway, the Captain behind the wheel, his close chum Max Detweiler in the back seat, and, to his right, in the passenger seat, the second love of his life, Baroness Elsa Schrader.

Von Trapp stole a peek at Max in the rearview mirror, noting as always how darn slick his friend looked, what with his greasy hair, his just-so mustache, and his toothy smile. For about the millionth time, the Captain thought, *He's one of my oldest and dearest, but I'd never buy a car from him. Never.*

He then glanced to his left, and drank in the breathtaking sight that was the Baroness. An Aryan ideal, Frau Schrader was blonde, blue-eyed, and bodacious, a delight to look at, to touch, and to hold. The Captain was so enamored with her face and body that he ignored the fact when she became angered, the whites of her eyes turned red, and, when she was really perturbed—which happened on a semi-regular basis—multicolored smoke poured from her ears.

After a particularly harsh bump, the Baroness cocked a thumb over her shoulder and said in a tone that if one were listening carefully, one might interpret as sarcastic, "Great route,

Georg. Those Alps sure are swell. Reeeeally swell. Sweller than Max's breath . . ."

"Those are not the Alps, per se," Georg interrupted.

"What do you mean?"

"This is the Untersberg."

"*Oy, Gott*, here we go with the useless trivia," the Baroness said. "Fine, I'll bite: Georg, please, for the sake of all that's good in the world, tell me what the Untersberg is?"

"The Untersberg," Georg said, "is a mountain massif of the Berchtesgaten Alps that straddles the borders of Berchtesgaten, Germany, and our very own town of Salzburg. The Berchtesgaten Alps are popular with tourists and Austrian Vampires alike because they're a mere sixteen kilometers to Salzburg. The first recorded ascent of the Berchtesgaten Alps was in the first half of the twelfth century by Eberwein, a member of the Augustinian Hydra Monastery at Berchtesgaten. As you may recall, the mountain lent its name to an 1829 opera by Johann Nepomuk, Baron of Poissl." He gave her a meaningful, love-lorn look. "I had them put up just for you, darling."

The Baroness said, "There's no way you could have had them put up for me, Georg. You said there was a recorded ascent in the twelfth century. I know for a fact that you were not alive in the twelfth century."

"Maybe I was," he said.

"No. You were not," the Baroness said in a tone that made it clear that she was right, and this topic was off the table. Then, in an overly cheery voice, she asked, "And what's this talk about Austrian Vampires? What do you know about them? Ha ha ha ha ha." (It should be noted that she didn't actually laugh. She literally said, "Ha ha ha ha ha," *sans* smile.)

Max said, "Yes, Georg, what do you know about Austrian Vampires? I'm always interested in new acts." Max was a concert promoter who fashioned himself an impresario put on Earth to make the dreams of artists everywhere come true. The rest of Austria, however, fashioned him to be an exploitative scumbag who took advantage of those so desperate to perform that they accepted Max's contract terms without question, terms that could be summed up in seven words: *Everything for me, and nothing for you.*

"I know nothing about Austrian Vampires," the Captain said. "This is becoming a ridiculous discussion, and unless you cease with this line of questioning, Max, I shall revoke my invitation."

"You didn't ask me to your villa," Max pointed out. "I asked myself."

The Baroness sneered, "As usual." (The Baroness and Max had a love/hate relationship, in that he loved her, and she hated him. That didn't stop them from making love once a week, couplings that inevitably ended in a plethora of pain and humiliation best not recounted here.)

Ignoring her, Max said, "I need some booze." He paused, then added, "For free."

"Max, you're a *ficken* sponge," the Baroness said under her breath.

The threesome rode in near silence for the next several minutes; the only noise heard from any of them was the tiny moan that escaped the Baroness's mouth when the Captain ran his hand high up her thigh. Soon, however, the quiet was broken by singing off in the distance.

Max stood up in the back seat and screamed, "Holy *scheisse*! What's that lovely sound?"

The Baroness leaned over to the Captain and whispered into his ear, "That's the sound of me becoming moist," and then she squeezed his man-parts, which almost led to an accident.

Von Trapp flicked her hand away, then told Max, "If I'm not mistaken, that's the Klopmannsteinberger Temple Young Young Young Girls Choir. Lord knows why, but they like to rehearse at the foot of the mountains."

"I bet it was Hammerstein's idea," the Baroness said.

Max leered. "Young Young Young Girls Choir, eh? They sound quite . . . chipper. Would you agree?"

"Chipper, no," the Baroness said. "Like a bunch of jailbait, yes."

"You say chipper, I say jailbait. You say to-*may*-toe, I say to-*mah*-toe."

The Choir sang, "Wrooonngggg mussssssicalllll, whorrrrrrresssssss!"

"My point is," Max continued, "I could take them to the Graz Gala of Gaiety and make them stars!"

"Stars who'll line your pockets."

"It isn't just about money, Georg. I'll also get . . . well, what I'll also get is between me and those singers. And don't give me that look, both of you—they're all sixteen going on seventeen. I think. I hope."

"You sicken me, Max Detweiler," the Baroness said.

Max grinned. "Funny, Elsa, if I recall, that's exactly the same thing you told me last weekend right after we . . ."

She spun around and glared at Max, the whites of her eyes as red as blood. "That will be enough out of you, Maxwell. *Enough.*"

The Captain laughed. "Oh, you two, always bickering like an old married couple."

The Baroness and Max exchanged a nervous look. "Old married couple?! What ever do you mean by that, Georg? Ha ha ha ha ha," Elsa said. (It should be noted that again, she didn't actually laugh. She literally said, "Ha ha ha ha ha," *sans* smile.)

"Good question," Max coughed. "What on Earth are you talking about, old friend, old buddy, old pal?"

"I was making a joke," the Captain said. "I make those once in a while, you know."

They simultaneously said, "Ha ha ha ha ha." (It should be noted *again* that they didn't actually laugh. They literally said, "Ha ha ha ha ha," *sans* smiles.)

The Captain stared at them both. "It wasn't that funny."

The "laughter" ceased abruptly. "You're right," Max said. "It wasn't."

"Not even a little bit," the Baroness said.

Max said, "Unless you want us to think that it was funny. If that's what you want, then yes, it was funny."

"*Very* funny," the Baroness added.

Shaking his head, the Captain sped by a meadow, in which seven pale children clad in some truly dreadful sailor suits were engaging in activities that, from this distance, appeared to be otherworldly. The fact that there was a young woman wailing away on a saxophone made the scene that much odder.

The Baroness stared at the children and swallowed hard. "Georg," she said nervously, "what do you think is going on over there?"

After a quick glance, the Captain said, "No clue. Street urchins? Street performers? Street sweepers? Street repairs? Whoever it is, they're wearing the *Hölle* out of those sailor suits. Nothing says class like a sailor suit. Man, woman, boy, girl, everybody looks good in . . ."

"I don't care for the looks of them," the Baroness interrupted.

Max said, "Me neither. It looks like a bunch of acrobats and saxophonists. Not my cup of tea."

"Not my cup, either," the Baroness said, glaring at the scene. "Not one bit."

"Now tuba sextets," Max said, "are a whole different story. The marvelous tuba sextet I've been trying for months to steal away from Herr Don von King . . ."

"Who's Herr Don von King?" the Captain asked.

"An underhanded promoter with bad hair. The kind of person who would rob you blind, and have you thanking him for doing so. The kind of person who would steal your grandmother's purse, then use the money to buy a kitten and kill it."

The Baroness mumbled, "Takes one to know one."

"Bite me!"

"You wish!"

"You wish that I wish!"

And so on.

Two montages and a pointless musical number later, they pulled into the von Trapp driveway. Gazing at the empty backyard, the Captain said, "I wonder where those brats of mine could be."

As the trio walked toward the front door, Max offered up a sardonic grin. "They must have heard I was coming and are off somewhere plotting ways to kill me."

The Baroness said, "I can't say I blame them."

Max said, "Nice mouth. Now, changing the subject, let me ask you both a question: Are you lovebirds ever going to make it official?"

"Apparently not," the Baroness said, glaring at Georg. "They're writing songs of love, Max, but not for me."

"Wrong musical, whore," Max whispered, so quietly that the Captain couldn't hear.

The Baroness, however, did hear. "Don't call me a whore!"

Georg asked, "Who's calling who a whore?"

"Forget it," Max said, then asked, "So what's the problem, Elsa? Why haven't you been able to tie down our Captain von Trapp? Are you not satisfying him in the bedroom? Tell me every teensy weensy, intimate, disgusting detail."

Her eyes flashed red, and a guttural sound came from, well, her gut. "Leave it, Max."

The Captain said, "I need a drink." And then, because it was a day that ended in the letter "y," he went into the house to get a drink.

"I won't leave it," Max said, once he knew the Captain was

out of earshot. "Do you do to him what you do to me? Like the thing with the paddle and the spikes?"

"No."

"How about the thing with the silk ropes, the feather, and the ball bearings?"

"No."

"The sauerkraut and the bratwurst?"

"No."

"The chains, the gasoline, and the matches?"

"No, no, and no."

Max shrugged. "His loss. So what *do* you do with him?"

"Not enough," she simpered.

"So why do you want to marry him? For that matter, why are you with him?"

"He's special, Max. Very, very special."

Max pointed at his own crotch. "You mean down there?"

"No, that's average at best. By *special*, I mean *rich*. When his wife bit it, er, passed away, she left him with a pile of loot, and all he does with it is buy booze and cars."

"Sounds good to me," Max said, then added, "When *your* last husband bit it he left *you* a pile of loot. So did the one before that. And the one before that."

The Baroness grinned. "Which is why I know *exactly* what to do with Georg's money."

"What's this about Georg's money?" It was Georg, drink in hand.

"Nothing," the Baroness sang.

The Captain took a staggering step toward Elsa, but came to a halt when he heard a light, rapid knocking on the front door. *It sounds as if somebody is throwing pebbles*, he thought, then turned back around, staggered through the living room, opened the door, and was promptly hit in the head with a boulder. "What the *Hölle!*" he yelled, rubbing the raw wound.

Rolfe said, "Oh. Captain. Apologies, mein Herr." He then offered up the Nazi salute, and goosestepped around the front lawn, chanting, "Heil Hitler! Heil Hitler! Heil Hitler!"

After Rolfe returned to the porch, von Trapp asked, "What can I do for you, young man?"

"You can Heil Hitler, is what you can do!"

The Captain shook his head. "There will be no Hitler heiling in this house, Rolfe." He peered at Rolfe's face; pointing at the numerous cuts, he asked, "What happened to you?"

"Military business, mein Herr. Is Liesl here?"

"I have no idea where Liesl is. But you best stay away from her. She's only sixteen, going on . . ."

"Going on seventeen, I know, mein Herr, I know. I have no interest in what I believe that you believe I'm interested in." He absently rubbed the biggest of his facial wounds and said, "I have other matters to discuss with her."

"As I said, she isn't here. Now is that all?"

"No," he said, reaching into his jacket pocket and pulling out an envelope. "I have a telegram for Herr Detweiler."

The Captain snatched it from Rolfe's hand. "All right. You have delivered your telegram. Now get out of my sight, you Nazi snot."

Rolfe nodded, raised his hand in salute, then resumed his

Heil Hitler chant, as he goosestepped his way off the property.

"Why were you so mean to him, Georg? He's merely a child."

He spun around; it was the Baroness. "I don't care if he's sixteen going on seventeen, or five going on six, or three-million going on three-million-and-one. He's a Nazi snot, and doesn't deserve my kindness . . . or, for that matter, anybody's kindness."

Max called from the backyard, "If the Nazis take over the world, the Nazis take over the world. What's going to happen is going to happen. Accept it. Embrace it. If you can't beat them, join them. Maybe those clowns'll do some good. I hear the trains in Germany are finally running on time. And look at your pal Rolfe. His hair is perfectly coifed. And his goosestep is a thing of beauty."

The Captain crumpled up the telegram and said, "Max, you're an idiot," then turned to the Baroness and said, "Right?"

"Right," Elsa said, "but he has a decent *schv—*" Before she could finish her thought, a high-pitched cry of *meeraydoe, meeraydoe, meeraydoe* came from the front yard. "Sounds like your children have arrived."

The Captain winced. "Indeed. Lucky us."

Led by Maria, the kids marched up the sidewalk, through the living room, and into the yard—almost goosestepping, but not quite—chanting, "*Doerayme, fahsola, teeraydoe. Doerayme, fahsola, teeraydoe.*"

The Captain called, "What in the name of *Gott* are you brats saying?" Then he turned to the Baroness and asked, "What are they saying?"

"I have no idea." But it looked to the Captain like she had plenty of ideas.

After the brats semi-goosestepped to their respective bedrooms, Maria wandered over to the Captain and said, "Welcome home, sir. I love you most of all!"

"You *what*?!" the Baroness cried.

She gave Elsa a closed-mouth grin and said, "You must be Baroness Schrader. So lovely to meet you."

When their eyes met, Maria's smile disappeared.

The two women stared at one another. The chilly day grew warmer, and the air in between them seemed to shimmer. Maria's skin became paler, and Elsa's eyes became redder. It seemed to go on forever. It seemed as if time had stopped.

The Baroness rose and took a step toward the Vampire. After a brief staring contest, she whispered, "I look forward to getting to know you. Getting to know all about you."

Even quieter, Maria said, "I couldn't agree more. And P.S.: Wrong musical, whore."

The staring contest continued, until the Baroness spun around, grabbed the Captain by the back of his neck, and gave him a kiss that left him drooling.

After the Captain adjusted his trousers and composed himself, he asked Maria, "Did you properly discipline the brats today, as we'd previously discussed?"

"As a matter of fact, no. You see, things have changed drastically since last night."

"Changed *drastically*? I was only gone for one scene, two montages and a pointless musical number—how could things have changed *drastically* in such a short amount of time? Best you educate me about these so-called changes."

"Fine," Maria said. "Take Liesl. She isn't a child anymore. One of these days you're going to wake up and find that she's dead."

"*Dead?!* Are you threatening my daughter, Maria? Do I need to report you to Mother Zombie?"

Backpedaling, Maria stammered, "I, um, I, um, I, um, I don't mean *literal* death, Captain. That's just a metaphor."

"For what?"

"For . . . for . . . for *aging*. Your children are all aging. Take Friedrich. He's a boy but he wants to be a man like you and there's no one to show him how. I'd love to give him some lessons, but fourteen is a tad young, even for me."

"How dare you talk about my son as if he's a piece of meat!" the Captain roared, grabbing Maria by the elbow and dragging her into the house.

Maria said, "But he *is* a piece of meat, sir. A tender, juicy piece of meat, so tender and juicy that he'll be eaten someday by some lucky girl, and he'll *love* it."

The Captain let go of Maria's arm, then covered his ears. "I won't listen to this anymore. Pack your things and go!"

Ignoring him, Maria said, "And then there's Brigitta, who's going to spread her wings and fly."

"Pack your bags!"

"And there's Kurt, who wants merely to feed, and all you do is mock his hunger. And you'd better stop that, because he's hungrier than ever, and you wouldn't want him to feast on something he shouldn't be eating."

"I! Said! Pack! Your! Bags!"

"And then there's Farta . . ."

"You mean Marta!"

"No, I mean Farta, who needs special attention—like *short bus* special—and Gretl, who needs a backhand across the jaw . . ."

"Pack! Bags! Now!"

"At the end of the day, they just want to be loved. Even though I've only known them for a short time, I love them a whole lot—more than you know—but they also need the love of a good man."

Just then, a chant came from upstairs: "The hills are alive. The hills are alive. The hills are alive." It grew louder: "*The hills are alive! The hills are alive! The hills are alive!*" And louder yet: "THE HILLS ARE ALIVE! THE HILLS ARE ALIVE! THE HILLS ARE ALIVE!"

The Captain looked toward the house. "What's that?"

Maria offered him a beatific smile. "It's chanting."

"I realize that, Governess, but who's chanting? Those voices sound, well, they sound dull. Hopeless. Dead."

"It's your children, Captain."

"My children? My brats? They usually sound so vibrant. Horrible and ill-behaved, granted, but vibrant nonetheless."

More chanting: "The hills fill my heart. The hills fill my heart. The hills fill my heart." Louder: "*The hills fill my heart!*

*The hills fill my heart! The hills fill my heart!"* And even louder: "THE HILLS FILL MY HEART! THE HILLS FILL MY HEART! THE HILLS FILL MY HEART!"

Maria smiled a toothy, fangy smile. "I taught them something to chant for the Baroness. She'll loathe, er, I mean *love* it." Her grin doubled, no, trebled in size. "It will change her life."

The Captain gawked at her fangs. He pointed, and tried to say something, but all he could do was gasp. After he more or less regained his composure, he sprinted inside and made a beeline for the ballroom bar, where he grabbed the nearest bottle of gin and a tumbler, poured three fingers into the glass, then dropped the glass onto the floor and took a guzzle from the bottle. He made the gin grimace, then said, "I didn't see what I just saw. *I didn't see what I just saw!* I DIDN'T SEE WHAT I JUST SAW!"

And then, convinced he didn't see what he just saw, he left the ballroom and climbed the stairs so he could visit his chanting children. Unbeknownst to the Captain, Maria was close behind.

Several minutes later, the Baroness burst into the house and ran into the living room, her hands plastered over her ears. *"What's that infernal racket?"* she cried.

The Captain staggered down the stairs in a daze that, to the keen observer, seemed to be different than his typical drunken daze, and said, "Maria has taught the children some chants. They would like us to go to the drawing room, where they'll demonstrate." He offered the Baroness his elbow. "Shall we?"

"Must I?" she asked.

"Yes. You must. If the brats are to accept you, you must humor them. At least a little bit."

She stomped her foot. "*Fine*," she snapped, then took a piece of tissue from her purse, ripped it in two, balled up each piece, and jammed them into each of her respective ears. The couple sat down, after which Max sauntered over and helped himself to a seat and a drink, after which the brats, led by Maria, marched in, chanting like no siblings—either mortal or immortal—have ever chanted before. For you see, the human musical scale consists of twelve notes, thus seven-part harmonies tend to sound cluttered; the undead musical scale, on the other hand, is made up of fifty-two tones, so seven-part harmonies like the ones the von Trapp Vampires were delivering are child's play.

As Maria led the brats through another snappy number, Max said, "They have potential, Georg. I can see them performing at . . ."

The Captain interrupted. "I can see them performing nowhere other than here. Keep your slimy hands and your slimier contracts away from my children."

Max shrugged. "They might like my slimy contracts, Georg."

Before the Captain could respond, the brats picked up a new chant: "We beat like the wings of the birds. *We beat like the wings of the birds!* WE BEAT LIKE THE WINGS OF THE BIRDS!" It was almost hypnotic.

Suddenly the Captain broke out into a blinding smile. He nodded and told the Baroness, "They beat like the wings of the birds. Nothing wrong with that," then hustled across the room in five long strides.

The chanting continued: "I go to the hills when my heart is lonely. *I go to the hills when my heart is lonely!* I GO TO THE HILLS WHEN MY HEART IS LONELY!"

After they finished belting out that particular lyric, the Captain cleared his throat and said, "The hills are alive! The hills fill my heart! We beat like the wings of the birds! I go to the hills when my heart is lonely!" He turned to the children and asked, "How was that? Was that acceptable?"

Brigitta gave her father a long, strong hug, burying her face in his shoulder. "That was wonderful," she said, then she opened her mouth wide and tried to thrust her fangs into the Captain's neck.

Maria noticed and wasn't the least bit happy about it, so before Brigitta broke skin, the Governess grabbed her hair, yanked her out of the embrace, and hissed, "Not in the house, Brigitta."

Oblivious to the near-bite, von Trapp stepped over to Gretl and patted her head. "Lovely chanting, darling. I never knew you had it in you."

"Thank you, Father," Gretl said. "In addition to entertaining her with our musical endeavors, we had intended to give the Baroness a welcoming bouquet of flowers—white wildflowers, to be precise—but for some odd reason, the flowers wilted the moment I picked them from the garden. I blame that on the inconsistent Austrian climate. One day it's too hot, and the next day it's too cold, so when a flower—or a plant of any kind, for that matter—is plucked out of the ground before it's strong enough to . . ."

The Captain cut off the overly-verbose dullard. "That's very kind of you to have thought of Elsa, Gretl. Now please, do shut up." He turned to the Baroness and said, "Wasn't that kind of my family to think of you?"

The Baroness folded her arms over her breasts, glared at Friedrich and Kurt, and hissed, "*Edelweiss.*"

At that, the boys grabbed their heads and dropped to their knees in obvious pain. Kurt said, "The ringing! It hurts! Make it stop, Father! Make it stop, Governess!"

The Baroness chuckled, pointed at the rest of the kids, then whispered, "Blossom of snow, bloom and grow!"

At that, Liesl, Louisa, Farta, Brigitta, and Gretl doubled over, so pained that they were only able to moan.

Elsa nodded. "Just as I suspected," she said. Then she snapped her fingers seven times in quick succession and stomped toward the door. The children stood up straight and tall as if nothing had happened. Right before the Baroness exited the room, she came to a halt and, without turning around, said, "Georg, you never told me how wonderful your children are."

"That's because they're not the least bit wonderful," he said. "Wait, let me rephrase that: They *were* not the least bit wonderful. Now they're quite wonderful. Or at least somewhat tolerable." He turned to Maria. "And I believe I have you to thank for that."

Visibly appalled, the Baroness took her leave, a dog-like growl oozing from her mouth. Maria took a peek at the children, then, once determining they were free of the Baroness's spell, she followed. Before she even made it five meters, the Captain grabbed her by the elbow and said, "Governess."

"Yes, Captain," she said, craning her neck to see where the Baroness was headed.

"I've behaved badly toward you. I apologize."

Still craning, she said, "Right, great, apology accepted. Now please let go of me."

The Captain bulled ahead as if Maria had said nothing. "I had no right to speak to you the way I've been speaking to you."

Still craning, she said, "Right, great, you'll be nicer, that's swell. Now please let go of me."

"And you have brought chanting into the house? And harmonized chanting at that! I never knew how wonderful the sound of words being delivered in unison could be."

"Right, great, the kids sound terrific. Now . . . please . . . let . . . go . . . of . . . me!"

"I guess what I'm saying is, welcome to the family!"

"Right, great, welcome to me." She yanked her arm from his; the sudden, strong movement caused the Captain to fall on his backside. "Sorry about that," she said. "I have to run."

And run Maria did. Right out to the backyard.

She looked to her left, then to her right. Seeing nothing, she took a deep breath, smiled a tight smile, skipped toward the lake, and called, "Baroness! I smell you! A word, please?"

The Baroness stepped out from behind an oak tree, her expression a combination of hunger, sensuality, and aggression. "Ah. The Governess. You and I, alone at last."

Maria said, "Indeed. I thought we should have a chat. I'd like to get to know you. Get to know all about you."

"I thought that was the wrong musical, whore."

In a single stride, Maria was two millimeters away from the Baroness. "What are you, Baroness Elsa Schrader? Where did you come from?"

"I could ask you the same question."

"You know exactly where I came from, Baroness. I came from the Abbey overseen by the great Mother Zombie. I came from the Abbey of the undead."

"Yet you're not a zombie yourself. Would you care to explain that?"

"I think you know what I am, Baroness."

"I think I do, but a certain someone doesn't."

"But if he did, I have confidence he would be quite pleased. Because I have confidence in me."

They stared at one another for what seemed like several minutes, then the Baroness broke eye contact and said, "The minute I laid eyes on you, I knew you were a stinking, rotten Vampire. I can smell your kind from ten kilometers away." She leaned into Maria and whispered into her ear, "And your reek in particular, Governess, is rancid. Like long dead animals."

"How kind of you to say," Maria said. "We cultivate that. So. Now you know me. Let me know you."

"You want to know me?"

"I do."

"Then know me you shall."

The Baroness lifted her right arm above her head. The sky turned pitch black, and the wind gusted so strongly that the largest pieces of the shattered gazebo flew around and about. The Baroness's skin gradually darkened until it was as black as the darkest night, then it began to glow as if lit from inside. The whites of her eyes burnt red, and her pupils disappeared entirely. Her fingernails grew . . . and grew . . . and grew some more, then, when they had reached three centimeters, their tips took the shape of a triangle, after which her breasts ballooned until they could balloon no more. A wing sprung from each of her shoulder blades, she began to grow . . . and grow . . . and grow some more, until she stood ten meters tall, at once hideous and beautiful.

As Maria took in the Baroness's new form, she felt a stirring in her lady-parts.

The Baroness-thing spit a ball of fire at Maria's head—which Maria neatly sidestepped—then said in an inhuman-sounding voice, "Care to hazard a guess what I am?"

Maria nodded. "I know *exactly* what you are. I've met your relatives many, many times over many centuries. You're a Succubus."

"Bingo."

"A daughter of Lillith."

"Third cousin once removed, actually."

"A seducer of men."

"You bet."

"An invader of dreams."

"Sure am."

"A thief of hearts."

"For sure."

"A follower of Sappho?"

"You wish."

"A collector of semen."

"And what a collection I have! As a matter of fact, Georg's is at the top of the pile."

"What are your intentions?" Maria asked.

"The same as yours, I bet: To marry Georg von Trapp and gain control of his fortune." She paused. "I might also kill those brats. That would do the world a lot of good." She paused again. "But not before I teach Friedrich a thing or two about Succubussing. That boy is one tender, juicy piece of meat."

Maria nodded. "I can't disagree with you there, Succubus. A bit young, but still."

"That's your opinion, Vampire. I mean, so what if he's only fourteen? If he's old enough to abuse it, he's old enough to use it. Am I right, or am I right?"

"I see your point, but I don't roll that way," Maria said. "But back to the business at hand. I have no interest in marrying the Captain. I have no interest in his fortune. At the Abbey, I did without; for that matter, I've *always* done without, and I'm fine. All I need to do is feed and perpetuate my kind, so I can't let you murder the kids. And in order that the children remain safe, I won't let you marry the Captain!"

"Try and stop me, Vampire." The Baroness then spit another gob of fire at Maria, and this time, Maria was unable to avoid it. As the Governess dropped and rolled, the Baroness-thing transformed back into the regular old Baroness and said, "Good luck, Vampire. May the best creature win."

# PART TWO

# CHAPTER 5

IN AUSTRIA, PUPPET shows are despised, and with good reason.

According to experts on the history of Austrian puppetry—of which there are hundreds, if not thousands—1831 was the first recorded instance of a puppet show gone awry. The performance took place in a rickety barn in Klagenfurt. The puppet master, a native Klagenfurtian named Florian Franzika, had put together a marionette show that, had it come off as planned, might well have been spectacular. He created eight marionettes, one matching each of the animals in his barn: Two Haflinger horses, three milking cows, a chicken, a rooster, and an underfed Alsatian. The idea was to have the living creatures interact with their puppet counterparts, but it fell apart two minutes into the performance, when the dog—who, it turned out, was rabid—attacked both Franzika and the dog puppet, at which point the puppeteer dropped one of the horse marionettes on one of the horses. The spooked horse then went on a bucking spree that killed six audience members, and injured eleven others. Franzika avoided injury, but was murdered in his sleep the following week by one of the widowers.

And then there was the Great Innsbruck Japanese Rod Puppet Fire of 1876, when fifteen of the delicate figures went up in flames, eventually burning down an entire city block, leaving sixty-one dead, and over ten times that many homeless. And then there was the controversial turn-of-the-century ventriloquist convention in Lustenau that ended in a bloody riot. (The less said about the 1905 Linz Muppet fiasco, the better.) Taking all that into account, it was understandable that the majority of native Austrians considered puppetry to be a cursed art . . . if they considered it to be an art at all.

But Brigitta didn't believe in the curses, so, after several hours of nagging, pestering, and harassment, she convinced her siblings to join her in organizing a puppet performance that would win over the Baroness. But remember, dear reader, we're talking about the von Trapp children, and there's no way these brats could do a normal puppet show. No, their performance had to be . . .

". . . memorable," Friedrich said, while the brats sat in a circle on the lawn in the backyard.

"Disturbing," Louisa said.

"Sensual," Liesl said.

"How on Earth can you make puppets sensual?" asked Farta, who, now that she was infused with Vampire blood, was discovering her own sensuality every hour, on the hour.

"You can make *anything* sensual," Liesl said. She pointed to the tree. "Like that." Then she pointed to a red-breasted robin. "Or that." Then she pointed to her lady-parts. "Or, naturally, that."

Kurt said, "I know you can make *food* sensual."

Friedrich said, "I know *you* can make food *anything*."

Kurt picked Friedrich up by the back of his neck and flung him into the middle of the lake.

Brigitta called, "Stop it, both of you!" She held up her index finger. "You know what? Let's ask Maria."

"Ask Maria what?" the Governess said as she wandered into the yard.

Louisa pointed at Brigitta and said, "This one wants to put on a puppet show for Father and the Baroness." The she pointed at Liesl. "And this one wants it to be sensual."

"Of course she does," Maria said. "As well she should."

"So," Louisa asked, "might you have any ideas?"

Scratching her chin, Maria said, "You say this is for the Baroness?"

Brigitta said, "And Father. The Baroness *and* Father."

"Right," Maria said, "for the Baroness." She clapped her hands. "Children, I have a remarkable idea, an idea that will turn this puppet show into one for the ages! A show that people will be talking about for years! A show that will become one of my favorite things, and one of your favorite things, too!"

Friedrich, who was dripping wet from his forced swim, wandered over and said, "Please, Governess, enough with the favorite things *scheisse*. Nobody likes your favorite things, *nobody*. If I trip on one more of your brown paper packages, I'll go insane."

Maria gave him a dismissive wave, then said, "How do you brats feel about goats?"

"Do you mean riding them?" Farta asked.

"Or sacrificing them?" Friedrich asked.

"Or eating them?" Kurt asked.

"No," Maria said, "I mean puppetizing them."

"Now *that*," Liesl said, "sounds interesting."

Maria leaned forward. "Here is what we're going to do." After she whispered her instructions to the brats, she said, "Meet me in the ballroom in two hours and thirty-eight minutes. And make sure you tell the grown-ups to join us."

Fast forward two hours and thirty-eight minutes. The now-completely vomit-free ballroom was as bright as the surface of the sun, and nearly as hot. On the far end of the room stood a newly constructed stage—ten meters high and seven meters wide, with a red curtain shielding the backstage area, and a platform for the novice puppeteers—in front of which sat two chairs. The Captain and the Baroness strolled across the floor, arm in arm, broad smiles plastered onto their faces, his sincere, hers not so much. After they sat down on the seats, the Captain draped his arm over Elsa's shoulders and said, "This is lovely, my dear, simply lovely."

The Baroness sighed. "Sure, Georg. Swell." She then traced a fingernail up his thigh. "But you know what would be lovelier?"

Von Trapp took a sip of his Sipsmith's. "What?"

Whispering into his ear, she said, "Your seed. Your seed is one of the loveliest things I've ever seen. Or tasted."

With heroic restraint, he gently took her hand from his leg.

"Not now, dear. Maybe later. Now is the time for the children."

She turned away and grumbled, "The children. Ever since I got here, it's all about the *ficken* children."

"I'm sorry, I missed that, Elsa. What did you say?"

"Nothing," the Baroness said. "Nothing at all."

Max appeared, then tapped the Captain on the shoulder and asked, "No chair for me, eh?"

The Captain looked around. "I suppose not." He pointed to the ground. "On the floor with you, Max."

Max blinked. "But . . . but . . . but I'm an *impresario*! Impresarios are never relegated to the floor."

Shrugging, the Captain said, "The Governess and the brats set this all up. *Kvetch* to them."

The Baroness checked her watch and asked, "When do you think this shindig will start?"

From behind the stage, Maria called, "Right now!" She stepped into view and said, "Thank you for your kind applause."

The Baroness said, "We're not applauding."

"Oh, Baroness, I love you most of all!" The two women-creatures glared at one another for a moment, then Maria continued: "Today, Captain von Trapp, and Max Detweiler, and Baroness . . . Baroness . . . Fader?"

Through gritted teeth, she hissed, "Schrader."

"Raider?"

Through gritted teeth, she yelled, "*Schrader!*"

"Seder?"

Through gritted teeth, she roared, "SCHRADER!"

"Right. Schrader. The von Trapp family players are proud to present to you an original play entitled 'The Lonely Goatherd.'"

The Captain applauded heartily, Max applauded half-heartedly, and the Baroness applauded no-heartedly, which is to say she clapped twice.

A lederhosen-clad shepherd was lowered from the top of the stage. He clumsily danced across the floor and crashed into the curtain. After a cry of *Scheisse!* the puppeteer regained control of his doll—or *her* doll; it could have been any one of the brats manipulating that thing—and the show improved exponentially. The shepherd did a *dessus,* a *pas de basque,* three *sissones,* and a speedy series of *épaulements,* before capping it off with a *fouetté jeté.* He sat down, folded his legs, and said, "I am but a lonely goatherd, unskilled except for my ability to yodel. My yodels are lusty and clear, and can be heard in remote towns throughout the land."

Max elbowed the Captain in his leg. When the Captain leaned down, Max said, "Those brats are pretty good. That thing looks real."

The Baroness said, "*Too* real, if you ask me."

The shepherd looked to the sky and continued: "A goat, my Lord, my kingdom for a goat!"

From behind the stage, a voice that was likely meant to be the voice of God, but missed Godliness due to its lack of boominess, commanded, "Yodel for me, my son! Yodel and ye shall receive a goat from yon!"

"As you wish," the shepherd said, then he cleared his throat and yodeled, "Lady oh the lady oh the lay hee hoooooooooooo!"

At that, the Baroness froze solid, so frozen that ice crystals formed on her eyelashes . . . although since her lashes were Aryan blonde and her eyes were as blue/gray as a lake in the wintertime, one might have believed the entire upper region of her face was frozen to start with. The Captain and Max were so absorbed in the show that they didn't notice she had stopped moving . . . and breathing.

A goat was then lowered onto the stage, bleating the entire way down. The Captain told Max, "Goodness, that beast reeks like feces. They even made certain it smelled like a proper barn animal. Those kids—their attention to detail was remarkable."

Max said, "It's remarkable, but I have one major quibble: The puppet strings are quite visible to the naked eye."

The Captain squinted at the goat. "Sure enough. Those *are* some thick wires. Looks like they nailed them right on in there. There's one in the left ear, and one in the right, and one in the tail, and one on each of the hooves."

Pointing at the shepherd, Max said, "There are less on that fellow. Just one in each cheek, one on each hand, and one on each foot. But they're manipulating him remarkably well."

"They certainly are." He paused, then added, "The show looks great, but I must admit, I can't say the same about this narrative. The plot isn't moving along."

Max said, "No, it most certainly isn't. Not to mention there's a significant lack of character development, and they clearly are not adhering to the three-act structure. This will all need to be addressed before we begin the tour. We might have to consider a script doctor."

"What tour?" the Captain asked. "And what's a script doctor?"

"Never you mind. Pipe down and let me do my job."

Before the Captain could tell Max off, a backdrop plunked down from the top of the stage, covering the red curtain; it was a crudely painted castle.

Max winced. "Terrible set design. Something else we need to work on."

The next puppet came from above; it was a handsome young Aryan man whose outfit could only be described as majestic. The puppeteer from above leaned the prince against the painted castle—making certain he didn't fall—then said, "Who am I, you might ask? Well, I'm a prince on the bridge of a castle moat heard."

Max asked the Captain, "How can you be on the bridge of a castle moat heard? For that matter, what's a castle moat heard?"

The Captain shrugged, "Whenever I ask one of the children a question like that, they always tell me the same thing: *Ask Hammerstein.*"

"Who's this Hammerstein?"

"No clue." He took a brief glance at the Baroness, then said, "Look at her, Max. She loves the show so much that she can't tear her eyes away from the stage." He shook his head and gave his friend a small, wistful smile. "Ah, those kids of mine, making certain my paramour is happy. It's moments like this that make all the trouble worthwhile."

"You know what would make it worthwhile?" Max asked. "Taking this act on the road. And a script doctor."

Two bearded male puppets with backpacks hopped to center stage from the wings. One of them said, "We're men on a road with a load to tote." And then they walked off.

Max said, "This is getting ridiculous. I can forgive a few plot holes here and there, but when multiple characters come in, deliver a line, then leave and are never heard from again, well, that's a problem."

"That's enough, Detweiler," the Captain said, then cuffed him on the back of his head.

After the bearded ones were clear of the stage, another backdrop whooshed down, this one, a crudely drawn beer hall. The two bearded men, now holding pints of lager, returned and plunked down at a table. ("See," the Captain told Max, "they came back. Now settle down.") Four bassoon players appeared behind the bearded men and tore into an odd arrangement of Franz Danzi's "Bassoon Concerto No. 2 in F-Major." (Several notes in, Max nodded in recognition. "Ah, Danzi," he said, "drinking music for the insane.") The men polished off their beers, at which point the Captain polished off his gin. ("Using spirits to get into the spirit," he told Max.)

Bearded Man Number One said, "We're men in the midst of a table!"

Bearded Man Number Two said, "We're drinking beer with the foam afloat!"

In unison, they yodeled, "Lady oh the lady oh the lay hee hoooooooooooo."

At which point Baroness Elsa Schrader's hair turned a bright, blinding green. The Captain and Max didn't notice.

A girl puppet with blonde braids—who, to Max's eye, looked a bit cheap and sleazy . . . but in a good way—bounded out from the wings, and straddled Bearded Man Number One. "I'm just a little girl in a pale pink coat," she simpered.

Bearded Man Number One asked Bearded Man Number Two, "Lay the lady?"

Bearded Man Number Two nodded. "Lay the lady. Hee hee! Hoo hah!"

Max whispered to the Captain, "*Now* we're getting somewhere."

Right when the girl leaned in to kiss Bearded Man Number One, a curvy woman who was mostly breast lumbered over to the table. The tempo of the Danzi Concerto picked up far beyond what the composer had intended.

The older woman—who was apparently the girl's mother—gave the scene a once-over, then said, "Little girl in the pale pink coat, I ask you, what are you doing?"

The girl smiled and said, "What do you think? Lay dee! Lady hee hoo! Lay the hoo hah!"

The Mother nodded and smiled her approval. "Hee hoo! Hoo hah!" She then straddled Bearded Man Number Two, and the puppet orgy was on.

Max's eyes widened. "Oh, my," he said, as the Mother stuffed her hand down Bearded Man Number Two's trousers, "this will alienate certain portions of our potential audience." He paused, then said, "But it might bring in a previously untapped crowd!" He clapped to the rhythm of the Danzi. "What a day this is, eh Georg?"

The Captain gawked at the performance, then said, "A part of me was anticipating another Austrian puppet disaster, but this, dare I say, is a triumph!"

After six more minutes of unbridled puppet sensuality, the two bearded men and the two women bopped off to stage left. At the same time, two goats bopped on from stage right. One goat sniffed the other goat's derriere; both the sniffer and the sniffee bleated happily. Then the goats positioned themselves so their faces touched; they rubbed each other's noses, then licked each other's lips. A few seconds later, one of the goats turned around, lowered itself to the ground, and raised its rear haunches. The other goat let out a disconcerting moan, then, as it approached the grounded goat, the Captain said, "And that ends our show! Great work, brats! Bravo, bravo!" He stood up, then kicked Max in the thigh and said, "Time for a standing ovation." To the Baroness, he said, "Care to join is, darling?"

Seven sharp, bullet-like cracks were heard from the backstage area. The noise snapped the Baroness out of her stupor, and her hair returned to its proper shade of blonde. She stared dazedly at the Captain and asked, "What happened?"

"What happened? Why, the children just gave us the show of a lifetime. Stand up for the curtain call."

One by one, the children stepped out from behind the stage; once they were in a line, they curtsied in unison. (Max mumbled to the Captain, "We'll have to work on that exit. All this curtsying makes Kurt and Friedrich look like nancy-boys.") The children then stepped to the side of the stage, and on came the puppets: The shepherd, the two goats, the prince, the girl in the pale pink coat, the two bearded gentlemen, the lusty daughter, and the lustier Mother.

The Baroness scratched her head, then elbowed the Captain in his ribs and asked, "Who's operating the puppets?"

Von Trapp said, "Why, the children, of course."

Max shook his head. "Georg, the kids are right there, in full view. How are they doing that?! *Mein Gott,* this show is fan-*ficken*-tastic!"

The Vampire stepped out from behind the curtain and waved her hand at the puppets, who immediately collapsed. She then said, "Lady oh the lady oh the lay hee hooooooooooooo," and the Baroness again froze solid. Looking the Captain squarely in the eyes, Maria said, "Gentlemen, the show isn't over. The show isn't complete. There's more, and what comes next might shock you. You might resist at first, but I ask you to give it a chance, because what I've done is a great thing for you and your family."

The Captain asked, "What are you talking about, Governess?"

Maria turned to the kids and said, "Brats, prepare for part two." After the kids obligingly scampered behind the curtain, she told the Captain and Max, "First of all, gentlemen, I'd like you to meet Dirk Vinizki."

The prince puppet popped up from the floor, then removed the nails and puppet strings from his various body parts, smiling as the wounds gushed blood all over the ballroom. "*Dankeschön,* gentlemen. I'm thrilled that you enjoyed the show. *Dankeschön,* Maria. I thank you for the opportunity." As he skipped out of the ballroom, he joyfully shouted, *"I have confidence!"*

Max watched the prince take his leave, then smiled and said, "Now *that's* what I call commitment."

The Captain, whose face was drained of all color, said, "I don't think that was a puppet, Max."

"Who cares?" Max said. "All that matters is it was a heck of a show."

Maria said, "As the pink-coated girl, give a warm round of applause to Mrs. Dirk Vinizki herself, Helga Vinizki!"

Like her husband, Helga stood up and removed the nails and the strings. Like her husband, she began to bleed profusely. Like her husband, she bound from the room screaming, *"I have confidence!"*

Maria then introduced the remainder of the cast, as well as the two goats. After all the performers had removed their, shall we say, *implements*, and vacated the room, Maria asked the men, "Any questions, kind sirs?"

The Captain pointed a shaky finger at the numerous blops of blood that covered portions of the ballroom floor. "Wh-wh-wh-what just happened?"

Max said, *"Genius* happened!"

Ignoring Detweiler, Maria explained, "What you have witnessed, Captain von Trapp, is the power of the *undead*. The power of the *nightflyer*. The power of the *Vampire*."

Blinking, von Trapp said, "Vampire?"

"Oh, come now, Captain, I know you noticed."

"Noticed what?"

"This," she said, then opened her mouth wide, displaying her fangs in all their gory glory.

Max fell to his knees. "Holy *scheisse!*"

Maria closed her mouth and shook her head. "Don't fear, Herr Detweiler. Any friend of the Captain is exempt from feeding." She glared at the still-frozen Baroness and added, "At least for now."

"No fear here," Max said, "just joy. With this sort of performance, top prize at the Graz Gala of Gaiety is *mine*! Er, I mean *ours*. Er, I mean *yours*."

"I'm afraid that won't be the case, Herr Detweiler. This is a one-time event. There will be no repeats. Enjoy it, imprint it upon your memory, and file it away for safekeeping. To repeat: No repeats."

"What if there's an occasion where you *have* to repeat it?" Max asked.

"*Have* to repeat it? What situation could possibly arise that would make a Vampire puppet-and-acrobatics performance . . ."

"*Mein Gott, there are acrobatics?!*"

". . . essential?"

Max shrugged. "Something might happen. You might find yourself in a sticky position that only a puppet-and-acrobatics performance can get you out of."

"That sounds ridiculous," Maria said.

"That sounds like foreshadowing," the Captain said.

"That sounds like it's time to bring on the Vampire acrobatics!" Max said.

"I agree," Maria said, then snapped her fingers seven times.

At the final snap, the Baroness's eyes popped open. She glared at Maria and said, "You. *You.*"

"Might you have something to attend to?" Maria asked. "Some seed-sowing, perhaps?"

The Baroness snarled at Maria, then smiled at the Captain. "I'll leave you alone with your children, darling. See you tonight." And then she gave him another one of those kisses that brought him to his knees and left him drooling. As she left the ballroom, she said to Maria, "Try *that* one on for size, Vampire."

The Captain crawled back to his chair and gasped, "Governess . . . you . . . may . . . begin . . . the . . . next . . . portion . . . of . . . the . . . performance." He looked at his lap and shook his head. "Another pair of trousers ruined," he mumbled.

Max sat down beside von Trapp and said, "Let the festivities begin!"

Maria beamed. "Gentlemen, may I present our first performer, Fraulein Liesl von Trapp!"

Liesl leapt out from behind the stage, clad in a Maria-like black cat suit. She said, "Thank you, Governess. I'm now going to demonstrate for you the quickness of the Vampire. But I must warn you: Don't blink, or you'll miss all the fun."

And then Liesl disappeared.

But she didn't really disappear; she was simply moving too fast for the naked eye to discern. Fortunately, we have the benefit of being able to describe each and every one of her actions in slow motion:

First, she zipped along the walls of the ballroom and opened each window.

Second, she hustled to the bar, fixed the Captain a drink, and placed it gently in his hand.

Third, she stole Max's wallet from his back pocket.

Fourth, she stripped the wallet bare.

Fifth, she replaced the wallet from whence it came.

Sixth, she jumped through one of the windows.

Seventh, she broke a pile of sticks from the big oak tree in the yard.

Eighth, she jumped back through another one of the windows.

Ninth, she made a little house from the sticks.

Tenth, she stood in front of her father and Max, and offered a demure curtsy.

All in twelve seconds.

The Captain poured his entire drink down his throat, belched, and said, "That was . . . that was . . . that was *remarkable*."

"Thank you, Father," Liesl beamed.

Max shrugged. "It was acceptable. Not as impressive as the puppet show."

Liesl said, "Is that so?" then she pulled the contents of Max's wallet seemingly out of mid-air. "Does this look familiar?"

Max peered at the items in her hand. "Money and paper. So what?"

"Look closer. And take a look inside your wallet."

Max pulled his billfold from his pocket and gave it a gander. An expression of utter anger flicked across his face, followed by an expression of utter glee. "Liesl, I apologize. You're a genius."

Again, she curtsied. "Thank you. Might I now present to you my little brother, Friedrich von Trapp!"

A bat flew down from one of the chandeliers and lighted upon Max's head. Max tried to swat it away, but the bat was far too slippery and tricky. After a minute or three of jousting, the bat landed on Max's left shoulder, at which point it transformed into Friedrich. "Greetings, Herr Detweiler," he said as he clumsily fell to the ground.

Max said, "You'll have to work on your landings, Friedrich."

"Maybe so," Friedrich said, "but my flying is all but perfect. I shall demonstrate."

And demonstrate he did.

Friedrich flew into all eight corners of the room—floor and ceiling—one, right after the other, right after the other. And then again, and again, and again. He moved through the room so rapidly, he created heat waves that made the air ripple. Finally he touched down daintily in front of the audience of two, then transformed back into his Friedrichian self and offered a bow.

The Captain clapped his son on the shoulder—a bit harder than he intended to; he was getting tipsier by the moment—and said, "Fine job, my boy. I knew you had it in you."

Friedrich said, "Really? You knew? Then why have you called me a useless tosser for all these years?"

"Heh heh heh. I was only kidding around, son. You know, jocular banter between a father and his boy."

"Right," Friedrich said, "jocular banter. Now without further ado, I'm pleased to introduce Louisa von Trapp!"

Louisa—who was wearing a cat suit of her own, although hers was red—was the only one of the children who actually did acrobatics: A Geinserschweiger double-back twist with a half-spin, a Linzerzen triple somersault, and a reverse Hansbroucken flip-flop, all capped off by the rarely attempted Wanzerschnagger-Belderschaden single-toed whirly. At the completion of her routine, the Captain and Max oohed, ahhed, and clapped appreciatively.

Louisa said, "And now, please enjoy the comedy stylings of Farta and Brigitta von Trapp!"

Vampires can fly. Vampires are flexible. Vampires can do magic. But Vampires are not funny. A few minutes into their act—just before the Captain was going to break his tumbler into shards and cut his carotid artery—a black cloud appeared above the girls' heads. The cloud then turned red, then blue, then orange, then white, after which a rainbow climbed up to the ceiling, after which the cloud floated to the chandelier.

And then the rains came.

The downpour that fell from the cloud was unlike anything the Captain and Max had ever seen. It wasn't a rainstorm, so much as it was a waterfall, and it took only several seconds before the two men were soaked to the bone.

Farta and Brigitta then told a series of knock-knock jokes that caused the rain to cease and the chandelier to explode, then curtsied and said, "Thank you very much."

The Captain and Max clapped, although with noticeably less enthusiasm. "My dears," the Captain said, wiping the water from his face, "that routine might need a little polishing."

Maria said, "If we ever give another performance—which we won't, despite the previous foreshadowing—I guarantee you it will be better. But it's a moot point, because we'll never give another performance. Unless it's absolutely necessary. But it will never be absolutely necessary. Anyways, I ramble. For our final act, may I introduce Gretl and Kurt von Trapp, who will read *Dracula*."

The Captain said, "You mean read *from Dracula*, correct?"

"No, Captain," Maria said. "Your daughter insisted upon reading the entire novel. So stretch out those legs and get comfy."

We'll spare you the details of Gretl's pompous reading of Bram Stoker's classic; suffice it to say that even with Kurt acting out all the characters—and acting them out quite well—Gretl's snotty voice made the whole thing difficult for one to sit through without repeatedly stabbing oneself in the eye with a pointed stick. Fortunately, Max was lost in dreams of glory, and Captain von Trapp was lost in a gin-induced stupor, so they suffered through the seventeen-hour-long performance piece none the worse for wear.

After some tired applause for Gretl and Kurt, the remainder of the children met on stage for a curtain call. "Well done, brats," the Captain said. "I'm quite impressed."

In unison, they said, "Thank you, Father."

He turned to Maria. "You certainly seem to have whipped them into shape, Governess."

Maris shrugged modestly. "They're your kids, Captain. All their good attributes come from you. They just needed a little push."

The Captain took Maria by the elbow and pulled her in close. Their eyes met, and in that silent moment, thoughts were exchanged, secrets were told, and hormones flew. They moved their faces toward one another, and they might have kissed had a voice not called from the doorway, "Is there anything you can't do, Governess?"

It was Baroness Elsa Schrader.

The Captain and Max chuckled. "Oh, Governess," von Trapp said, "I have confidence that you could do anything you set your mind to. And I have confidence that you'll be with us for a long, long time."

As the children cheered their Vampire mother, the Baroness said, "Not if I have anything to say about it." And then she barked out a series of sharp, sinister laughs that would have made Bela Lugosi proud.

# A TRANSCRIPTION OF NPR'S "BOOK WEEK," NOVEMBER 1, 2012 LIVE FROM THE 92ND STREET Y HOST: ARIEL PORTNOY

**ARIEL:** *Good evening, everybody. Thanks to all of you in the audience for coming out on this snowy day, and thanks to all of you listening to us on your local NPR outlet . . . especially those tuning in on Chicago's WBEZ. Now I'm certain everybody out there's thinking about next week's big election—as am I—and I don't know about the rest of the country, but I need a break from all these serious issues, which is why I'm thrilled that we're devoting today's entire show to the acclaimed, no,* revered *comedic novel* My Favorite Fangs: The Story of the von Trapp Family Vampires *by Alan Goldsher. We have a wonderful panel on the stage here at the 92nd Street Y on Manhattan's Upper East Side, so first off, please join me in welcoming the author of nine books including his new memoir-in-essays,* Frankly Speaking: An Old School Monster in a New School World, *Dave Frankenstein. Good to have you back on the show, Dave.*

**FRANKENSTEIN:** *Great to be here, Ariel. And I apologize to those of you in the audience who suffer from seizure disorders. I missed the weather forecast, and didn't bring my hat, which meant snow on my ear sockets. And as all my fellow monsters know, when those things get wet, they blink like mother-you-know-whats.*

**ARIEL:** *That's great, Dave, that's great. To Dave's left, making his Book Week debut, book critic for the* New York Observer, The Blob. *Thanks for joining us, Mr. Blob.*

**BLOB:** *Thanks for inviting me, Ariel. I'm a long-time listener, and I'm thrilled to be here. And please, call me The.*

**ARIEL:** *Will do, The. Finally, off to Dave's right, please give a nice round of applause to a gentleman who flew in all the way from Cairo to be here, author of the international sensation* A Crypt With No View, The Mummy.

**MUMMY:** *Thanks, Ariel. All of Egypt sends their regards. We loves ourselves some* Book Week. *Mmmmmmmmmmmmmmmhhhhhhhhhhhhhhhhh. Grrrrrrrrrrrrrrrrrrrrrrrrr. Unnnnnnnnnnnhhhhhhhhhhh.*

**ARIEL:** *Glad to hear it, Mummy. So let's dive right in.* My Favorite Fangs. *Transylvania meets the Great White Way. Any opening comments?*

**FRANKENSTEIN:** *I'll field this one, Ariel. It's a nice piece of work—very nice—but, like most of today's paranormal parodies, it has some inherent flaws, the most obvious one being that the characters' voices sound nothing like their on-screen counterparts. Me, I'm wanting Goldsher's Maria to sound like Rogers and Hammerstein's Maria, but most of the time, well, it's almost like they have nothing in common.*

**BLOB:** *I'll agree with Dave that the book characters and the film characters are radically divergent—as is the majority of the plot, for that matter—but that's part of the fun.* Viva la différence! *Throwing in subtle sprinkles of lyrics and dialogue is exciting for both casual and hardcore fans of the original film. And it's also completely legal.*

**FRANKENSTEIN:** *I can't argue with that. But I do have a quibble, and this one is, well, this one's a biggie. Over the last few years, the huge majority of these paranormal parodies has utilized Vampires or Zombies, and nothing else, and that's flat-out exclusionary.*

**ARIEL:** *Terrific point, Dave. Anybody care to comment? The?*

**BLOB:** *Dave's absolutely right, but frankly, I don't have an issue with that, because . . .*

**FRANKENSTEIN:** *Because there's no way that any author would use The Blob as source material, so you have no expectations.*

*Robots comprised of dead people's body parts offer the parodist myriad possibilities. Admittedly, Zombies and Vampires are ideal for this sort of thing, because they have templated mythologies that you can plug anything into, i.e.* The Sound of Music, *or the* Beatles . . .

**ARIEL:** *If I may interrupt, regarding the Beatles, Dave is, of course, referring to Goldsher's 2010 outing,* Paul Is Undead: The British Zombie Invasion, *the acclaimed remix novel in which Lennon, McCartney, and Harrison were Zombies, and Starr was a Ninja. The entire* Book Week *staff—heck, the entire NPR nation—was appalled that didn't get a National Book Award nomination.*

**FRANKENSTEIN:** *As was I. But as wonderful as that was, and as wonderful as* My Favorite Fangs *is, Goldsher could have gone to the next level. He could have included a piecemeal monster such as myself, or even a Mummy, or, yes, even a Blob. Heck, he could've even done something with an NPR host!*

**ARIEL:** *Ah, that's hilarious. Great stuff, Dave, just great. But I should point out that Alan did have a Succubus in there.*

**MUMMY:** *Alan had to have a Succubus in there. Dddddddddrrr rrrrrrrrrrrrrnnnnnnnnnnnn. Maria couldn't have a human rival, because there's no way a human could take a Vampire in any kind of battle. No way, no how, no sir, no hhhhhhhh-hhnnnnnnnnnnnnn.*

**BLOB:** *But why a Succubus? Do you know any Succubi? Because I sure don't. I do, however, know plenty of Blobs. Even female ones.*

**FRANKENSTEIN:** *Of course you do. And I know plenty of robots, and Mummy here probably knows plenty of his kind, but, as Blob said, none of us know any Succubi, because—are you ready for this?—Succubi don't exist. That being the case, why didn't Goldsher use an existing entity . . . like me? Heck, he could've even interviewed me for verisimilitude. I'm easy to reach on my Web site . . . which, by the way, is Dave.Frankenstein.com. Plenty of great merch on there. For instance, I'm offering autographed copies of* Frankly Speaking *for only ten bucks, while supplies last. And if you order today, half of the proceeds will go to National Public Radio.*

**MUMMY:** *Must be nice to have a Web site. For that matter, it must be nice to have fingers that aren't permanently wrapped up in gauze so you can type on a laptop and add content to your Web site. Nnnnnnnnuuuuuuunnnnnnhhhhhhh.*

**BLOB:** *Hey, quit complaining. I don't even have limbs.*

**FRANKENSTEIN:** *Which explains why there aren't too many Blobs around. I mean, how in God's name do you guys reproduce?*

**BLOB:** *We lay eggs.*

**FRANKENSTEIN:** *Where do they come from? I don't see any exit holes.*

**ARIEL:** *Gentlemen, let's get back to the book. Throughout the novel, there are numerous mentions of the great saxophonist, John . . .*

**BLOB:** *Listen, Frankie-boy, I may not have limbs or genitals, but I can handle myself in a fight.*

**FRANKENSTEIN:** *Is that right? You want to go at it? Right here on the 92nd Street stage? Hell, I'll wipe the floor with you the way John Irving wiped the floor with Susan Orlean.*

**ARIEL:** *If I'm not mistaken, that was the other way around. But regardless, we won't be having any fights today. It's not . . .*

**MUMMY:**  *Rrrrrrrrrrrrrrrnnnnnnnnnnnnnnnmmmmm-mmmmmmmmmmmmppppppppppppppppppp-poooooooooooooooooooooooommmmmmmmmm-mmgggggggggggggrrrrrrrrrrrrrrr.*

**FRANKENSTEIN:** *Hey, no fair using chairs, you Mummy freak! Just fists.*

**BLOB:** *I don't have fists, Frank. But I have this!*

**FRANKENSTEIN:** *That's it? That's what you've got? That's the best you can do? Didn't feel a thing.*

**MUMMY:** *Hey, watch it, Frank. Lllllllllllllllllllllllllllllllllllllllnnn nnnnnnnnnnnn.*

**ARIEL:** *Gentleman, if I can ask you all to sit . . . ow! Jesus Christ, Dave, watch it with the kicking!*

**FRANKENSTEIN:** *Sorry. Who knew that if you kick a Blob, your foot goes right through?*

**BLOB:** *Nobody knows that. Which is why Goldsher needs to do a book with Blobs.* The Great Blobsby. The Blobber in the Rye. Wuthering Blobs. *I could go on forever.*

**MUMMY:** *Nnnnnnnnnnnnnnnnnooooooooooooooooooo. Please. No. Don't.*

**ARIEL:** *I'm afraid we're . . . ow . . . going to take a quick . . . ow . . . break, but when we get back . . . ow . . . we'll be . . . AH-HHHHHHHHHHHHHHHHHHHHHHHHHHHHHHHHHH-HHH! Goddamn it, guys, this is a major clusterf—*

**IRA GLASS:** *And now, a very special edition of* This American Life.

# CHAPTER 6

THE BRAINCHILD OF a failed Austrian composer named Rudolf Schteinmetz, the Graz Gala of Gaiety debuted in 1925. Initially, it was strictly a musical event, and the majority of the participants were *a capella* singers. Audiences stayed away in droves—solo vocal versions of Austrian folk tunes had not yet caught on; that wouldn't happen until the last revolting days of the thirties had come and gone—so Schteinmetz decided to allow any type of performing artist to participate: string quartets, forty-member choirs, solo bassoonists, oompah bands, clowns, gymnasts, magicians, hypnotists, synchronized goosesteppers, and, beginning in 1932, Vampires.

Every year since 1929, Max Detweiler had brought multiple acts to the Gala, and each year, his acts finished out of the top three. As a talent scout, Max's primary problem, musically speaking, was that he had what his fellow Austrians liked to call *ohren aus zinn*, or ears of tin. What sounded beautiful to

Max sounded cacophonous to the average music fan, and vice versa. After years of failure, he came to the realization that, at the very least, he should hedge his bets and mix things up, so from 1936 on, Max came to the Gala with a variety of diverse acts in his back pocket. His non-musical talent scouting proved to be equally questionable, and the only client of his who ever sniffed one of the top three prizes was a contortionist who could bend himself into a pretzel. Unfortunately, one of that year's entrants was *another* contortionist who turned himself into the spiral, and there was no way the Gala judges would award prizes to two contortionists, so Max and his talent went home empty handed.

When Max saw the von Trapp Vampire extravaganza, he knew he finally had a winner.

The morning after the command performance, Max stood in the middle of the living room and yelled, "Attention, everyone! I have an announcement to make! Out of bed, everybody, rise and shine! Uncle Maxie has some news!"

The Captain was the first von Trapp to lumber down the stairs. Holding his head with his right hand and rubbing his bloodshot eyes with his left, he grumbled, "Why is the house spinning?"

"The house is perfectly still, Georg."

"So you say. What are you doing up this early?"

"Well, Georg, yesterday, after yet another long and desperate search, I've finally found a most exciting entry for the Graz Gala of Gaiety."

"And this announcement couldn't be put off until after breakfast?"

"Since when do you eat breakfast? You're usually too busy expelling last night's libations to enjoy a plate of bacon and eggs."

The Captain—whose face had taken on a greenish tinge—placed his hands over his stomach and winced. "Don't discuss bacon or eggs right now, Max, please."

"Fine, but only if you get your brats down here. I'd like them to hear this, too."

"If you want to wake them up, you're more than welcome to. Me, personally, I think it would be smart to let those little Vampires sleep. I have no idea what kind of mood in which they'll awaken. What if they're cranky and hungry? I have no urge to get bitten."

"Get them now. They have to get up eventually."

"Do they?" the Captain asked. "I'm not sure about that. My Vampire mythology is hazy at best. Maybe they sleep all day. Maybe they sleep all night. Maybe they sleep all week. Maybe they don't sleep at all. All I know for sure is that it's too early for *me*."

He turned to head back to his bedroom, and almost crashed into Maria, who was skipping cheerily down the stairs. Peeking over the Captain's shoulder, she said, "Why, good morning, Mr. Detweiler! A pleasure to see you."

"Him?" the Captain asked, pointing at Max. "A pleasure?"

"I love him most of all!" Maria said.

The Captain rolled his eyes. "Of course you do." He then turned to Max and asked, "The children are not performing at the Gala—end of discussion. Which begs the question, who'll you be taking advantage of at this year's extravaganza?"

Max frowned. "My best bet is Glockenspiel the Clown. He juggles."

The Captain smirked. "Sounds like a winner, Max. Who else?"

"Gerhard Grosz. He plays glockenspiel. And that's it."

"Wait," von Trapp said, "let me get this straight. All you have in your stable is a clown named Glockenspiel, and a gentleman who plays the glockenspiel, and nothing else?"

Max shrugged. "Austria's talent pool is drained. This is why I need your family, Georg." Max dropped to his knees. "Please, Georg," he begged, "I need this."

"Alright, fine, if you get up off the floor, you may speak with the children. I'll leave the decision to them."

As Max rose, Liesl flounced down the stairs and asked, "What decision, Father?"

The Captain said, "Get your brothers and sisters, darling."

"Will do." She blinked her left eye four times, then clapped once; three seconds later, the rest of the von Trapp brood was standing on the stairs, positioned tallest to shortest.

"Oh, my goodness," Max said. "That was astounding."

"What was astounding?" Friedrich asked.

"The precision, the accuracy, the speed. If you can bring that to the stage, I'll win, er, *we'll* win for certain!"

"Win what?" Louisa asked.

Maria said, "Why, the Graz Gala of Gaiety! Does that sound appealing?"

Brigitta asked, "Maybe. What do we win?"

Max grinned. "The admiration of your peers." The Captain cuffed him on the back of his head. "Oh," Max said, "right, two hundred shillings." Another cuff. "I mean five hundred shillings. Minus my commission." Another cuff. "What was that for?" Max whined.

"I'm certain you'll do something in the future to merit it." The Captain then said to his children, "Show of hands: Who wants to perform at the Gala?" Six von Trapp arms shot up in the air. The lone dissenter: Gretl. "What's the problem, little girl?" the Captain asked.

Gretl looked Max in the eye. "I've seen how you do business, Max Detweiler, and I don't like it one bit. You don't give your clients the individual attention they deserve, you take a 10-percent cut, when the vast majority of the managers in Austria take only 7.5 percent, and you have *ohren aus zinn*, and I don't know if it's a wise idea for me and my family to leave our careers in the hands of somebody who has *ohren aus zinn*." She turned to her siblings. "Am I right, or am I right?"

Louisa said, "Do shut up, Gretl."

Maria gave Gretl the sweetest smile one Vampire could give another, then said, "Louisa is right, darling. It's best for you to shut up." Addressing all the children, she continued, "Say yes, brats, just say yes! Show the world what you're all about! Perform your feats of strength! Suck blood for the masses! Suck blood *from* the masses! Demonstrate that you have confidence in you!" She paused, then looked at the Captain. "But before we make a final decision, we need to make an addition, because I think the act is missing something."

The Captain said, "What?"

Maria pulled her saxophone case out of nowhere, opened it up, took out her axe, offered it to the Captain, and said, "This."

"Your horn?" von Trapp said. "So what?"

Max cocked an eyebrow. "I think the Governess is offering you her mouthpiece, if you know what I mean." Leering at her bosom, he said, "If it were me, I'd accept."

Maria bared her teeth and hissed at Max, who promptly grabbed his chest and fell to his knees. "You best show some respect, Mr. Detweiler."

Max moaned, "*Glurg . . . glurrrrg . . . glurrrrrrg . . . ,*" and then he collapsed. The brats applauded happily.

Maria then held out her sax to the Captain. "Please, sir?"

He shook his head. "No, no, no, no, no, no, no!"

"I'm told that a long time ago you were quite good."

"Who told you that?"

After Liesl raised her hand, the Captain mumbled, "Brat."

"I heard that," then she bared her teeth in the exact manner with which Maria had bared hers just seconds before.

The Captain held up a calming hand and said, "Sorry, sorry, sorry." He then told Maria, "That was a very, very, very long time ago."

Maria glided into the Captain's personal space and ran her fingertip over his lips. "It looks to me like you still have it, sir," she breathed.

Friedrich glared at Maria and whispered, "Get a room."

"What was that, son?" the Captain asked.

"I said, kick out the jams, Father."

"Well, if you insist." He snatched the instrument from Maria's grasp, jammed the mouthpiece into his maw, then blew a series of arpeggios that left the Governess beaming.

A shrewish voice from upstairs interrupted the impromptu recital: "*Mein Gott*, what the *fick* is that infernal racket?" It was, naturally, the Baroness.

The Captain pulled the sax from his lips and called, "Apologies, darling!" He chuckled nervously and said, "Women, eh?"

Liesl leaned over to Friedrich and said from the side of her mouth, "He's whipped."

Friedrich nodded. "*So* whipped."

Baroness Schrader stomped from the bedroom and down the hallway. "A *concert*? At *this* hour? *Must* you?" Her eyes flashed redder than they had ever flashed.

After blowing a dejected D-minor Dorian scale—the saddest of all scales—the Captain said, "Every morning, this is how you greet me, and I thought for once that you would be happy to meet me." He said to the children, "Apologies, brats. Elsa is usually small, and white, and clean, and bright when she awakens."

"I'm small, and white, and clean, and bright when I'm not awakened by the sound of two elephants mating." The Baroness pointed to Max. "What happened to him?"

Maria said, "He brought it upon himself, you know."

She ran down the stairs, knelt down next to Detweiler, and put her ear to his chest. After listening for a moment, she glared at Maria and said, "You Edelweissed him."

If a Vampire could blush, Maria would have done so. Looking away, she said, "Why, Baroness, I have no idea what you mean. What a funny word. Is it even a word? Did you say *made of ice*? Or *paid the lice*? Or *gay device*?"

"You know *exactly* what I said, Vampire," The Baroness growled. "You know *exactly* what I mean." She turned to the brats. "You see, children, Vampires have more powers than you can ever imagine. Some of them you demonstrated yesterday, and some of them will take you years to perfect. Edelweissing, for instance, is out of your reach right now."

"What's Edelweissing, darling?" the Captain asked.

The Baroness pointed at the still-prone Max. "This. Your Vampire friend has the ability to leave him in this state, a state in which he'll bloom and grow in the ground forever. Or she can release him."

"Maria," the Captain asked, "will you release him?"

She said, "Fine," then snapped twice and whispered, "Blossom of snow, blossom of snow, blossom of snow."

At that, Max's eyes popped open. After collecting himself, he pointed at the saxophone and said, "You want to join the act, Georg? Make it the von Trapp Family Vampire Octet."

The Baroness pounded the floor, causing the entire house to shake. "Oh, this is wonderful, just wonderful. Let's just fill this house with music, as if we have nothing else to do." She stood up and glared at von Trapp. "How about we just go ahead and throw a grand and glorious party, while we're at it?"

The Captain said, "I think that's a wonderful idea, Elsa!"

Kurt said, "Hoorah! A party! With food!"

Freidrich said, "Hoorah! A party! With girls!"

Liesl said, "Hoorah! A party! With boys!"

Louisa said, "Hoorah! A party! With bare necks!"

Farta said, "Hoorah! A party! With human blood!"

Brigitta said, "Hoorah! A party! With pockets to pick!"

Gretl said, "Did you know that the average Austrian imbibes 57.9 liters of beer per year, and 25 percent of this imbibing occurs at parties?"

The Captain said, "A wonderful idea, darling, simply wonderful!"

The Baroness glared at Georg and the brats, then said, "I was being sar*cas*tic."

Grand and glorious parties used to be a regular thing at Chez von Trapp, but these shindigs soon began getting out of hand—injuries, arrests, fires, et cetera—so the Captain decided it would be best for all if he left the gala hosting to someone else. The last time they had a soiree, Liesl was a child, Friedrich was a baby, the other five brats were mere twinkles in the Captain's eye, and Mrs. Agathe von Trapp was still alive and kicking, and boozing it up like a good Austrian wife should.

That final party—a celebration of Agathe's cousin's sisters's nephew's birthday—began at noon on a Saturday and ended at midnight the following Monday, and what a gathering it was:

The food was plentiful and sumptuous, the booze flowed freely, there were twelve profane shouting matches (six of which led to bloody fistfights), eighteen of the guests—as well as both of the party's hosts—passed out and/or vomited into the piano, and somebody set fire to the gazebo. All in all, an evening to remember.

This time, however, the Captain vowed the affair would remain festive yet controlled. He limited the drink menu to red wine and lager, he called for it to be black tie mandatory (figuring that people would be less likely to engage in physical battle when dressed in their finest finery), and for the entertainment, he hired a string orchestra rather than a brass band. In his mind, this was the blueprint for a sedate, classy affair.

And at first, he was right. At first, it was success. The string quartet set the mood perfectly, sawing their way through a medley of waltzes by Austria's favorite son, Johann Straus, the "Philomelen-Walzer Op. 82" a particular highlight. (Or maybe it was the "Huldigung der Königin Victoria von Grossbritannien Op. 103." Or possibly the "Wiener Gemüths-Walzer, Op. 116." Frankly, dear reader, it's difficult to tell those interminable Austrian waltzes apart.) Women wearing flowing ball gowns and men clad in crisp tuxedos twirled around the room, contented grins plastered on their faces.

It was around midnight, and Captain Georg von Trapp and Baroness Elsa Schrader were standing on the ballroom's balcony, right above a red Austrian flag dangling over the railing, staring indulgently at the revelers. As the Captain absently rubbed his finger across the flag, the Baroness elbowed him in the ribs and pointed to a balding, heavyset, barrel-chested gentleman standing in the middle of the floor, staring up at the both of them. The man waved at the Captain, a wave that turned into a Hitler *heil*-ing Nazi salute.

The Captain said, "Who invited him?"

"I did," the Baroness said.

"You invited a *Nazi* into my house? And a Nazi radio host at that. *Why?*"

She pulled Georg's iPhone from her cleavage and said, "He was on your contacts list."

He sighed and said, "Okay, come on, let's get this over with." He walked toward the stairs.

Following him, the Baroness clapped and grinned. "Oh, goody, this'll be fun."

The Captain and the Baroness caught up with the bearish Nazi at the bar. Offering his hand, von Trapp grumbled, "Colonel Wilde von Beckbaw. Good evening."

Von Beckbaw stared at the Captain's hand as if it were a rancid piece of smoked fish—then again, even today, most smoked fish in Austria is rancid, so that might not be the best metaphor—and took it gingerly. "Captain von Trapp," he said, his lip curling in distaste.

Nodding at his Succubus, the Captain said, "This is Baroness Elsa Schrader."

Von Beckbaw removed the Baroness's clothing with his eyes; the Baroness aided him by sticking out her chest. He gave her cleavage an obvious leer, then said, "I feel like we've met, Baroness."

"Maybe we have, Colonel von Beckbaw. Maybe we have . . . in your dreams!" As they shook hands, she said, "Heil Hitler, right? Is that how you say it?" And then she laughed a laugh of enchantment.

Von Beckbaw wiped some newly sprouted dots of sweat from his forehead and cleared his throat. "You say it beautifully, Baroness. More beautifully than Mrs. Hitler herself. You should come on the show sometime."

Fanning her face demurely, the Baroness said, "Why Colonel von Beckbaw, you're making me blush." (That was a patent lie, as Succubi, like Vampires, don't blush.)

After barking three barrel-chested laughs, von Beckbaw turned serious. "Von Trapp," he said, "when is the last time you heard me on the radio?"

"I believe it was 1932."

"That was the year I premiered."

"Correct," Georg said.

"It's quite a good show, von Trapp," von Beckbaw said. "I think you might enjoy it."

"Too much propaganda."

"Propaganda is essential to the Nazi movement."

"That doesn't mean it's enjoyable to listen to. I prefer that young woman out of Innsbruck, Rachel von Meadow. That gentleman based in Klagenfurt, Kiefer Ollberrmann, also has some interesting things to say."

"My dear Captain," von Beckbaw said, "they're also spewing forth propaganda. Oftentimes louder than me."

"Yes," Georg said, "but it's my team's propaganda, and our

propaganda can beat your propaganda with one ganda tied behind its back." Then, under his breath, he added, "Right wing freak."

Von Beckbaw sneered at the Captain, then pointed at the Austrian flag on the balcony and said, "Quite the display of nationalism you've got going on here at the mansion, I see. One of those things in the ballroom, one of them outside, and no Nazi paraphernalia to be seen. I was really hoping I'd see, oh, I don't know, maybe a lanyard Swastika, or a bust of Hitler made from those wooden ice cream stick thingies. Why, I bet you never even wore the *von Beckbaw Show* t-shirt I sent you. If I didn't know better, I'd say you were a . . . a . . . a . . . a *Democrat!*"

As the Captain said, "Um, I am," the Baroness laughed, and laughed, and laughed, and with every second of laughter, each man at the party became more and more aroused. They grew short of breath, their legs turned to jelly, and their man-parts became engorged with blood. Even the gentlemen out on the terrace—one of whom was Kurt von Trapp—were not immune.

As Kurt was adjusting his pants, Brigitta wandered over, peeked through the window, and said, "Check out all the hotties."

Kurt covered his crotch and said, "They're not hotties! They're, um, they're *coldies!* Why would you think that *I* think they're hotties? I don't even like women!"

"You don't like women?" Brigitta blinked. "Is there something you're not telling us, brother dear?"

Louisa sauntered by and threw in her two shillings: "Me, I think you're scared of them."

"I'm not scared of *anybody*," Kurt said. "Why should I be? I have these." He bared his fangs.

"How does having those," Louisa asked, "keep you from being frightened of girls?"

That throaty, enchanting female laugh again came from the ballroom, and Kurt shuddered and moaned, then wiped some newly sprouted dots of sweat from his forehead and cleared his throat. He turned his back to his sisters, untucked his shirt, carefully positioned it over his beltline, then said, "Alright, fine, right now, right this second, I'm a little scared of women. But not the way you think I am."

Gretl joined the group, peered in the window, and said, "I think the men at the party look beautiful, too."

Louisa said, "How would you know what's beautiful and what isn't? You're only five."

"Yes, I'm only five," Gretl said, "but that doesn't mean I don't understand the concept of male attractiveness. My hormones don't yet race through my body, but I have eyes, and my eyes work perfectly, and I'm no fool . . ."

Liesl wandered over, stuck her hand on Gretl's chest, and shoved. As the little girl flew into the lake, the rest of the von Trapp brats applauded. Liesl then curtsied, reached out her arms, and did an awkward solo waltz.

Brigitta gawked at her sister. "Um, Liesl, who are you dancing with?"

"Nobody."

Brigitta asked, "Who are you *pretending* to dance with?"

"I bet it's Rolfe," Louisa said. "Speaking of beautiful-looking men, that one has a package that . . ."

Liesl roared, *"Never mention the name Rolfe Mueller in my presence again! Never, ever, ever, ever, ever!"* She took a calming breath, then added, "If you do, I won't be responsible for my actions."

"Boy, somebody is in a mood. Probably that time of the month." Brigitta called out to the lake, *"Gretl, do Vampires get premenstrual?"*

Gretl called back, *"I don't know."*

The three girls stared at one another. Louisa said, "There's actually something on this Earth that Gretl doesn't know?"

"Who knew?" Brigitta said.

Liesl said, "I suppose there's a first time for everything."

Friedrich wandered by, bent down on one knee in front of Liesl, and said, "May I have this dance?"

Smiling, Liesl said, "That's very kind of you, Friedrich."

"Wait," Louisa said, "Friedrich is doing something *kind*?"

"Goodness, this *is* an evening of firsts," Brigitta said.

Ignoring her sisters, Liesl said, "I'd be thrilled to cut some rug, brother dear."

Friedrich said to Louisa and Brigitta, "Could you crack the door, so we can hear the muzak, er, music?" Louisa obeyed.

As the strain of another Straus waltz floated from the house—and we don't know which one it was, dear reader, because, as previously noted, they all sound the same—Friedrich and Liesl chuckled and twirled as if they had not a care in the world.

"Another first," Brigitta said. "Liesl and Friedrich laughing together about something that doesn't involve them doing violence upon one of our bodies."

And speaking of laughing, it was then that the Baroness produced another of her man-enchanting chuckles. Friedrich heard the laugh loud and clear, and, as was the case with every other man within earshot, dots of sweat sprouted from his forehead, he grew short of breath, his legs turned to jelly, and his man-parts became engorged with blood . . . right against his older sister's thigh.

Friedrich let out an involuntary moan—and an even more involuntary emission of his seed—after which Liesl screamed, "*Ewwwwwwwwwwwww*," then picked up her brother and threw him into the lake, where he landed right next to Gretl.

Once Friedrich came up for air, Gretl said, "What did you do to her?"

"Got excited against her leg. You?"

"I talked."

Friedrich nodded. "I could see that setting her off." He pulled his sister from the water and put her on his shoulders. "Come on. We should get into some dry clothes."

By the time they returned to the shore, there were two new developments: Maria had arrived on the scene; and the string quartet had dived into a familiar-sounding folk song. Maria smiled. "Ah, the Ländler. I love this dance most of all."

Kurt asked, "What the *fick* is the Ländler?"

Maria turned to Gretl. "Would you care to field this one, my dear?"

Gretl stared sullenly at Liesl. "No. If I do, she'll hurt me, I just know it."

Liesl said, "Go ahead, shrimp. I promise I'll be nice."

"Really? You promise?" Liesl nodded, then Gretl smiled. "*Wonderful*. So. The Ländler is a folk dance involving stomping and hopping that was popularized in the nineteenth century. The dance is quite herky-jerky, and this odd rhythmic attack is reflected in the music, which many consider to be reminiscent of the compositions of . . ."

Before she could complete the sentence, Liesl shoved her into the lake.

After they heard the splash, Brigitta said, "Governess, do you know the Ländler?"

"Of course I do," Maria said, smiling. "I learned it from Beethoven, before I took away his hearing."

Liesl asked, "Wait, you made Beethoven deaf?"

Maria blinked. "What? No. Of course not. That's simply ridiculous. Who told you that?"

"You did. Two paragraphs ago."

"What do you mean, paragraph?"

"Forget it," Liesl said. "Just do the stupid dance, already."

Here's a little-known fact about elderly Austrian Vampires: They're completely devoid of rhythm. Now the Ländler is filled with awkward motions to begin with, but in Maria's hands (and feet), it became a spastic dance of death. Literally. By the time she got to her second stomp-and-hop variation, every duck in the lake had met its maker.

Needless to say, the von Trapp brats loved it.

When Maria finally ran out of steam some fifteen minutes later, she opened her eyes and found herself surrounded by von Trapps . . . the family patriarch included.

The Captain clapped and slurred, "Brrrrravo, Messina . . ."

"Maria, sir."

"Right. Maria. That was one *Hölle* of a display. Never seen anything quite like it. Elsha . . . I mean *Elsa* . . . I mean the *Baroness* most certainly doesn't move like that."

Their eyes met. "You like the way I move, sir?"

"I do, Melody."

"Maria, sir."

"Right. Maria. I like the way you move a whole lot." He then took her by her waist and pulled her close. They stared deeply into each other's eyes; when their respective parts brushed against one another, they smiled.

The Ländler music came to a halt, and the children scattered. The Captain looked around, surprised. "Brats," he called, "you don't have to leave! Nothing is happening here!"

They heard somebody say, "It doesn't look like nothing to me."

It was the Baroness. The red-eyed Baroness. The red-eyed Baroness who had multi-colored smoke pouring from her ears.

Maria and the Captain separated. "It isn't what it looks like," the Captain said.

"What do you think I think it looks like?" the Baroness asked.

"What do *you* think that I think that you think that I think it looks like?" the Captain countered.

Ignoring him, the Baroness said to Maria, "That was lovely dancing, Maria, simply lovely." She took the Governess by the elbow. "You must teach me how to Ländler. Dare I say, you're the finest female Ländlerer I've ever seen." The Baroness squeezed Maria's arm, causing Maria to imperceptibly flinch. "Come with me. A Ländler lesson is in order. That's to say you and I, Vampire, are going to dance."

Maria's eyes found the Captain's. She said, "Your ladyfriend wants a dance lesson."

"So I see." He asked the Baroness, "Darling, Maria is a Vampire. Do you think this is a wise idea, to dance with the undead?"

The Baroness's ear smoke turned red. "I think it's a *wonderful* idea. The best idea I've had all evening. Now go get a drink or three, and I shall see you posthaste."

After the Captain took his leave, the two women strolled over to the lake, saying nothing. Finally, when they reached the sand, the Baroness spoke: "Reveal your true self, Maria, and I shall do the same."

Maria said, "I am what you see, Baroness." She paused. "I can take off my dress, if you would like," she said.

"I will if you will," the Baroness said.

They stripped off their respective clothes, and even though their bodies were drastically different—where Maria was tall, lithe, and muscular, Elsa was short, soft and curvy—each was perfect. Had Colonel von Beckbaw gotten a gander of their pulchritude, his conservative-leaning, Bush-loving, working-folk-hating brain fluid would have oozed from his conservative-leaning, Bush-loving, working-folk-hating ears, and his conservative-leaning, Bush-loving, working-folk-hating heart would have exploded in his conservative-leaning, Bush-loving, working-folk-hating chest.

Maria said, "Now that you're bare, I defy you to once again take your true form, Baroness. Or should I call you Lillin, daughter of Lillith and Adam?"

Cocking an eyebrow, the Baroness said, "I see you know your Succubus history."

"Not really," Maria said. "After I found out what you were, I looked up Succubus on Wikipedia."

"Wikipedia?" the Baroness asked.

"Never mind. Just shut your mouth and take your true form."

"If you insist." She lifted her right arm above her head. The sky turned bright blue, and the wind gusted so strongly that a miniature tsunami formed in the lake. The Baroness's skin gradually darkened until it was as black as the darkest night, then it began to glow as if lit from inside. The whites of her eyes burnt red, and her pupils disappeared entirely. Her fingernails grew, and grew, and grew, then, when they had grown to three centimeters, their tips took the shape of a triangle, after which her breasts ballooned until they could balloon no more. A wing sprung from each of her shoulder blades, and she began to grow . . . and grow . . . and grow some more . . . until she stood ten meters tall, at once hideous and beautiful.

"I can't lie," Maria said. "That's one impressive transformation. Puts my bat thing to shame."

The Baroness roared, "Let's begin the dance, Vampire!" She crouched into a defensive stance. "Strike the first blow!"

Maria shrugged. "If you insist." Then she cocked her fist and threw a haymaker at the Baroness's midsection.

She hit air. The Baroness was gone.

From directly behind her, Maria heard a casual chuckle. "Did this Wikipedia of yours tell you that Succubi can move like a will o' the wisp?" And then she kicked Maria on the small of her back; Maria fell facedown into the sand with such force that her head was buried entirely. "Did this Wikipedia of yours tell you that Succubi can kick like a flibbertijibbet?"

The Vampire extricated her head from the Earth, spit out a mouthful of sand, and said, "No. But it did tell me that there are two kinds of women in the world: Those who *fick,* and those who get *ficked*. And I'm about to *fick* you like you have never been *ficked* before."

Maria hopped up and, anticipating the Baroness's next move, kicked just to the left of her head. Sure enough, the Succubus leaned into the kick, and found herself on the ground, on her back, staring up at the sky. The Baroness rolled to her left and onto her side, narrowly avoiding Maria's heel. Pushing the ground with her wings, the Baroness raised herself to a standing position, and backhanded Maria in the face, opening a gash on her cheek that oozed a thick, blue substance that, when it dripped to the ground, turned the sand into rock. Maria snatched up one of the newly-formed stones and hurled it at the Baroness's face. The Baroness ducked and leaned right, but Maria again anticipated her move, and the rock struck her in the ear. Again, the Baroness fell onto the sand, her wings splayed out on either side of her. Maria leapt seven meters in the air and landed squarely on the Baroness's left wing. The Baroness let out a screech that caused every male within a ten-kilometer radius to spew their seed, and every woman in the same range to drip from their lady-parts... Maria included. The warm feeling down below so overtook the Vampire that she lay down on her back, spread her legs wide, raised her hips, and touched *that* area. With some difficulty, the Baroness pulled herself to a sitting position, and found herself face-to-lady-parts with Maria. She was so disconcerted by the Vampire's hand-action that she transformed back into her human form.

"This isn't over, Maria," the Baroness said.

Breathing heavily, Maria gasped and moaned, "You're correct." *Gasp.* "It isn't over yet." *Moan.* "But give me about ten seconds." *Gasp.* "Oh, there it is." *Sigh.* "It's now over." *Contented smile.*

Baroness Elsa Schrader limped away, shaking her head and muttering, "How the *Hölle* do you solve a problem like Maria? How the *Hölle* do you solve a problem like Maria? How the *Hölle* do you solve a problem like Maria?..."

# INTERLUDE #3

*C*AN'T LIE, DRAC," *Handsome Boy said. "All this Vampire-on-Succubus sexual subtext ain't a bad thing."*

*"It's not subtext," Dracula pointed out. "It's text."*

*"The Vampire-on-Vampire lesbian sex was pretty hot, too," Felt Face said. "One, two, three, four. I've popped four boners."*

*"Do Muppets have the ability to pop boners?" Brown Cape asked.*

*"Don't know and don't care, because I'm not a Muppet. Can cartoon cereal characters pop boners?"*

*"Don't know and don't care, because I'm not a cartoon cereal character." Brown Cape stood up and said, "I'm grabbing a drink. You guys want anything from the fridge?"*

*"Blood," Dracula said.*

*"Ditto," Handsome Boy said.*

*Felt Face said, "One, two. Two. In other words, make mine a double."*

*After Brown Cape returned with the libations, Dracula asked,*

"Which begs the question, does all this sex and sexual tension advance the plot?"

Handsome Boy said, "Plot advancement? Ha! Even the characters in the book bitch about plot advancement, or lack thereof. The sex is strictly for the sake of titillation."

Brown Cape said, "Maybe it's a metaphor. Or an allegory. Or a simile. Or a homonym. Or a synonym. Or a . . ."

"Oh, cut the crap, General Mills," Handsome Boy said. "You're making an ass out of yourself."

"How's that?"

"One, because you didn't read the book, and B) because you have no clue what any of those literary devices mean."

"Apparently," Brown Cape sneered, "neither does the author."

"Guys, guys, guys, settle down," Dracula said. "Believe it or not, General Mills here is right. It's all a bunch of metaphors . . . ham-handed metaphors, granted, but metaphors nonetheless. The point is, in the movie, Maria and the Baroness are vying for the Captain's affection, but it's all hiding beneath a veneer of faux-politeness. Goldsher's using sex to heighten and exaggerate the rivalry."

"So it's not really a metaphor," Handsome Boy said. "It's heightening and exaggeration."

"Heightening and exaggeration," Felt Face said. "I count one, two. Two of the most important properties of parody."

Dracula pointed at Felt Face. "What he said. I stand corrected. Now wait'll you check out the sex stuff at the end of chapter seven . . ."

"*Screw that,*" Handsome Boy said. "*Let's just watch the movie and call it a night.*"

*Throwing his book onto the coffee table, Dracula said, "You want to watch the movie? Fine, we'll watch the movie."*

*As the host searched through his DVD collection, Handsome Boy looked at his watch and said, "Get moving, bloke," then, under his breath, added, "Can't let that Jacob arsehole start sniffing around Bella."*

# CHAPTER 7

MARIA WAS EXHAUSTED, as exhausted as she had ever been, even more exhausted than after her feeding frenzy of 1697, a frenzy that lasted three months, and lead to the deaths, and/or the undeaths of 201 people, thus turning the tiny town of Gosch into Austria's first Vampire colony.

That exhaustion was physical, but this, this was mental. Overseeing the von Trapp children, even for this brief amount of time, was all-consuming, plus, the Captain was childlike in his own right, and there was only so much babysitting Frau Alice and Alfred could do by themselves. So Maria was compelled to help when and where she could ... which, for the most part, meant cleaning up the Captain's empty bottles, empty glasses, and regurgitate.

And then there was the Baroness. Ah, the Baroness, the Succubus from *Hölle*, the nemesis she'd never asked for. (*Why would anybody want to be my nemesis?* Maria wondered. *I'm a nice creature, always kind to everybody ... except for the periodic disembowelment, but I never disemboweled anybody who didn't more or less deserve it.*) As far as Maria knew, she had never said or done anything to merit Elsa's ire—*Alright, stepping on the Baroness's wing wasn't necessarily the kindest of gestures,* Maria admitted to herself, *but she started it.* And sure, she had had that nice moment with the Captain down by the lake after the Ländler, but there had been no kissing or fondling involved, so that shouldn't have upset the Baroness. *Maybe she's simply insecure,* Maria thought. *But why on Earth would a Succubus be insecure about keeping a gentleman pleased? Pleasing gentlemen is theoretically their expertise.* It was all very confusing . . . and exhausting.

Maria opened her bedroom window, taking in the stars and their awful beauty, wishing she were back at the Abbey, where life was far less complex. Yes, the Abbey had its downsides—Cinnamon and Brandi, for instance, were busybody tattletales, which Maria always found odd, because one would think that centuries-old Zombies would have more to keep their minds occupied than reporting her comings and goings to Mother Zombie—but she had her cramped, fetid room, and she had Mother Zombie beating her regularly, and she had easy access to the Untersberg, so all in all, it was a lovely place for a Vampire to spend her undeath.

On the other hand, there were certain aspects of the von Trapp mansion that made for a nice existence. There was . . . there was . . . there was . . . well, truth be told, aside from the wonderful acoustics in the ground-floor bathroom—acoustics that allowed for some quite fulfilling saxophonics and fantasies about John Coltrane—there was only one thing that got Maria excited: Captain Georg von Trapp.

There was something about the old lush that caught Maria's fancy. It wasn't his looks—he was probably a handsome man back before he became a single father and started drinking gin for breakfast. It wasn't his money—like most Vampires of her era, Maria cared little for material goods, and besides, if there was something she really wanted, she could kill its owner and steal it. No, it was the Captain's bearing: The way he staggered across the floor, the way he spoke down to people, the way he handled his children with a drunken iron fist. It all added up to the kind of flawed man that any female Vampire would happily allow into their lady-parts time and time again.

Bored with looking at the stars, Maria began to disrobe, but she was so tired that stripping was proving to be problematic. And then, a light knock at the door: "Good evening, Vampire. May I come in?" Then, without receiving an answer, Baroness Elsa Schrader opened the door and walked across the threshold. "It seems you're having some trouble with your outfit. Might I lend you a hand?" Cat-like, Maria hissed, and bared both her fangs and nails at the Succubus. The Baroness held up her hands in what appeared to be a conciliatory manner. "I come in peace, Maria. I mean you no harm. I'd just like to speak. Can we do that?"

Maria relaxed a bit. "Speak about what?" she asked suspiciously.

"This. And that. And the other thing."

"Baroness, I most certainly don't love you most of all."

"Georg seems to love *you* most of all."

Maria looked away. "What do you mean by that?"

"Oh, come now, Vampire. We're both women. We're both otherworldly creatures. We're both immortal. We have both been there and done that. Let's not pretend we don't notice when a man notices us."

"Frankly, Baroness, I *don't* notice when a man notices me."

"Well *I* do, and I notice when a man notices somebody else other than me, and I've noticed on more than one occasion the Captain noticing you."

"The Captain notices everything and everybody. I don't stand apart."

"A pale, slender female with legs up to *here*, perky breasts, and the sharpest fangs in Austria? You stand apart, Maria, whether you like it or not." The Baroness walked across the room. "Come on, let me help you disrobe." Before Maria could say a word, the Succubus removed the Vampire's dress in six seconds flat, then gave Maria's backside an unabashed gawk. "I know Georg notices that derriere of yours, and I can't say that I blame him. It's quite a sight."

"You can credit that to the Pilates."

"Credit that to the *what*?"

"Nothing. And for the record, I haven't done a thing to attract the Captain's attention."

"You don't necessarily have to, my dear. Men like women who like them." She stole another glace at Maria's rump and shook her head appreciatively. "Plus he probably likes that thing."

"Wait," Maria said, turning back around, "you think he's in love with me?"

"Surely you have noticed the way he looks at your face. And your teeth. And your chest." The Baroness leered at Maria's bare breasts. "And I can't say that I blame him there, either. For a lady who's many, many centuries old, you are tight as *fick*."

"Pilates."

"What?"

"Forget it." Maria went to her closet and put on her nightgown, rerunning that evening's interaction with the Captain in her head. *Maybe the Baroness is right*, she thought. *Maybe he's interested in me.*

As if the Baroness had read Maria's mind—which she wasn't able to do; despite many centuries of research and development, Succubi have no extrasensory perception—Elsa said, "Maybe he *is* interested in you, but I wouldn't take it too seriously. Like all men, he has a wandering eye. He'll move on to another soon enough. Familiarity breeds contempt." She stepped toward Maria and whispered into her ear, "But maybe to play it safe, you should go back from whence you came." She then took a nibble of Maria's earlobe and breathed into her ear in a manner that few beings—be they Vampire or mortal, be they male or female—could resist. "Pack now," she added, moving her hand under Maria's robe and tweaking her left nipple.

Maria's breath quickened. "I should go back from whence I came," she said in a Zombie-like tone. "I should pack now."

The Baroness licked Maria's neck, then said, "Return to the Abbey."

"I shall return to the Abbey."

The Baroness rubbed her thigh against Maria's lady-parts. "Leave immediately."

"I shall leave immediately."

The Baroness gently pulled Maria's hair. "You love me most of all."

"I love you most of all."

The Baroness ran a finger down the center of Maria's backside. "Don't say goodbye to the Captain or the brats."

"I shall not say goodbye to the Captain or the brats."

The baroness ran her lips along Maria's neck. "Write a goodbye note and leave it on the table."

"I shall write a goodbye note and leave it on the table."

The Baroness then put her hand on Maria's neck and pulled her into a kiss. Defenseless at this point, Maria opened her mouth wide and let Elsa's tongue explore her fangs. The kiss intensified, and their intermingled saliva created a scent that would have brought a eunuch to orgasm. The Baroness broke off their embrace and said, "Nice meeting you, Maria. Climb every mountain."

"Nice meeting you, Baroness. I shall climb every mountain."

"Oh, also, don't let the door hit you on the way out."

"I shall not let the door hit me on the way out."

After she left the dazed Vampire's room, Baroness Schrader walked down the stairs and into the drawing room, head held high, a broad grin plastered on her stunning face. She blew a kiss at the Captain and said, "Hello, darling," then nodded at Detweiler and sneered, "Max."

"Well," von Trapp said, rising from the sofa, "you seem a lot more chipper."

"I feel a lot more chipper, my dear. Almost as if I lived through a silver-white winter that melted into spring."

Max said, "You always struck me as being impervious to weather."

The Baroness's grin grew wider, and she said, "Oh, Max, I love you least of all!" She turned to the Captain. "And speaking of your Governess, dear, it's lovely having her around, just lovely. It would be a shame if she disappeared."

"Why would she disappear?" the Captain asked.

Giggling, the Baroness said, "Never mind." She cupped her hands over her mouth and yelled, *"Alfredddddd! Champaaaaaaaagne! Nowwwwwwwwww!"*

"*Shh,*" the Captain hissed. "Inside voice. You'll wake the children. And Malia."

"Maria," Max corrected.

"Right. Maria. She has worked hard this week, and she deserves a good night's sleep."

The Baroness nodded. "She works hard for the money, that Governess of yours."

"She does," Max agreed. "So you'd better treat her right." He asked the Baroness, "Was that even in a musical?"

"No. It was on plenty of soundtracks, though."

Von Trapp asked, "What's a soundtrack?"

Before she could answer, Alfred arrived with a bottle of champagne and three glasses. Elsa took the tray from the butler's hand and placed it on the table, then filled all three glasses, and chugged straight from the bottle until it was empty. She belched lightly, then said, "Hmm, what's this?"

"What's what?" the Captain asked, eyes raised to the ceiling.

She cuffed him on the back of his head, then pointed to an envelope that had materialized on the marble table at the front of the room, the Baroness said, "*That*, dummy, *that.*"

The Captain staggered over to the table, opened the envelope, and read aloud:

> Dear Captain von Trapp: This is to inform you that I'm taking leave of you and your family. You're lovely people, but the Untersberg beckons me, and I can't ignore its pull. I must climb every mountain, so it's with much regret that I say so long, farewell, *auf wiedersehen*, good night. If you wish to contact me, you know where to find me. Yours, Vampire Sister Maria of the Zombie Abbey. P.S.: Tell Friedrich I shall find him in exactly one hundred years, and I will teach him about doeraydoeraydoeraydoeray. He'll know what I'm talking about.

The Captain dropped the note on the table, speechless, clearly in shock.

Max said, "*Scheisse.* She was the only one who could whip the brats into performing shape. I guess my chances of winning the Gala rest on the shoulders of Glockenspiel the Clown."

The Captain said, "And my chances of love rest on the shoulders of . . ."

The Baroness said, "*Me!*" She downed all three glasses of champagne, then ran across the room, took the Captain's hand, and said, "Join me in bed, Georg. I believe it's high time we sowed some more of your seed."

As was always the case, Georg couldn't resist.

After yet another bout of satisfying seed-sowing that shall not be described here—because let's be honest, how many seed-sowing scenes does one really need?—the Captain tottered back downstairs and fixed himself a drink. And then another. And then another. With each minute that passed, he became drunker and sadder, and this cycle of seed-sowing and drinking went on for a week after the Governess's departure.

This was arguably the Captain's longest, most intense sex-and-booze bender to date, although some von Trapp aficionados would claim that the March, 1935, alcohol-and-*fick* onslaught was worse. Depressed about his lack of female attention, the Captain spent a week having only liquid breakfasts, liquid lunches, liquid dinners, and liquid ladies of the night. The only thing that enabled him to (sort of) function was that he didn't mix his drinks—it was an all-gin-and-prostitute rampage.

The post-Maria drinking festival, conversely, was a mix-and-match affair. The Captain enjoyed whatever booze or babe he could get his hands on: Gin, Baroness, lager, champagne, hooker, lager, Baroness, scotch, lager, vermouth, Baroness, hooker, hooker, lager, red wine, lager, white wine, hooker, Baroness, hooker, lager, lager, and lager. (The explanation for all the lager? The Captain believed that the heaviness of the drink

matched the heaviness of his heart.) This all led to epic hangovers, which led to epic headaches, which led to more drinking, which led to more epic hangovers, et cetera.

On the eighth day after Maria's departure, von Trapp, Max,
and the Baroness sat on the veranda overlooking the lake, Elsa
and Detweiler sipping some smoothies, the Captain drooling
into a tumbler filled with a mixture of gin, scotch, vermouth,
and goat's milk. The children were nearby, playing some sort of
ball game that involved a lot of bouncing and counting, and
each bounce and subsequent utterance was like a chisel in the
center of the Captain's brain. He roared, *"Brats, can you please
take that to the other side of the house?"*

"Sorry, Father," Friedrich said. "The lay of the land by the
water is more conducive to our game." Then, whispering, he
added, "Plus if the ball gets away from us, there's always
the chance we can knock the Baroness's skull into the lake."

"What was that son?"

"I said, um, if you all come and play with us, there's always
the chance we can dock the Baroness's hull in the lake!"

The Baroness turned to the Captain and said, "Tell that brat
I don't have a boat, Georg."

Louisa then wound up and whipped the ball at the Baroness's head. Kurt yelled, "Think fast, Schrader!"

Schrader thought fast. But not fast enough.

It turned out that Louisa had not only magnificent aim, but
an arm with a whip action similar to that of American baseball legend Cy Young, which enabled her to hurl a ball at 61
kilometers per hour with pinpoint accuracy. Had a baseball

talent scout seen what Louisa could do with the ol' horsehide, he would have signed her in a heartbeat. (If Max Detweiler had more than half a brain, he would have made Louisa a solo entrant for the Graz Gala of Gaiety.) Long story short, Louisa von Trapp nailed Baroness Elsa Schrader right in the side of her noggin.

Succubi's heads are as hard as diamonds, so the Baroness was more thrown by the surprise of the blow than the blow itself. After rubbing her temple to make certain everything was where it was supposed to be, she picked up the ball and yelled, "This looks like fun, kids! May I join in?"

In unison, the brats said, "No! *Fick* off!"

She turned at the Captain and said, "Georg, are you going to let your children use that sort of language?"

The now-unconscious Captain didn't answer.

The Baroness shook her head and told Max, "Keep an eye on Georg. Make sure he doesn't choke on his own sick. I'm going to show these brats who's the *real* ballplayer in this house."

"Are you sure that's a good idea, Elsa?" Max asked.

"No. No, I don't think it's a good idea. I think it's a *great* idea."

"Do you not recall the performance after the puppet show last week? They're a, shall we say, *talented* bunch. The kind of talent that even the likes of you can't compete with."

With a dismissive wave, the Baroness said, "I have age and experience on my side."

"If you say so."

Farta called, "Are you going to give us our ball back, Baroness?"

"Not only am I going to return your ball, but I'm going to join the game."

The children all groaned. "We already told you to *fick* off." Brigitta said.

"I will not *fick* off. Trust me, this'll be fun."

Liesl nodded thoughtfully, then said to her siblings, "You know what? I think she's correct. I think it *will* be fun. Baroness, please throw me the ball."

Elsa wound up and awkwardly tossed the sphere across the lawn. She got some giddy-up on the ball—she *was* otherworldly, after all, and what she lacked in technique, she made up for in sheer strength—and had it smacked an unsuspecting mortal on the side of the head, it would have caused significant damage. But Liesl was a Vampire, with Vampire strength, Vampire quickness, and Vampire cunning, so she knew where the Baroness was going to throw the ball before the ball even left the Baroness's hand. All of which was why Liesl was able to, in a single, blurry-fast motion, catch the ball with one hand then heave it back toward the Baroness, who never saw it coming.

*KLONK!*

The blood jetted from the Baroness's broken nose in a single stream, and the kids all ran toward it as if it were a sprinkler on a hot summer day, mouths open, tongues a-wagging. They drank—or ate, depending on how one looks at it—every drop of the Baroness's hemoglobin, including those drops that fell onto the lawn. Benevolent Vampires, the brats shared with one another, and by the time the Baroness got the bleeding under control, all seven were equally sated.

Her white dress splattered red, the Baroness sat down beside Max, who stared off at the lake and said, "Ah, the country is so restful this time of year." He pushed a glass toward her. "Here, have another smoothie. Fresh mango. Yummy, yummy, yummy."

She knocked the glass off the table. Even when it shattered loudly on the floor of the veranda, the Captain didn't stir. The Baroness said, "There must be an easier way to make this one big, happy family. I can see it Max: Me, Georg, the kids, happy, rich, and ruling the world."

"The thought of you being their mother is hi-*fickin*-larious." Max smiled beatifically. "Elsa Schrader taking care of seven angry Vampire brats. I *love* it. How do you plan to raise these kids by yourself?"

"Two words: Boarding school. They'll leave in September and return in June. I can handle them for three months out of the year."

Max shook his head. "As demonstrated just now, you can't even handle them for three *minutes* out of the *day*. Besides, Georg would never let you send them away, not now that they're incrementally nicer than they have ever been. Face it, Elsa: You can be your most devious self, but if you manage to get Georg to marry you, those brats are yours."

All five of the von Trapp girls wandered over. Brigitta asked, "Uncle Max, when do you think Father will regain consciousness?"

Max leaned over his friend, said, "Now," then backhanded him across his right cheek.

The Captain popped up, blinked, and got a gander of Elsa's swollen nose. "What the *Hölle* happened to you?"

Pointing at the kids, she said, "*Them*. They happened to me."

"Hmm," he hmm'd with a tiny smile, then took the smoothie from the Baroness and asked, "What is this?" He sniffed at the drink and made a disgusted face. "It smells spoilt."

"That," the Baroness said, "is because your nose is out of whack, as the only thing you have smelled this week is libations. This is a smoothie, with real fruit in it. So drink it up, because you'll need your strength for tonight."

"What's tonight?" he asked.

She cleared her throat and hocked up some red and yellow sputum, then wiped some drying blood from her upper lip and said, "You and me. Alone together. In your bedroom. With candles. And I have a new item of clothing I think you'll enjoy." And then she spat again.

He looked at the two globs of mucus on the ground and curled his upper lip in disgust. "I think I'll take the night off, Elsa."

Brigitta repeated, "Father, I don't think our Governess is coming back."

Still staring at the Baroness's gloppy discharge, "What, you mean McMillan?"

"Maria."

"Right. Maria." He gave his daughter a sad, sad look, and said, "Yes, I suppose it's true, yes. She shall not return."

Brigitta said, "I can't believe it, Father. Why would she go?"

The Baroness said, "Can we stop talking about her? She bores me."

Louisa said, "She didn't even say goodbye."

"Can we stop talking about her?" the Baroness repeated. "She bores me."

"She did in her letter," the Captain said.

"What letter?" Farta asked.

"*There was no letter,*" the Baroness screeched, "*Now can we stop talking about her? She bores me.*"

"She wrote something about climbing every mountain, and teaching Friedrich about *doeraydoeraydoeraydoeray . . .*"

Liesl said, "Gross."

". . . and that we would know where to find her."

"Alright," the Baroness said, "now that that's out of the way, CAN WE STOP TALKING ABOUT HER! SHE BORES ME!"

Gretl said, "I have a question, Father. Who will take care of us now?"

The Captain ran his hand over his mouth, and said, "Well, darling, you're not going to have a minder . . ."

"Thank *Gott*," Louisa said.

". . . but you'll have a new munder. Er, I mean *mother.*"

"We will?" Liesl asked.

"We will?" Friedrich asked.

"They will?" the Baroness asked.

The Captain draped his arm over Elsa's shoulders. "Yes, darling, they will. You've made it clear that you want to be married to me, and I don't think I'll be able to do any better than you . . ."

"Gosh, thanks."

". . . so what the *Hölle*, let's tie the knot."

The Baroness pumped her fist and shouted, "*Yes!* That's what I'm *talkin'* 'bout! In your *face*, Lillith! How ya like me *now*, bitches?!" Then she cleared her throat and calmly said, "It would be my honor, Captain Georg von Trapp, to be your wife. Forever. And ever. And ever. Until the end of time."

Hearing the commotion, Friedrich and Kurt wandered over. Friedrich asked, "What happened here?"

Louisa told him, "Father and the Baroness are getting married."

"Oh," Friedrich said, then, unmoving and unblinking, stared at the Baroness. She met the boy's gaze, but could only hold it for a few seconds.

She surveyed the brats—all were staring at her, unmoving and unblinking. "So," she said almost nervously, "how does a girl go about getting some welcome-to-the-family hugs around here?"

In unison, the von Trapp children hissed at the Succubus, turned on their heels, and walked down the driveway and out the front gate.

After they were out of sight, the Captain turned to Elsa and Max, and said, "Well, I think that went smashingly. Who wants a drink?" And then he passed out.

# CHAPTER 8

I N   T H E   M I D S T of putting together a Power Point presenta-
tion to use as a recruitment tool, Mother Zombie was jolted
from her reverie by a sharp noise from the Abbey's entrance.
Irked, she began a long shuffle to the Abbey's front gate; when
she finally arrived some thirty minutes later, the Abbey's over-
seer asked Zombie Sister Cinnamon, "What was all the brou-
haha?"

"Well, these seven brats—actually, it was six brats, and one
pompous, snotty, pretentious girl twerp—wanted to visit everybody's favorite flibbertijibbet."

"Speaking of which," Mother Zombie said, "Bring her to me."

Thirty-six minutes later, Maria was sitting in front of
Mother Zombie's desk, wearing her favorite black cat suit, rubbing her head. "Mother, why did Cinnamon pull me in here by
my roots? All she had to do was tell me you had summoned me
and I'd have rushed over. What's it with you Zombies and all
the unnecessary violence?"

"Never mind that. Tell me why you have returned. If it's for a good reason, I shall let you stay. If it's for a bad reason, well, there are plenty of families looking for Governesses. Why were you brought back to us?"

"I wasn't brought back, Mother Zombie. I left of my own accord."

"Why?"

"I was scared."

"You? *Scared*?! You're a Vampire! What do you have to fear, except for a stake to the heart?"

Maria said, "I don't know how many times this has to be reiterated to the reader, but this stake to the heart business is malarkey. Everybody knows the only thing that can kill a Vampire is . . ."

No longer laughing, Mother Zombie said, "*Shh*. I hate Vampires as much as the next Zombie does, but if the world finds out how easy it is to stop you, your kind will be extinct in a matter of weeks . . . and that will end Stephenie Meyer's career before it even starts."

"Who's Stephenie Meyer? And why does she spell Stephanie as Stephenie?"

"Never mind. Tell me what you were frightened of."

"Fright is not the right word, *per se*. Maybe confusion. Mixed with nervousness. Combined with alarm. With a touch of exhaustion. Not to mention the boredom. And a smidgen of back pain. I also somehow caught a case of the crabs. So I needed to be away from all of that; thus, here I am."

"Maria, our Abbey isn't a place that Vampires can use as an escape from their problems."

"Well, it *should* be," she pouted.

"Well it isn't. So you'll have to face them again."

"*No!* I can't face him. I mean, *them*. I can't face *them*."

"Him, who?"

"Him, nobody."

"*Him, who?!*"

"Him, Captain von Trapp," Maria sighed.

Mother Zombie made a face. "Are you in love with him or something?" She snorted. "In love with Georg von Trapp. Ridiculous."

"Sometimes when I looked at his red cheeks, his bloodshot eyes, and the tiny veins on his nose, I'd get fluttery. Does that equal love? I have no idea." She paused, then said, "The Baroness said I loved him."

At that, Mother Zombie perked up. "Which Baroness?"

"Elsa Schrader."

"Schrader, Schrader, Schrader, hmmm . . ." After a thoughtful minute, Mother Zombie opened up her bottom desk drawer and removed a dusty, musty oversized book. She wiped the dirt from the cover and riffled through the pages, stopping about three-quarters of the way through, then moved her finger down the page and said, "Ah, here we are. Elsa Schrader, Succubus, born in the year 913, stopped aging at thirty, can cloud the minds of men and women alike, best known for her temper, her jealousy, and—and this is a direct quote—her awesome rack."

Maria nodded. "That's her, alright."

"Did you tell Captain von Trapp about your feelings for him?" Mother Zombie asked.

"Not purposely. We had one moment where . . . where . . . where *something* happened. We were dancing, he held me close, and there was a look in his eye . . . but that might have been the booze."

"More importantly," Mother Zombie said, "did you let Baroness Schrader see how you felt?"

"She could tell. She knew. It was she who made me go. She clouded my mind, just like the book said. I'm mortified to return, so I want to stay here. I'll follow Zombie Law. No more leaving the Abbey without your consent. No more singing in the mountains. No more turning into a bat and sneaking into your chambers and watching you touch your rancid lady-parts . . ."

"*What?!*"

"A joke. Just know that Maria shall not be a problem."

Mother Zombie stood up and paced the room. "Maria," she said, "the love of a man and a woman is holy, too, even if the man is weak, and the woman is a filthy Vampire. You have an enormous trove of love, and you must find out how the Devil wants you to spend your life."

"My life is now pledged to Zombie Law. The love of another is no longer an option."

"Maria, if you love this man, it doesn't mean you have to ignore Zombie Law. Go back to the von Trapp mansion. Find out one way or the other."

"Oh, Mother Zombie, please, let me stay," she begged. "I'll do anything!"

"Will you burp Foxxxy?"

"Of course!"

"Will you clean Foxxxy's daily discharge?"

"Yes!"

"Will you clean Foxxxy's *nightly* discharge?"

Maria gulped, then, with considerably less enthusiasm, said, "Yes."

"Will you change Foxxxy's diapers?"

Maria gagged a little bit, then said, "I guess."

Mother Zombie shook her head. "I'm not sure about this, Vampire. Changing Foxxxy's diapers isn't how you climb every mountain. Dealing with Foxxxy's discharge floor clean isn't how you follow every byway. Burping Foxxxy isn't how you ford every stream . . ."

"What's fording a stream, Mother?"

"No clue. Ask Hammerstein. Anyhow, do you get my point?"

Maria said, "Are you trying to say that if I want to find my dream, if I want to give all the love I can give, if I want to search high and low for happiness, I have to . . ."

"You have to *leave.*"

"I was going to say *follow my heart.*"

"Right. That too. But more importantly, *leave.*"

"I suppose I could go and . . ."

Zombie Sisters Brandi, Jazzmine, and Cinnamon burst into the room. Brandi hurled a suitcase at Maria—Maria ducked, and it hit Mother Zombie smack in the face, knocking her onto her hindquarters—then said, "Leaving so soon? We packed your belongings."

Jazzmine said, "Do you remember where the front gate is? I shall show you, so you won't get lost." She handed Maria her saxophone case.

Cinnamon said, "There's a carriage waiting to take you back to the von Trapps. So you get out there and climb every mountain, Maria!"

Mother Zombie pulled herself up from the floor and said, "It's probably best for you to waltz your way out of here, Vampire, because no matter how hard you try, and no matter how good your intentions are, nobody causes a problem like you."

Several hours after the Zombies foisted Maria out onto the street, the von Trapp brood arrived home from the Abbey, where they were greeted by their Father. "So," he said, clutching a lager in his right hand, and a tumbler of gin in his left, "the prodigals return. Care to tell me where you disappeared to? I announce my engagement, and you take your leave without so much as a congratulations." He checked his watch. "Also, you're tardy for supper."

Friedrich pointed at the Captain's lager. "Looks like you went and started without us."

Ignoring his eldest son, the Captain said, "Which one of you is going to be the first one to tell me where you were? Brigitta?"

Brigitta said, "As if."

"Louisa?"

"No way, Jose," Louisa said.

"Friedrich?"

"Give me some of that gin, and we can discuss it."

Liesl said, "Where do you think we were, Father?"

"Rolling drunks?" the Captain guessed.

Kurt said, "Rolling drunks is so last year. We're Vampires now, Father, and Vampires are far too elegant and classy to roll drunks." He paused. "We prefer to feast on the weak of mind and heart. Like I said, elegant and classy."

"So is that where you were? Feasting on the weak of mind and heart?"

Farta said, "Well, that wasn't our primary objective . . ."

". . . but we got hungry, so it happened anyhow," Kurt said.

"Very well," the Captain said. "Since you have obviously stuffed yourselves full of millions of blood corpuscles, you can't be hungry anymore, so I'll just have to tell Frau Alice to dispose of your dinners."

Kurt said, "*Schiessen.* I'm still hungry."

"Of course you are," Liesl said.

The Captain said, "Ta ta, brats," and traipsed into the house.

"*Schiessen,*" Kurt repeated. "We should have told."

"He would have killed us," Farta said.

"He can't kill us, silly," Louisa said. "We're already dead."

"But he can starve us to death," Kurt said. "I feel horrible. And hungry."

Brigitta said, "Remember Fraulein Maria's ridiculous list of things that are supposed to make us feel better when we're feeling blue?"

Liesl said, "*Mein Gott,* I almost forgot all about that. Brown paper packages? *Hah!*"

Friedrich said, "That was bad, but the worst was bright copper kettles. And she was so specific about it: Not just kettles, but *bright copper* ones. Dull black ones won't make you feel better, but bright copper ones will."

"What about blue satin sashes?" Farta asked. "There's nothing, but *nothing* you can do with a sash that will make you feel better . . . except maybe choke the Baroness."

At that, the children laughed, but a call from the end of the driveway quickly interrupted their merriment: "Kettles and sashes are wonderful, wonderful items, and if they don't make you happy, well, you don't know what happy is!"

The children turned around, and were greeted by the sight of a woman, an exquisite woman with glossy brown hair, piercing brown eyes, and alabaster skin. The woman was wearing a tighter-than-tight cat suit, and wasn't the least bit ashamed . . . but why should she have been, for you see, her body was perfect: muscular arms, a graceful neck, firm breasts, a flat stomach, and strong thighs—the kind of flawless form that many a mortal would kill for.

Let's not forget her fangs.

The children ran to their Governess/creator, arms opened wide, the sun reflecting off of their bared teeth. Maria dropped her suitcase and saxophone, and fell into the brats' embrace. After the hug ran its course, Maria said, "Someday, kids, someday you'll understand the joy of brown paper packages."

"I seriously doubt that," Liesl said, "but it's lovely to have you back."

"Lovely to be back. What did I miss?"

Brigitta said, "Nothing big . . . unless you think that Father and the Baroness getting married is big."

"Oh," Maria said. "Wow. Gone from the mansion for only twenty-ish pages, and look what happens."

Just then, Georg von Trapp walked out onto the porch. Louisa, seeing her Father, waved and jumped up and down, up and down, up and down. "Father," she cried, "Father, look who has returned!"

The Captain walked over, staggering only a little. He nodded at the Vampire, then somberly said, "Maria."

She nodded back. "Captain."

"You're looking well."

"As are you."

Without taking his eye from hers, the Captain said, "Kids, go in and eat your supper."

Beaming, Kurt said, "I thought Frau Alice threw it out!" and then turned into a bat and flew into the house.

Giving his chunky brother an exasperated look, Friedrich said, "We're staying right here, Father. This is unmissable stuff."

Liesl said, "However, we'll leave if you two get naked."

"Nobody's getting naked," the Captain said.

Maria mumbled, "I wouldn't be so sure of that." Then she told the children, "Go inside, brats. Immediately. Thank you."

In unison, they said, "Yes, Governess."

After the kids were in the house, the Captain said, "You're looking well."

"Yes," Maria said, "you mentioned that."

"Ah. Right, then. So. Well. Um. So. Um. Well . . ."

"Spit it out, Captain."

*"You left without so much as a goodbye to me or the children, and I don't care if you're a Vampire, or a Werewolf, or a Blob, but delivering that sort of news with a note is flat-out rude behavior, and I don't abide by rudeness!"*

"Ah. Right. Well, you might want to talk to your *fiancée* about the way I left."

"Oh. Fiancée. You know about that."

"I know about that," Maria agreed.

"Why should I ask Elsa about? . . ."

"Ask Elsa about what?" asked Elsa, who had slipped into the yard undetected.

"Nothing, darling. As you can see, Maria has returned."

The Succubus glared at the Vampire. "I see. How wonderful. How delightfully droll." She asked Maria, "So are you here to stay, or did you just pop by for a visit?"

"That's yet to be decided."

The Baroness took a step toward Maria. "And how will it be decided?"

Maria took a step toward the Baroness. "I haven't decided yet."

The Baroness took another step toward Maria. "Have you decided when you're going to decide? Because I can help you make your decision."

Maria took another step toward the Baroness; their noses were practically touching. "How would you decide to help me make my decision?"

The Baroness took yet another step toward Maria; their mouths lightly grazed. "I haven't decided yet."

The Captain took the Baroness by her elbow and said, "Alright, darling, let's get you inside." As he tugged his fiancée toward the house, he said, "Welcome back, Governess."

"Lovely to be back, Captain. Lovely to be back, indeed."

Knocked for a loop by Maria's reemergence, Captain von Trapp passed on his usual dinner cocktails in favor of a smoothie, so by the time ten o'clock approached, he was stone sober. *Hmm,* he thought, *this nighttime sobriety isn't all that horrible,* as he stood on the balcony outside of his bedroom, watching Maria watch the lake. *My goodness, that's one good-looking bloodsucker. I never imagined I'd be attracted to a being who could kill me without a second thought. I wonder what making love to a killer would be like. It might be like making love to a Nazi. Not that I've ever thought about making love to a Nazi. I'm just saying.*

He briefly pictured Maria in a skintight S.S. uniform, and his imagination might have taken him a couple steps farther down a road best left unexplored had the Baroness not burst into the room. "Darling," she breathed, "I think you should turn around."

Reluctantly, he tore his eyes from Maria's pale form and was greeted by a sight that would have melted many a mortal man's mind: Elsa was wearing a gauzy red negligee that hugged her upper body, flowed over her waist, and ended just above her knees. Her breasts peeked over the décolletage, almost as if they were shy, which they most definitely were not, as witnessed by the erectness of their nipples. Her feet were encased in a pair of shoes that were all points—pointy toe, pointy heel, pointy bottom, pointy top—and shaped her legs perfectly. As for the Baroness's hair, it was ironed flat, and hung down to the small of her back, and, in the candlelight, resembled spun gold. Her face was flawless and her eyes glowed a mellow shade of red.

As did her lady-parts.

She asked the Captain, "Do you like my new outfit, Georg? I put it together just for you."

Having seen this sort of display dozens and dozens of times over the last year, the Captain wasn't quite as impressed as one would expect . . . but he was still impressed. "It's lovely, my dear."

"What's your favorite part?" she asked, closing the distance between the two.

He gave her a general, noncommittal gesture and said, "I guess the thing over by the thing next to the thing."

"What *thing*, darling?" she pouted.

"The *whole* thing," he said, then snuck a peek over his shoulder and out the window.

He heard the sound of thin fabric falling to the floor, then Elsa's commanding voice: "Look at me, Georg. Look at me now."

After von Trapp turned around, he was careful to keep his eyes above her chin, because if he caught a glimpse of her naked body, his blood would vacate his brain and migrate to his man-parts, rendering him unable to do what he had to do. Their eyes remained locked for several minutes or several hours, during which point, Georg made a decision. "It isn't you, it's me," he said. "I *love* you, but I'm not *in love* with you. I believe we would be better off being friends rather than lovers. You deserve better than me. I need to love myself before I can love somebody else. I'm so enamored with you that it scares me. I love you like a sister . . ."

"Oh, for the love of *Gott*, enough with the crappy break-up clichés, just say it: You want to *fick* the nanny." She shook her head. "Typical middle-aged Austrian male behavior. You turn fifty, and you want the fast cars—cars that go thirty kilometers per hour, perhaps even forty—and the young women . . ."

"Maria is many centuries old."

"You know what, Georg," the Baroness said, donning her negligee, "you can have her. And you know what else? I was going to leave you anyhow, but you beat me to the punch. I don't need you, or your money, or your brats, or your *schvantz*. And you know why? Because I get all the *schvantz* I need from Max Detweiler."

The Captain nodded. "So I've heard."

Elsa blinked. "He told you?"

"Of course he did. Bros before hoes."

"*What* before *what?*"

"Forget it. You were saying? . . ."

"What I was saying was, *good-bye.*"

As Baroness Elsa Schrader sashayed out the door, von Trapp took one more appreciative look at her backside, then forgot what she looked like immediately after he turned his attention back to the Vampire by the lake.

# CHAPTER 9

THE NIGHT WAS CHILLY, but Maria was toasty, so toasty that she slipped out of her cat suit and tiptoed into the lake to cool off. What with the water being so freezing, she only went up to her ankles. (One might wonder how or why freezing water would bother a being whose body pumped ice-cold blood. Well, one best not ask too many questions, lest one wants to suffer the wrath of the Vampire community.)

A quiet voice from behind whispered, "Hello."

Startled, Maria spun around, bared her fangs, hissed, and lunged toward whoever or whatever had crept up upon her. Fortunately for our story, the Captain stumbled on a pebble and fell down on his rump, so Maria missed biting his neck by a mere sixteen centimeters.

Once she got a gander at who she had almost killed, she was despondent. "Oh Captain, my Captain," she said, "I apologize ever so much."

Von Trapp stood up, brushed himself off, and said, "I've been watching you from my balcony, Maria."

Maria liked that. She asked, "Was there something you were watching for in particular?"

He rubbed his temples and then, with his eyes seemingly adjusted to the dark, noticed her naked body. "I, um, I, um, I, um . . ." He pointed to the ground. "Might I sit down?"

"Well, being that you own this land, sir, you may do as you please." Maria noted that the Captain wasn't eyeing her body, which at once pleased her *(What a gentleman!)* and upset her *(Does he not like my rack?)*.

Once the Captain got himself into a comfortable position in the sand, he said, "You have not told me the true reason you left us and returned to the Abbey."

"Well," Maria fudged, "you see, there's only so long one can go without being in the presence of Zombies. They're such lovely, loving creatures, and as welcoming as you all have been, there's little more gratifying in this world than a Zombie hug."

"Is that the truth?"

"Sure. Why not?"

"Alright. Then why did you leave the Abbey and return to us?"

"Easy: I missed the children."

"*My* children?" he asked, incredulous. "Those brats? *Nobody* misses my children." After she didn't respond, he added, "Is there anything else you missed?"

Maria looked at his neck, and wondered how he would taste. *Probably like yearning, heartbreak, old money, and booze,* she thought. "What I missed doesn't matter." She stood and walked back toward the water. "All I want is the best for you and your family. But I'm sure you'll be fine, what with your future wife, Mrs. Baroness von Succu-Trapp taking care of you."

Hoisting himself up off the ground, the Captain said, "There isn't going to be a Mrs. Baroness von Succu-Trapp."

"Wait, what?" she asked, unconsciously wading into the water.

The Captain pulled off his shoes, socks, and trousers, then joined her in the lake. "The Baroness and I have called off our engagement."

Maria blinked. "Oh. I'm sorry."

"Are you?" the Captain asked, his teeth chattering.

"Of course I am. As I said, all I want is what's best for the von Trapps, and if the best means that you marry that . . . that . . . that . . ." She trailed off, then, after a deep breath, roared, *"Baroness Schrader is a scum-sucking wench, and the sight of her fills my stomach with bile, and my undead soul with disgust, and I want to send her to the Tenth Ring of* Hölle, *a Ring reserved for gold-digging sex addicts, a Ring where she would live all eternity with a red-hot poker buried in her backside, which is exactly, exactly, exactly what the scum-sucking wench deserves!"* She paused, then added, "That said, I'm sure you two would have been very happy together."

"No, we wouldn't have been happy, as I have eyes for another."

"You do?"

He took a step toward her. "I do."

"And that person would be? . . ."

He took another step, gently touched her cheek, leaned in, and parted his lips ever-so-slightly. Before their mouths met, he said, "Could we get the *fick* out of this lake? The shrinkage situation could prove to be problematic."

Once they were back on dry land, they kissed, and it was as magical as Maria could have hoped: Lips mashing lips, tongues wrestling tongues, teeth colliding with fangs. When they came up for air some five minutes later, the Captain asked, "Is *that* why you came back?"

"No," she said, "*this* is why I came back," then she cupped his man-parts through his undershorts. After a moment, she said, "Goodness, you weren't kidding about the shrinkage."

"Give me a second here, Maria. I'm not as young as I used to be." When his man-parts finally became properly engorged some forty minutes later, he said, "Oh, can this be happening to me?"

She squeezed him tightly, and asked, "Why would it *not* be happening to you?"

Breathing heavier by the second, he said, "Well, Maria, I had a wicked childhood. I had a miserable youth."

"Is this really the time to discuss your childhood?" Maria asked, her lady-parts singing an aria of their own.

"Of course it isn't." He gently touched her breast, then added, "Here you are, standing there, loving me, whether or not you should. At some point in the past, I must have done something good."

She squeezed his ever-growing man-parts. "I know that in the present, you're doing something good, alright."

Legs wobbling, he asked Maria, "Do you know when I first started loving you?" Maria shook her head. "That time in the ballroom, when we were projectile vomiting."

"Ah, good times, good times. Do you know when I first started loving you?"

"I don't."

"When you first berated me for breaking your whistle." After another squeeze, she whispered into his ear, "I like being berated. That's something I'd like to explore with you further." The Captain shuddered as his man-parts exploded in glee, after which Maria rinsed her hand in the lake and said, "I guess the shrinkage problem is a problem no more."

The Captain jumped into the lake and dived underwater, oblivious to the cold. When he came up for air, he said, "Obviously it will be difficult to track down your parents, so is there anybody who I should ask for your hand in marriage?"

Maria said, "Mother Zombie would be the logical choice, but she isn't exactly what you would call a fanatic of the human race, so I don't want to go down that particular road just yet. But you know who we *should* ask? The brats."

Nodding, the Captain said, "You're probably right. But what if they say no?"

"Than I shall turn their undeath into death."

"You can do that?"

"Sure. Why not?"

The Captain grinned. "Works for me."

In order to keep the story from stalling, the brats immediately gave the union their blessing, so, just like that, Vampire Sister Maria of the Salzburg Zombie Abbey and Captain Georg von Trapp of the Salzburg von Trapps were officially engaged, after which the Captain set a wedding date for the following evening, again to keep the story from stalling. Being that it was impossible to find a proper venue for such an event on such short notice, Maria suggested they get married at the one place in Salzburg she knew wouldn't be booked: The Abbey.

"There?" Liesl asked during an impromptu meeting of the von Trapp women. "Really?"

"It's ideal," Maria explained, "full of history, and statues, and dust, and Zombie discharge."

"That sounds awful, Governess," Farta said.

Maria patted Farta's hair. "Never you fear, my dear. I shall make sure the discharge is cleaned from their floor in time for the wedding."

Liesl asked, "More importantly, will you make sure that the Zombies don't make a meal of our brains? Our yummy, yummy Vampire brains?"

"I shall do my best," Maria said, "but I offer no guarantees."

Louisa said, "I suppose I can live with that . . ." Cocking a thumb at Gretl, she continued, ". . . so long as she enters the building first."

Before the annoying little insect could launch into a treatise about how simple it is to survive a Zombie attack, Maria said, "The only person who might eat somebody's brain on my wedding night would be Kurt, because, as we all know, the little porker will eat anything. But I shall make sure that he has been properly fed." She clapped once, then said, "Now let's begin the beginning of the wedding montage!"

And what a beginning of a wedding montage it was! All 173 Zombies from the Abbey—as well as several from the Abbey's Vienna franchise—were in attendance, as was a small contingency of Vampires from Romania, none of whom Maria had ever met in her life (Vampires are always game for a good party, even if they know neither the bride nor the groom.), as was John Coltrane, there strictly for symmetry's sake. (Like all comedians know, comedy comes in threes, and to this point, he has appeared in only two chapters. Plus, as most are aware, jazz musicians never turn down free food.)

Maria's dress was a sight to behold: The top was identical to her favorite cat suit in color (black) and cut (tight), but the bottom was unlike anything Maria had ever worn in either her life or her undeath. The shiny black crinoline—which matched the cat suit-like portion of the dress to a "T"—billowed into an ornate dome that covered the bride's shapely legs. The gown's heavy train was seven meters long, and required the help of five zombies to carry down the aisle. (Mother Zombie picked her five speediest minions to handle the task, which she hoped would mean that the march to the altar would end before sunrise.) The processional—maid of honor Liesl, followed by flower girls Farta and Gretl, followed by best man Max, followed by the semi-sober bridegroom, followed by the nervous bride—staggered down the aisle, sickened by the sight of the wedding guests. (Haters of most everything human, the Zombies felt the exact same way.)

Once the wedding party was arranged in proper order beneath the statue of The Being Whose Name Shall Not Be Uttered, Mother Zombie stepped to the pulpit, gave the bridal party a loving look, then said, "We're gathered here today to answer one question: *How do you solve a problem like Maria?*"

Maria said, "Excuse me?"

Ignoring her, Mother Zombie continued. "When I first laid eyes upon this Vampire all those centuries ago, I asked myself, how do you find a cloud and pin it down? The answer to that is, of course, you can't. Does anybody know why?"

Gretl raised her tiny hand and said, "A cloud is a *visible* mass, but not a *tangible* mass. In other words, you can see it, but you can't touch it. Well, that isn't *exactly* the truth: You can *touch* it, but you can't *feel* it, because—since it's composed entirely of water droplets and/or frozen ice crystals—there isn't anything to feel. And if there isn't anything to feel, there isn't anything to pin down."

Mother Zombie beamed. "That's exactly how I'd have put it, little girl, *exactly*. Well answered."

Gretl whispered to Farta, "I like her."

Farta whispered back, "Do shut up, Gretl."

"When I got to know her a bit better," Mother Zombie continued, "I asked myself, *How do you find a word that means Maria?* Well, we at the Abbey came up with three: Flibbertijibbet—which means whore, will-o'-the wisp—which is another kind of whore, and clown—which, of course, means *clown*."

"Wait a minute," Maria said.

"As I look out into this chapel, I ask you, is there something you would like to say to her?"

In unison, the Zombies yelled, "*Whore!*"

Maria said, "Hold on a second."

"As I look out into this chapel, I ask you, do you feel there's something she ought to understand."

Again: "*Whore!*"

"Come on, guys," Maria said, "this is my *wedding*."

"But now, as I look at the human faces we have with us—faces that look quite dinner-worthy—I know the answer. I know how to solve a problem like Maria." Mother Zombie paused, fixed the audience with a steely gaze, then said, "You marry her off to a rich mortal. Problem solved."

Maria said, "Thank you, Mother Zombie. That was nice. Sort of."

"The pleasure is mine, dear. Now, by the power invested *in* me *by* me, I pronounce you mortal husband and Vampire wife." Maria closed her eyes and leaned in to kiss her new husband—who, for some reason, was slumping over, or at least seemed to be noticeably shorter—but before her lips made contact with her betrothed, Mother Zombie roared, "*Stop!* Don't engage in such foulness in our Abbey! Kissing horrifies us, so if you want to see a roomful of Zombies emit foul discharge from every orifice in their body, I'd keep your mouths to yourselves."

So Maria, eyes still shut, reached out her arm and squeezed the hand of her betrothed . . . a hand that seemed small . . .

and soft . . . and cold, cold, so very, very cold, as cold as that of a Vampire's. She opened her eyes and stared at the face of her new husband: Friedrich von Trapp.

Maria gasped, "Friedrich? . . . Where is Georg? . . . How did you? . . . I don't understand . . ."

Friedrich touched his finger to her lips and said, "Best not to ask too many questions. Best to just accept and embrace the fact that we're now married. Best to cut to the remainder of the wedding montage."

And thus began the conclusion of the oddest, least romantic, most multi-orgasmic wedding montage in the history of wedding montages.

# INTERLUDE #4

*D*RACULA HIT A BUTTON *on his universal remote and turned the lights back on.* "Okay, now that you've seen most of The Sound of Music, *does this book make more sense?"*

*"You know what makes sense to me, Drac?" Handsome Boy asked. "That this Goldsher character is doing the same thing that the* Twilight *lot is doing: Trying to entertain people while making a buck."*

*"You told us at the last meeting that* Twilight *wasn't about money," Brown Cape noted. "I thought you said it was pure and uncynical."*

*"Yeah, well you can watch the bottom line while you're being pure and uncynical," Handsome Boy said.*

*"One," Felt Face said. "I count one line of bullshit."*

*Brown Cape said to Felt Face, "You're surprised? This limey bastard flip-flops like he's Bill Clinton . . ."*

*"Hey, lay off of Clinton," Dracula said. "Best U.S. president since Kennedy."*

"... *and he'll contradict himself to make some point that he disagreed with twenty minutes before.*"

"*One,*" Felt Face said. "*I count one flip-flopper.*"

Handsome Boy grabbed his crotch and said, "*Two. I count two bollocks you can suck.*"

"*You know what?!*" Dracula roared, "*I give up! This is the worst book club I've ever been to in my entire existence, and I've had a long-ass existence, so I've been to a whole heap of book clubs. Screw it, I'm pulling the plug and joining Dave Frankenstein's discussion group! Sure, he's a pretentious fop who sounds like an elitist jerk whenever he's on NPR, but at least he reads the frickin' books!*" Dracula gestured at Felt Face and said, "*Let's go. I'll drive you home,*" then he nodded at Handsome Boy and Brown Cape and said, "*Watch the rest of the movie or not. Read the rest of the book or not. I don't give a crap. Just make sure you lock up on your way out.*"

After Dracula and Felt Face made their exit, the two remaining book clubbers stared at the door for a bit. Eventually Handsome Boy picked up Dracula's copy of My Favorite Fangs and said, "*You know what? This thing's growing on me. Want to see how it ends?*"

"*Why not? My cereal will keep for a while.*"

Handsome Boy put his arm over Brown Cape's cartoony shoulders and said, "*I'm sure it will, mate. I'm sure it will.*"

PART THREE

# CHAPTER 10

IT WAS TWO WEEKS after Friedrich and Maria got hitched, and Max Detweiler was gawking at some drab buildings, some bright streetlights, and some empty kiosks, then said aloud, "*Mein Gott.* What the *fick* happened here?"

"Here" was the town square where the Graz Gala of Gaiety had been held for the last five years, and "What the *fick* happened?" might better have been phrased as "*Who* the *fick* happened," and that "Who" would refer to the Nazis. In Galas past, the square had been decorated with balloons, streamers, flowers, and a few incongruous piñatas. This year, however, it was all red flags with swastikas and crudely illustrated tributes to Adolf Hitler. Again aloud, Max said, "Call me crazy, call me nutty, call me kooky, but I don't equate Hitler with the Gala of Gaiety."

Waiting to begin a run through of their performance—which Max had dubbed "Vampirecrobatics"—the von Trapp children were huddled up by the stage, looking ill at ease. Max wandered over and said, "What's going on, brats? Why the glum faces?"

Louisa said, "We're not prepared for tonight, Herr Detweiler. My human-to-bat transformation is wonderful, but my bat-to-human won't win us any prizes."

Friedrich said, "You have got that right, sister dear. Mine is perfect in both directions, but the rest of you are going to mess it up for all of us. How can we synchronize our transformation if you have no control? It's all about control."

Kurt said, "You may be ready to go with transformation, Friedrich, but your centrifugal force is down significantly. You don't move as fast as even Farta. Talk about blowing the synchronicity."

Liesl said, "Can we just eat the judges and go home?" Pointing at the biggest of the Nazi flags, she said, "Because I don't like the looks of this one bit."

"Apologies, kids," Max said, "but we're committed. If we pull out, we'll . . ."

He was interrupted by a tap on the shoulder. "What's this about pulling out, Herr Detweiler?"

Max turned around and found himself face-to-chest with Colonel Wilde von Beckbaw, who was decked out in his best Nazi finery. "Oh. You. Good morning."

Von Beckbaw's arm popped up in a Nazi salute. "Heil Hitler."

Max's arm popped up and he scratched his cheek, mumbling, "Heil my *schvantz*."

"Apologies, Herr Detweiler," von Beckbaw glowered, "but

my hearing seems to be going. Probably all that time I spend on the radio. Did you know I have a radio show?"

"So I've heard."

"Quite. In any event, could you repeat what you just said, please?"

At the top of his lungs, Max roared, "HEIL MY *SCHVANTZ!*"

Von Beckbaw stared at Max. Max stared at von Beckbaw. After a tense minute, von Beckbaw burst out laughing. "Oh, Herr Detweiler, always the jokester, just like my good friend, Herr Stern. And your timing couldn't be better. I need a chuckle, because this Gala of Gaiety is lacking gaiety. I hear there are Vampires on the premises, and you know how we feel about Vampires."

Gesturing to the kids, Max said, "You knew we were going to be here, Colonel von Beckbaw, so don't act surprised. You should be thrilled the brats came. Best act of the night. I guarantee victory." He paused. "Or would you like us to leave? We'll gladly be on our way, but that will leave the show about fifteen minutes short, and we all know how much Herr Hitler likes his punctuality. I can hear him now: '*The trains run on time, but a gala doesn't?! Kill von Beckbaw!*'"

Von Beckbaw sniffed. "He wouldn't kill me. Der Fuhrer is a benevolent dictator who would never, never murder one of his men, especially one who does such a good job recruiting for the party. Castration, maybe, but not murder." Glaring at the children, he said, "Fine, they can perform. But I can't be held responsible for the audience reaction."

Max said, "We'll take our chances. Now if you'll excuse us . . ."

"One more thing before I leave you to your duties, Herr Detweiler," the Colonel said. "Have you been to Captain von Trapp's house lately?"

"Why?"

"I was curious if he'd done up those Nazi arts and crafts I'd suggested. Maybe a macaroni Hitler head, or a swastika made from sticks and feathers. Why, even a crayon drawing of me would suffice. All he has on display in there is that hideous Austrian flag. It makes me shudder." And then, as if to prove his point, he shuddered.

"The Captain is away celebrating Friedrich's honeymoon, Colonel von Beckbaw."

"Wait, what?"

"Friedrich pulled a switcheroo at the altar, but the bride chose to spend her post-wedding week with Captain von Trapp." Max cocked his thumb at Friedrich, who was playing a game of pocket pool, a dreamy look plastered on his face. "Can you blame her?"

Ignoring Friedrich, von Beckbaw leered, "Georg is one lucky duck, bagging the Baroness. That girl oozes Aryanism, if you know what I mean."

"I know what you mean."

"Conservatively speaking, I'd make her scream liberally, if you know what I mean."

"Again, I know what you mean."

"I'd love to park my blue state in her red state, if you know . . ."

"Okay, okay, okay, Wilde. I get it." Figuring it would be pointless to not mention that von Trapp had broken ties with the Succubus, Max said, "You're correct, though. The Captain is a lucky duck, indeed. Now please go. We must prepare."

Ignoring Max, von Beckbaw asked, "When will the Captain return?"

"No idea. He's M.I.A. Radio silence."

"I can't fault him there. If I were with that luscious piece of *arsch*, I too would remain out of contact with the rest of the world. When he returns, tell him I expect to see him wearing that nice von Beckbaw t-shirt. If not, there will be consequences."

"Is that so? What kind of consequences?"

"My American counterparts tell me that there's a trend in the States in which one takes a scoop of dog *scheisse*, places it in a paper bag, leaves it on the victim's front stoop, and sets it on fire. The beauty of this is when the victim stamps out the fire, his foot will be covered with . . ."

"I get it, Colonel von Beckbaw," Max said. "Nazi ingenuity never fails to impress."

"Yes, quite," von Beckbaw said. "So we shall see you tonight. All there's to say now is farewell, and . . ." Another Nazi salute. ". . . Heil Hitler! Heil Hitler! Heil Hitler!" Von Beckbaw then goosestepped across the square, knocking over a mere three pedestrians.

Max shook his head, then turned to the kids and said, "Alright, brats, we must go home."

"No run-through?" Kurt asked.

"No, chunky butt. We shall be spontaneous! We shall improvise! Our talent will win out! Singers, instrumentalists, and magicians, beware: The von Trapp family Vampires are coming to get you! Now, in the car, brats."

All the kids, save for Liesl, piled into Max's brown jalopy. Right as Liesl was about to step through the door, a tall blond man in a brown S.S. uniform tapped her on the shoulder and said, "Good afternoon, Miss Liesl von Trapp, Vampire."

Liesl turned around. "Good afternoon, Rolfe Mueller, Private in the Nazi Undeath Squad."

Louisa poked her head out the window. "What's the Nazi Undeath Squad?"

"Never mind," Liesl said. "If you'll excuse us, me and Rolfie have to have a chat." She walked ten meters from the car; Rolfe followed.

Rolfe said, "I haven't forgotten our night at the gazebo."

"Nor have I," Liesl said.

"It was a revelatory moment for me."

"As it was for me."

"I look forward to a repeat performance."

"As do I."

"The ending, however, shall not be the same."

"No, it shall not," Liesl hissed. "It shall be worse for you. Much, much worse."

Rolfe made a fist and snarled, "If we weren't preparing for the Gala of Gaiety, I'd perform right here."

She pointed at his crotch. "Somehow I doubt that."

Still snarling, Rolfe pulled an envelope from his pocket and threw it at Liesl; it bounced harmlessly off of her chest and fell to the ground. "Give this to your traitor of a father when he returns from his vacation. And tell him we left a little gift for him at your house."

Liesl asked, "How do you know he's on vacation?"

"The Nazi party is all-knowing and all-seeing! We know what you're going to do before you're going to do it!" He paused. "Plus I ran into him at that dive bar by my house, and he told me."

Heading back to the car, Liesl said, "Get out of my sight, Rolfe. Next time I see you, I'll end you, whether we're at a Gala, a gazebo, or an Abbey filled with Zombies. And that's a promise."

He gave Liesl a Nazi salute, said, "Heil Hitler, and death to the undead!" then goosestepped off into the afternoon.

When she stepped into the car, she asked Max, "When are Father and Maria returning?"

"I have no idea," Max lied. In actuality, Max knew the Captain's plans to a "T," for that morning, von Trapp had called Max to give him the details of his trip, because—you guessed it, dear reader—the plot needed advancement.

For the entire two weeks after the wedding, Maria and Georg drove around Austria in the Captain's Austro-Tata, stopping to eat at every intriguing-looking restaurant, to drink at every intriguing-looking watering hole, and to sleep (and consummate, and re-consummate, and re-re-consummate their relationship) at every intriguing-looking hotel. The Captain, Max learned, found making love to a Vampire—especially one he was desperately in love with—far more fulfilling than sleeping with a Succubus. At times, his carnal relations with the Baroness felt more like a contest than an expression of their feelings, a test of who could go faster, farther, and weirder. With Maria, the bedtime games were playful, comfortable, and warm, the only difficult issue being that Maria had to be extremely careful with how she used her mouth; one too-hard nibble, and the Captain would join the ranks of the undead (or the castrated), and, as everybody knows, in every Vampire story, all undead heroes (or antiheroes) have to have a mortal guide, and said mortal guides have to have a full helping of franks and beans. If Maria Vampire'd the Captain, Max Detweiler would be called into mortal guide duty, something Max undoubtedly wanted no part of.

The happy couple returned from their vacation the day of the brats' aborted rehearsal. When the Captain pulled his car into the driveway, he was greeted by the sight of two items that had not been at the house when he and Maria had departed: A charred paper bag filled with dog *scheisse* on the porch, and a bust of Adolf Hitler's head made from bottle caps. He told Friedrich's wife and his snuggle bunny, "My, my, my, those Nazis are experts with psychological warfare. Good thing I'm of sound mind, or the statue and the *scheisse* would have brought me to my knees." Yes, dear reader, he was being sarcastic.

Maria said, "You shouldn't joke about this, Georg." (Now

that they were married, she called him by his given name . . . unless they were in bed, where she continued to call him "Sir.") "Today it's arts and crafts and feces, but tomorrow it could be bullets and bombs."

"They wouldn't dare, Maria," the Captain said. (Now that they were sleeping together, he called her by her proper name . . . unless he was really, really schnockered, then he continued to call her random three-syllable names that started with the letter "M.")

"And why do you say that?" Maria asked.

"Because I'm a Captain?"

"A Captain of what? You have never quite made it clear."

"Well I *can't* make it quite clear, because *Hammerstein* never quite made it clear."

"Oh, that rapscallion Hammerstein, always there to take the blame." At that, the couple doubled over with laughter.

Max and the brats then pulled into the driveway. After they trooped out of the car, Max pointed at the house and said, "My, my, my, those Nazis are experts with psychological warfare. Good thing I'm of sound mind, or the statue and the *scheisse* would have brought me to my knees." Yes, dear reader, he too was being sarcastic. "I can't bear to be in the presence of this sordidness a moment longer," he said, then hopped back in his car and toodled off.

The kids then heaped upon Maria a bunch of hugs and *Oh-we-missed-you-ever-so-much* platitudes that were so inane and treacly they shan't be repeated here, after which they marched into the house . . . save for Liesl, who fished an envelope from her cleavage and handed it to her father. "From Rolfe," she said, her voice oozing with contempt.

As the Captain nervously played with the envelope, Maria said, "From the tone of your voice, my dear, methinks thou art missing young Rolfe."

Liesl said, "Gross."

"It's acceptable to have feelings for him, Liesl."

"But I don't . . ."

"You're sixteen going on seventeen, and when children reach that age, their bodies go through all sorts of changes."

"Maria, you don't understand . . ."

"Shush, let me explain: When a girl and a boy love each other very, very much, there are certain ways they can express their love on a physical level. Soon enough, physiological changes occur that can lead to what's known as *arousal*."

Pointing to her father, Liesl hissed, "First of all, we're *not* having this conversation in front of *him*. And second of all, I'm well aware of what arousal is, and have been since I was twelve going on thirteen, and you of all people should know that. And third of all, I'm a Vampire, and Vampires are aroused all the time, regardless of their age, so none of this applies . . ."

"Oh. Right. Good point."

". . . and fourth of all, I am *not* missing Rolfe." She looked at the Captain to make certain he wasn't paying attention to them—which he wasn't; he was apologizing to Friedrich for banging the boy's wife for the previous two weeks—then whispered, "Rolfe is a member of the Nazi Undeath Squads."

Maria nodded. "No surprise there. I always had the feeling he was a weasel."

"He's a weasel, but he's a *strong* weasel, and I believe he's getting stronger by the day. And he wants to kill me." She paused. "And I want to kill him."

Still nodding, Maria said, "When a girl Vampire and a mortal boy hate each other very, very much, certain physiological changes occur, and that can lead to what's known as *murder*." She draped her arm over Liesl's shoulders. "You do what you have to do. If you're compelled to kill him, then kill him."

"Good."

"If you're compelled to wrestle with his *schvantz*, then wrestle with his *schvantz*."

"Gross."

"Whatever choice you make," Maria said, "you have my full support."

The Captain turned from Friedrich and asked, "Full support for what?"

Maria said, "Never you mind, my love. Now what does that note say?"

He tore open the envelope, removed and unfolded the letter, cleared his throat, then read, "Captain von Trapp, stop. At the request of Herr Adolf Hitler, you are hereby ordered to report to your Naval base at Berngdenschnockenvanderplatz to begin active duty, stop. Refusal will result in punishment by Herr Adolf Hitler, stop. Punishment will include, but not be confined to, imprisonment for you and your family, seizure of your property and assets, and more dog *scheisse* on your porch, stop. Sincerely, Admiral von Schreiber of the Navy of the Third-and-a-Half Reich." He threw the letter on the ground, and said, "I don't understand. I'm almost fifty-one years old, I'm a Captain in name only, and von Beckbaw is well aware that I'm not a Nazi sympathizer. Why me?"

"That's an excellent question," Maria said, "and it makes me realize that there are certain aspects of this plot that make absolutely no sense. Holes galore."

"What plot?" Liesl asked.

Ignoring her, Maria continued, "Sometimes I think that our storyline is there as an excuse for the musical numbers."

"What musical numbers?" the Captain asked.

Ignoring him, Maria said to herself, "Hammerstein. You rapscallion." Then she turned to Liesl and said, "Tell your brothers and sisters that we're taking a ride."

"Where?" Liesl asked.

"Make something up."

"What about the Gala? We go on in a few hours!"

"*Fick* the Gala!"

"Okay . . . Mother."

Maria beamed. "Oh, sweetheart, you called me Mother. This is one of my happiest moments of the last three-hundred years. I love you most of all! Now *go*." After Liesl was out of earshot, Maria said to her husband, "So. Darling. Three questions: First, are you familiar with the acronym A.W.O.L.?"

Cocking an eyebrow, the Captain said, "Go on."

"Second, how would you feel about a trip to the United States?"

Cocking his other eyebrow, the Captain said, "Continue."

"Third, can any of the brats drive a car?"

Smiling, he said, "Well, Maria, it appears that your new husband might be of some use to us after all."

The day he turned fourteen, Friedrich von Trapp was bitten by the car bug. He took to sitting in the garage for hours at a time, basking in the presence of his Father's fleet of autos, perched behind the wheel of the blue Austro-Tata, wishing he could put the key in the ignition, fire up the engine, and drive . . . *somewhere. Salzburg is a town full of losers*, he would think, *and I want to pull out of here so I can win!*

Loathe to let any of his brats touch any of his cars, the Captain was having none of it. "You're far too young to drive, Friedrich. And you're also far too . . . well . . . how can I put this gently . . . what's the right word, *das richtige wort* . . . oh, yes, I've got it . . . *insane*."

"Please, Father!"

"No!"

*"Pleeeeeease!"*

*"Nooooooo!"*

And so on.

Eventually, Friedrich took matters into his own hands, and began stealing the Captain's keys when he was passed out after an evening of drinking—practically a nightly occurrence. It turned out that, like many thugs-in-training, Friedrich had a natural aptitude for cars, so when the Captain caught him executing a perfect three-point turn on his way out of the garage—and in the tank-like Steyr, yet—he couldn't help but be impressed.

All of which was why Friedrich was tabbed to drive the getaway car.

That evening, after the sun was fully set, the Captain and Maria went through each and every room in the house, turning on each and every light, so if one wandered by and saw the brightness, one would assume that somebody was home. Once the house was deemed acceptably bright—and once Detweiler finally dragged his slimy ass back to the mansion—the Captain, Maria, the brats, and Max all tiptoed to the garage. Max said, "It breaks my heart that there will be no Vampirecrobatics at the Gala. Nobody was going to beat us, *nobody*! The Ernst von Schwingenbottom Players performing the works of Baron Eligius Alfred Joseph von Münch-Bellinghausen? *Please*. Harpsichord master Werner Belschpradt von Schinglehoffer? *No, no, no*. The Kirkis Müll? *Garbage*. We had it in the bag." He sighed. "Maybe Glockenspiel the Clown will give the performance of his lifetime. Or maybe I'll have to wait until next year."

The Captain looked at his watch. "Are you done, Max?" he asked. "I appreciate that you're upset your Gala dreams are being put on hold, but let's keep our priorities straight. You're losing a medal, and we could lose our lives. Got it?"

"Got it."

"Good. Now get to that Gala and win one for grand old Austria!"

"How about I win one for my grand old bank account?"

"Fine. Just win. Good night." After Max drove off, von Trapp turned to Friedrich, who was nestled in the driver's seat, and said, "Alright, son, just like we talked about. Put it in drive."

Friedrich said, "Already done," after which all the brats got behind the car and pushed.

"Not too hard, kids," the Captain said. "We can't make any noise, nor can we lose control of the car."

Louisa said, "Father, what if somebody comes by to question Frau Alice and Alfred?"

"They won't say a word, darling," the Captain said. "Your Governess put them both in a state of suspended animation."

Liesl turned to Maria. "We can do that?"

Nodding, Maria said, "It takes some practice, but yes."

Farta asked, "What's suspended animation?"

Maria said, "Would you care to field this one, Gretl? I suspect a pompous little snotburger such as yourself would know everything there is to know about suspended animation."

Even though she had super Vampire strength, Gretl was a tiny girl, and pushing the car had exhausted her to the point that she could barely speak . . . but that didn't stop her from trying. "Suspended animation . . . *(huff)* . . . is . . . the . . . slowing . . . *(puff)* . . . of . . . life . . . processes . . . *(gasp)* . . . by . . . external . . . means . . . without . . . *(whew)* . . . termination . . . and . . . *(snarf)* . . . I . . . can't . . . go . . . on . . ."

Smiling, Liesl—who was pushing the car with her pinky—said, "Oh no, shrimp, don't stop now."

"Yes," Kurt said, "continue. This is fascinating!"

Gretl coughed.

"No more?" Brigitta said. "Quite a pity that you can't continue, because . . ."

"Alright, brats," the Captain said, "enough." As they approached the bottom of the driveway, he said, "Now shut your fang-holes and listen: We need to push this past the gate, then another half-a-kilometer to the North. After that, Friedrich will spark the ignition, and we'll . . ."

The von Trapps suddenly found themselves on the bright end of ten flashlights. One of the flashlight holders asked, "Is there something wrong with your car, Captain von Trapp?"

The Captain squinted, then frowned. "Ah. Wonderful. Colonel von Beckbaw. Thank you for the welcome home gifts."

"Quite," the portly Nazi said, stepping toward the car. "It's a pity, however, that you were not home when we dropped the dog *schiesse,* thus you were not able to enjoy the full experience."

"Full experience?" the Captain asked.

"In general, when we place the *schiesse* upon the victim's doorstep, it's lighted with a match, which means . . ."

Friedrich leaned out the window and said, "I get it! It means that you have to stamp out the fire with your foot, and you get dog *schiesse* all over your shoe. *Mein Gott,* that's *brilliant.*" He turned to Maria and said, "Oh lovely wife of mine, can we get a dog?"

"Maybe for Christmas, darling."

Brigitta said, "I want to name him Hammerstein!"

Von Beckbaw clicked his heels together and said, "Silence! *Mein Gott*, Captain, do your brats ever shut up?"

"Never," von Trapp said. "It's like living with seven conservative radio show hosts."

"Touché," von Beckbaw said, then he strolled over to the car, pulled a gun from his waist holster—a Luger P-08, to be precise—held the barrel to Friedrich's temple, and said, "Start it, brat."

"The . . . the . . . the . . . the car is broken. And I . . . I . . . I don't know how to drive."

Von Beckbaw cocked the trigger. "I said, *start it*."

Friedrich sighed, then turned the key and fired up the engine.

Smiling, von Beckbaw said, "*Wunderbar*. Now. Care to tell us where *we* are headed?"

"We?" the Captain asked.

Von Beckbaw's smile became wider. "What with all your car trouble—not to mention an inexperienced driver behind the wheel—you might need an escort. After all, Admiral von Schreiber will be quite disappointed if you don't report for duty tomorrow."

"The disappointment would be mutual, Colonel von Beckbaw. But this evening's mission is of vital importance to the cause."

"Hmm, intriguing," von Beckbaw said. "What's the mission?"

"*Vampirecrobatics!*"

At that, von Beckbaw's minions all gagged. Von Beckbaw shook his head. "Apologies, Captain. My men become upset when they hear talk of the undead. This is why they march with me, rather than with the Undeath Squads." Absently picking his nose, von Beckbaw continued: "Ah, the Undeath Squads. Such a fine collection of soldiers. Brave. Cunning. Strong. Why, they could kill any stinking Vampire in the country without even batting an eyelash. *Any* Vampire." He gestured at the brats. "I'm certain that the family of a Naval officer would be spared such a fate. Understand?"

"Yes, Colonel von Beckbaw. I understand."

"Good, good. Now what are these Vampirecrobatics you speak of?"

"The children's act for the Gala of Gaiety. That's what it's called. Vampirecrobatics."

"Ah, yes, I almost forgot: The family von Trapp is slated to close the Gala. What with all the excitement of you trying to shirk your military duties—and the fantastic opportunity of my being allowed to shoot you on sight should you disregard our orders—it nearly slipped my mind." He checked his watch. "We'll have no problem arriving in time for your performance. And you know how much we Nazis love our punctuality!"

"*Everybody* knows how much you Nazis love your punctuality," Liesl said.

"Quite." Von Beckbaw turned to his troop and said, "Alright, men, one car in front of Captain von Trapp, and one behind." Looking at Maria, he said, "And I shall ride with the family."

Maria smiled, then a stream of blood jetted from her front

fangs, splattering von Beckbaw's men's oh-so-perfect Nazi uniforms. "It would be our pleasure to have you in the car, Colonel von Beckbaw," Maria growled. "An absolute delight."

Von Beckbaw blanched. "Um . . . er . . . um . . . maybe I shall ride with my men. They sometimes need extra supervision. So I shall see you at the Gala."

Spitting a mouthful of hemoglobin at von Beckbaw, Maria said, "Not if we see you first. Gala of Gaiety, I love you most of all!"

Despite Maria's proclamation of love, experts would later say that year's Gala of Gaiety was the worst in the event's history. The Ernst von Schwingenbottom Players butchered Baron Eligius Alfred Joseph von Münch-Bellinghausen's "Ingomar the Barbarian: Der Fechter von Ravenna" to the point that they were hooted off the stage. Werner Belschpradt von Schinglehoffer's rendition of Thomas Arne's "Six Favourite Concertos for Harpsichord" was a cacophonous mess. The Kirkis Müll lived up to their name—translated, Kirkis Müll means *Garbage Circus*—by delivering a performance that included a collapsed human pyramid, a fire eater who left the stage smoldering, and a lion tamer who began the show intact, and finished it *sans* her left ear and right foot. With one more act to go, it appeared that Max's very own Glockenspiel the Clown— who came off looking quite good, if only because he didn't harm himself or anybody else during his performance—was in the best position to take home the top prize.

After the Gala volunteers swept the performance area clean of blood, charred skin, and broken dreams, the Master of

Ceremonies stepped to stage center and called, "Ladies and gentlemen, from here in Salzburg, may I present the von Trapp Family Vampires, and their exhibition, Vampirecrobatics!"

As the brats trooped to stage center, the Vampire-hating audience's chorus of disapproval—boos, hisses, curse words—could be heard in the Alps.

Liesl, who looked as if she was ready to massacre the entire front row, said, "We're as glad to see you as you're glad to see us. Now let's start the show! First up, performing a move he has dubbed The Reverse Edelweiss, Kurt von Trapp!" As she wandered stage left, there were more boos, more hisses, and more curse words.

After the audience settled down, Kurt did a neat front flip, landing lightly on his hands and launching into an impressive hand-walk. When he finished circling the stage for the third time, he did a quadruple backward flip, landing lightly on his feet. He raised his hands to the sky and said, *"You look happy to meet me!"*

More boos. More hisses. More curse words.

"Er, I mean, *bless my homeland forever!*"

Less boos. Less hisses. But the same number of curse words.

"Alright, forget it. Now I'd like to present a girl who's small, and bright, and clean, and—most importantly to this audience— white. Please welcome Gretl von Trapp!" He then took his place by Liesl off to the side.

Gretl cartwheeled her way around the stage, ultimately jumping three meters into the air, spinning in a perfect tight spiral. The next jump: Four meters. The jump after that: Five.

With every jump she spiraled faster and faster, until she was a small, bright, clean, white blur. Her final jump concluded with a perfect toe-landing that visibly impressed the audience.

After Brigitta and Farta executed twenty-eight consecutive synchronized back walkovers that left even the most undead-hating Gala attendee breathless, a consistent refrain began to float through the crowd: *Hate Vampires, love these von Trapps.*

With six of the seven von Trapps on the side of the stage, Liesl said, "To close the show, we would like to present my little brother Friedrich with a demonstration that will at once amaze and terrify you."

Quietly, and with a sense of dignity and poise rarely seen in a fourteen-year-old hellion, Friedrich said, "If you're faint of heart, I suggest you close your eyes. But if you're brave, watch this." And then, in half-a-blink of an eye, Friedrich transformed into a bat.

And then back into a human.

And then back into a bat.

Then human.

Then bat.

Then human.

Then bat.

With each transformation, the seated audience gasped with appreciation.

With each transformation, the soldiers standing on the perimeter of the crowd—the majority of whom were part of Hitler's most elite Undeath Squad—became angrier and angrier.

Especially Private Rolfe Mueller.

After his twentieth transformation, Friedrich said, "On behalf of my family, I thank you from the bottom of my heart. So long, farewell, *auf wiedersehen*, and good night, Cleveland!"

At once, the crowd yelled, *"Who's this Cleveland you're saying goodnight to?!"*

Friedrich said, "It isn't a who, it's a where, and it's located . . . ah, forget it. Judges, vote von Trapp!" He ran into the awaiting arms of his siblings, after which they all trotted offstage, where they were met by their Father, their Mother/creator/wife, and Max.

The all huddled up, and Max said to Maria, "Everything is ready?"

She nodded.

He said to the Captain, "You know where you're going?"

"No," he said, then put his arm around Maria. "But she does."

"Yes, that she does." Turning to the children, he said, "Brats, you know what needs to be done?"

At once, they said, "Yes, Uncle Max."

"And you have your good walking shoes?"

"Yes, Uncle Max."

"Alright, then." He offered a sad smile, then said, "The Gala results will be in any second now. Good luck."

The von Trapps and Max fell into a tight group hug that was cut short by a shout from center stage. The noticeably pale Master of Ceremonies said, "Goodness. My, my. What a way to end this year's Gala of Gaiety, eh? Good thing acts aren't eligible to perform two years in a row, I say." At that, the crowd delivered a hearty round of applause. "Alright, the judges have tallied the votes, and I'll announce a winner momentarily. But first, let me get a big Heil Hitler!"

"Heil Hitler!"

"I can't hear yooooooou!"

*"Heil Hitler!"*

"Let them hear you back in Berlin!"

"HEIL HITLER!"

"Fan*tas*tic! And now, the third prize goes to . . ." He opened the envelope and made a somewhat disgusted face. ". . . the Ernst von Schwingenbottom Players." A shell-shocked troupe of actors trooped onto the stage and accepted a tiny trophy from an Amazonian Aryan woman, after which Ernst von Schwingenbottom himself said, "This is quite unexpected . . ."

A loudmouth in the front row yelled, "No *scheisse*, you hack!"

Von Schwingenbottom's thin face fell. He mumbled, "Thanks," and led his dejected players to the wings.

"That was wonderful, Ernst," the Master of Ceremonies said. "The second prize goes to . . ." He opened the envelope and made a slightly less disgusted face. ". . . Glockenspiel the Clown!"

Glockenspiel, accompanied by Max Detweiler, bound across the stage to accept their trophy to lukewarm applause. Glockenspiel said, "Thank you, Aryan Nation! I'd like to give special thanks to . . ."

Max jumped in front of the clown and said, ". . . me! He'd like to give special thanks to me! Because I found him! And I molded him into what you see now! No more of this *ohren aus zinn* business! See you next year, suckers!"

Smiling despite himself, the Master of Ceremonies hustled

the twosome offstage, then said, "And now, the moment you have all been waiting for: The winner of this year's Gala of Gaiety is . . ." He opened the envelope and winced. ". . . the von Trapp Family Vampires." He ripped the paper into a million pieces, pointed offstage, and grumbled, "Come on out and accept your award, von Trapps."

Nothing.

"Hello? Von Trapps? Come on out here and take what's rightfully yours!"

Still nothing.

In the third row, a certain balding, barrel-chested Nazi talk show host who we all know and hate pushed down the aisle and hoisted himself onto the stage, then stumbled into the backstage area. After a couple of minutes, he sprinted back out and roared, *"They're gone! The von Trapps are gone! An officer has deserted his Navy! There are Vampires on the loose! S.S. Unit 415, congregate at the West entrance, and Elite Undeath Squad, congregate at the East!"*

As the Nazi military scrambled to their respective positions, Colonel von Beckbaw said, "I want all nine of those *arschlochs* dead by sunrise."

# CHAPTER 11

Housed on what the majority of Austrians agreed was the most rancid corner in Salzburg, the nameless Abbey was an eyesore, so painful to look at that nobody looked at it . . . including Nazis, which was why Maria decided it would be the perfect place for her family to hide out until the heat was off, and then they could head to the United States.

When Mother Zombie met Maria *et al* at the front gate, she was exceedingly polite, more polite than the Vampire had ever seen. Mother Zombie herded the von Trapps into the Abbey and told Maria, "I hear the sirens. I estimate they're about three minutes away."

"How in the Devil's name did they track us so quickly?"

Liesl said, "Those Undeath Squads know what they're doing. I don't know how well they handle themselves on the battlefield, but they can track our kind down like they're bloodhounds. Frankly, I'm surprised we managed to get away at all."

"You *did* get away," Mother Zombie said, "but it will all be for naught if the Squad storms the Abbey and captures you." She paused. "You realize if you're caught, they'll do *things* to you. Things like imprisoning you in a Vampire concentration..."

Captain von Trapp said, "Mother Zombie, I'd prefer we don't discuss that in front of the brats. Please lead us to the hiding place."

From the other end of the room, Zombie Sister Brandi called, "Follow me! This way."

Maria *et al* trotted over to Brandi, who shuffled toward the hiding place as quickly as she could. But if you'll recall, dear reader, Brandi is a slow, slow zombie.

"Can we pick up the pace?" Friedrich whispered to Maria.

"You have to have patience with these creatures, husband dear."

"But if we don't hurry, we'll..."

"All the way back in 1377, my old friend William Langland said to me, 'Patience is a virtue,' and that was one of the most profound moments in my life. Patience equals strength of character. Patience demonstrates maturity. Patience means... *oh, for* fick *sake, Brandi, can you not move faster*?!"

"For your information, missy," Brandi said, clearly offended, "we're here." She pointed to a fence at the far end of the courtyard. "Climb over that and duck down. They'll never find you."

Maria said, "I apologize for yelling at you."

"Apology accepted... *whore*." And then she shuffled away, and that was the last Zombie Maria von Trapp ever saw.

Once the family was situated, Gretl said to Maria, "Mother,

I don't like any of this, and I could use a distraction. Can we talk about our favorite things? Right about now, brown packages with string don't seem so bad."

"No. We must be quiet."

"How about the Vampire alphabet? Maybe we can discuss how to *doedoemee* the *rayrayso* so it will be able to *fafalala* the *lalafafa*."

"Please, not now, Gretl."

"What about . . ." She was interrupted by a scream coming from the direction of the front gate: *"Major Erich Hassler, Nazi Undeath Squad! I demand entry into this Abbey!"*

Mother Zombie let out a mournful Zombie moan that would have had normal mortals seeing stars. The members of the Nazi Undeath Squad, however, were hardly normal.

Another scream: *"To repeat: Major Erich Hassler, Nazi Undeath Squad! I demand entry into this Abbey! If my request isn't granted immediately, I shall be forced to use force."*

Gretl said, "Forced to use force? Talk about ridiculous word choice."

The eight other von Trapps whispered, "Do shut up, Gretl!" Unfortunately, eight whispers add up to one yell.

"I heard that," Major Hassler said. "It came from the courtyard! Squad, advance!"

The von Trapps heard the gate crash in, followed by the sound of quick, well-organized, shiny-booted footsteps. One of the voices said, "Major, I smell them! They're to your left!"

Friedrich asked Liesl, "They can smell us?"

"Apparently so," Liesl answered.

"Did Rolfe smell you?"

"Not the way I wanted him to, brother dear. Not the way I wanted him to."

Another scream from about ten meters away: "Found them, Major! Behind that fence."

"Good work, Schmitt," the Major said. "Men, take your positions!" More shiny-booted footsteps, then silence. "Okay, Vampires," the Major continued, "there are two ways we can do this: You can walk out of here undead, or you can get carried out of here dead-dead. Your choice."

Friedrich yelled, "You'll never take us, you fascists *ficks*!"

"I'll give you until the count of three to come out with your hands up, your mouths closed, and your fangs hidden. If we don't see you at three, we'll engage, and I don't believe you want that. One . . ."

No movement.

"Two . . ."

No movement.

"Three! . . ."

And then, movement. And lots of it.

Friedrich ripped a wide hole in the fence, wide enough so all the brats could file out two at a time. The two boys, Farta, and Gretl went left, and the other three girls went right. Captain von Trapp tried to follow, but Maria shoved him onto his backside. "Stay here, Georg. This isn't your fight. Stay put."

"But this is my family . . ."

"I said *stay put*!" Knowing better than to argue with a Vampire preparing for battle, the Captain stayed put. "No matter what happens," Maria said, "I love you more than the sound of music that comes from my saxophone." She kissed him on the cheek, then added, "I also sure as *Hölle* love you more than I do my new husband, Handsy McGrabbington." She then entered our battle, already in progress.

There were twenty Squad members situated in a half-circle, each holding a jerry-rigged machine gun that would slow down even the strongest, oldest, most experienced Vampire . . . but only if they managed to land a shot. When the von Trapps burst from the fence, the Nazis opened fire, but Maria and the brats could *move*. They dodged the bullets with relative ease, and in seconds, were face-to-face with Hitler's finest.

Maria lashed out at a Squad member, fingernails first. She faked right, fooling him for a split second, and in that split second, she was able to tear off his ear, break six of his ribs with her left index finger, and bite his neck into gristle; she looked as if she were a starving German shepherd, and he were a piece of schnitzel. She then yanked off his left arm, threw it at the approaching Squad member, and yelled, "If you don't get your Major to call off your men, you'll suffer the same fate! Or worse!"

The Squad member called, "Major, I need back-up! I never saw anything like this in basic training!"

Maria smiled, her fangs a veritable blood factory. "You most certainly have not, young man. You most certainly have not." And then she attacked.

It was gruesome.

On the left side of the yard, Kurt, occupied with two Squad

members, wasn't faring as well as his creator. He had taken a bayonet to the thigh, and even though the bleeding stopped seconds after the blade ripped through his leg, he was still in unimaginable pain. But when he saw Maria tear off her second Nazi arm of the battle, he felt a surge of strength unlike anything he had ever felt in his life. *I'm incorrigible,* he thought, *and nobody can beat me! I'm* doeraymeefahsolateedoe! He then jumped straight into the air, did a half turn, and landed on one of the Squad members' heads. When the Squadder fell to the ground, Kurt snapped his neck as if it were a twig, then, for good measure, bit off his ear and took a satisfying suck of blood.

A second Squadder backed off in order to refill the magazine of his gun, but he backed right into Friedrich, who pulled him into a headlock, then cracked his skull open with his elbow. Pointing at the man's exposed brain, Friedrich bellowed, *"Food for the Zombies! The Zombies shall feast tonight!"*

The Major then sent seven of his Squad members to take Farta, Brigitta, and Gretl, a questionable strategy, because one would think that was overkill, that three well-trained soldiers could take out three little girls. It turned out the strategy was indeed bad.

The Major should have deployed more men.

The girls worked as a three-headed monster, moving so quickly that the Squadders couldn't get a bead on them, let alone hit them with a fist, a knife, or a gunshot. When two of the men crashed into each other and fell to the ground, Farta leapt into the air and landed feet-first onto their heads, destroying both of their faces. A still-hungry Kurt appeared out of nowhere, and drained both of their bodies.

By the time the dust settled, the entire Squad was dead, and Louisa was the only von Trapp girl who had suffered an injury, and it was a minor one at that: A Squadder, in the throes of death, had pulled off her both of her earlobes. As the family caught their breath, Maria put an arm around her daughter and said, "No earrings for you, I guess." Louisa just laughed, and buried her head in Maria's chest.

Right when they were ready to call it a night, in came the reinforcements. Or, more accurately, the reinforcement. Just one.

Rolfe.

"I know you're there, Liesl," he called from the front gate. "I can smell you!"

Liesl yelled, "We killed twenty of your men. One more won't bother us a bit. But we won the Gala, and we offed a whole lot of your compatriots, thus I'm in an exceedingly good mood, so I'll let you walk away."

*"Never,"* he said, stepping over the threshold and rushing to the battleground.

Liesl met him halfway. "Ah, Rolfe, Rolfe, Rolfe, we meet again. Does this bring back memories? Remember the gazebo? Remember my body?" She ripped off her cat suit, and the second she saw his eyes fall to her breasts, she made her move, a move so swift, and cunning, and nimble, that it can't be described in mere words. All you need to know, dear reader, is that it took Liesl von Trapp six seconds to dismember Private Mueller.

Raising both of Rolfe's legs to the sky, Liesl cried, "I have confidence in me!" She turned to her brothers, her sisters, her Father, and her Mother, and, even louder, roared, "*I have confidence in me! Do you hear me, world*: I HAVE CONFIDENCE IN ME!"

Beaming, Maria said, "On that note, let's make our way to the United States."

Gazing at the Nazi body parts strewn about the floor, Captain von Trapp said, "On that note, I could use a drink."

The next morning, the von Trapp family learned that at the very top of the Alps, the sky is bluer, the air is crisper, and the birds sing louder. They also learned that Vampires who have recently engaged in an intense battle despise blue skies, crisp air, and loud birds.

Glaring sullenly (and hungrily) at the picaresque tableau, Kurt said, "Golly gee, this sure is swell, fording every stream, following every rainbow, and climbing every mountain. Most fun I've ever had."

Gretl said, "This is no mere mountain, dear brother; this is the Untersberg, a mountain massif of the Berchtesgaten Alps that straddles the borders of Berchtesgaten, Germany, and our very own town of Salzburg. The Berchtesgaten Alps are popular with tourists and Austrian Vampires alike because it's a mere sixteen kilometers to Salzburg. The first recorded ascent of the Berchtesgaten Alps was in the first half of the twelfth century by Eberwein, a member of the Augustinian Hydra Monastery at Berchtesgaten. As you may recall, the mountain lent its name to an 1829 opera by Johann Nepomuk, Baron of Poissl."

After a moment of silence, the entire von Trapp family said, "Do shut up, Gretl."

Gretl glared at her siblings and her parents, then—just before transforming herself into a bat and flying toward the sun—she said, "I do hate you so. All of you. Very, very much. You," she said, pointing at Liesl, "you're, simply put, a whore. And don't tell me that you behave that way because you're sixteen going on seventeen thousand. You're old enough to know better. And you," she said, pointing at Friedrich. "I'd like to take a *doeraymee* and jam it up your *fasola*, then turn it sideways so you'll never *teedoeray* again. And you," she said, pointing at her Father, "always drinking beer with the foam afloat . . ."

"Gin," the Captain said.

*"Shut up!"* she roared. "And you three," she said, pointing at Brigitta, Louisa, and Farta, "every morning you greet me, and you look happy to meet me, but I know the truth. I know that given the opportunity, you would jam a stake through my heart while I sleep. And you," she said, pointing at Kurt, "somewhere in your youth or childhood, you must have done something good, but I can't think of it. And you," she said, pointing at Maria, "are the worst of all. You know what my favorite thing is?"

"Kittens?" Maria asked.

*"No!* Not kittens, or raindrops, or kettles, or snowflakes, or white dresses, or ponies, or brown paper packages—get it

through your thick skull that *nobody's* favorite thing is a brown paper package. *My* favorite thing is the thought of never seeing any of you *arschlochs* again. So so long, farewell, *auf wieder-sehen*, goodbye. Adieu, adieu, to you, and you, and you, and you, and you, and you, and you, and you."

And that, dear reader, is the right musical.

# EPILOGUE

U TILIZING THEIR VAMPIRE ingenuity—as well as several well-placed bribes—the entire von Trapp family made it to the United States safe and sound ... save for Kurt. The chunkiest von Trapp child was concerned that American food wouldn't be to his liking, so much so that he stayed put. He avoided the Nazi Undeath Squads without much problem—it's considerably easier to hide when you don't have six irksome siblings, a sax-playing Vampire, and a semi-recovering alcoholic in tow—by remaining deep in the bowels of the Untersberg. Over the intervening decades, he became a master Vampire chef, so skilled that undead of all shapes and sizes— Vampires and Zombies alike—would come from kilometers around to sample his blood orange blood soup, his blood sausages, and his offal in blood sauce, as well as dozens of other blood-soaked delicacies. In early 2012, the BBC got wind of this phenomenon, and, knowing that in this age of *Twilight*, anything involving Vampires was a guarantee for killer ratings, offered Kurt his own cooking show, which, according to sources within the network, will begin production in 2014.

After what her siblings came to call The Meltdown on the Mount, Gretl von Trapp wasn't heard from for some seven years—even now, we can't account for her whereabouts during this disappearance—before resurfacing in New York City, where her pretentiousness wasn't only tolerated, but encouraged. In 1951, she and four of her pretentious Vampire friends started a pretentious group called, pretentiously enough, the Algonquin Vampire Triangular Table. The A.V.T.T. was written up in several pretentious periodicals, and there was talk of a book deal, but it soon became clear to the entire group that there was no way five pretentious Vampires could coexist as a cohesive unit for a significant amount of time, so they pulled the plug. In 1984, Gretl launched a pretentious magazine called *Blitzkrieg Bop*, which—much to the chagrin of music fans who bought it expecting articles about the burgeoning punk rock scene—was a monthly examination of how World War II affects contemporary paranormal creatures. Today, with her magazine thriving among WWII and Vampire obsessives, Gretl lives in the Williamsburg section of Brooklyn with her paramour, a pretentious rapper/Vampire fetishist who goes by the name of Undead Orville.

Soon after landing in America, Friedrich von Trapp became bored with Maria and infatuated with baseball, so after he divorced her—leaving her free to tie the knot with the Captain . . . which is what should've happened in the first place, but somebody who shall remain nameless made me change who married who in the eighth draft *(Editor's note: Jesus Christ, Alan, let it go. The switcheroo at the altar was funnier anyhow.)*—he spent his every waking hour learning the history and fundamentals of the sport. In the winter of 1952, he migrated to the Midwest, where he managed to land a workout with the St. Louis Browns. When the team got a gander of the curveball he had been working on for the past decade-plus, they decided to overlook both his lack of documentation and his fangs, and ink him to a contract. He had a wonderful rookie season, going 19–6 with an ERA of 2.56, but in spring training of 1953—after a winter that saw him drink a mere three pints of blood—he went on a rampage that literally killed the Browns entire minor league system, so the team cut him, and he never played professionally again. Today, Friedrich runs a Vampire softball league, as well as a website called VampireBaseballNerds.com, geared toward, you guessed it, Vampire baseball nerds. He has only five subscribers, but the membership fee is exorbitant, so he has enough money to pay for his studio apartment in suburban St. Louis. Most impressively, since he arrived in the U.S., he has murdered and/or Vampire'd over six thousand mortals, yet has not raised suspicion within the law enforcement community.

And speaking of the law enforcement community, Liesl von Trapp changed sides, if you will, and became a do-gooder, a decision she made in 1961 after reading about the infamous Tijuana Undead Slaughter. So appalled was she by the 3,958 needless murders committed by a gang of Mexican Vampires who went by the overlong moniker of *Los Mercaderes de la Muerte Unmuerte* (that's The Undead Death Merchants to you and me) that she moved South of the border and became the country's most feared Vampire bounty hunter. The American government learned of her work in 1964, but waited ten years to invite her into the fold, an invitation that she declined . . . and declined again the following year . . . and the year after that . . . and the year after that. Finally, in 2009, she moved to Washington, D.C., after accepting an offer to head up her own division within the Central Intelligence Agency. Her current whereabouts are unknown, but one can assume she's scouring the United States, kicking some paranormal booty.

When telling a story either via film or book, it's often said that unless one wants to lose and/or confuse one's audience, one has to be careful not to have too many main characters; thus in an ensemble piece, everybody can't carry equal weight, and some folks have to take a backseat. Well aware that their parts in our tale were considerably smaller than those of their siblings—and also well aware that their personalities were nowhere near as developed as the rest of the cast—Louisa, Brigitta, and Farta von Trapp decided to team up for all eternity in hopes that the three of them as a unit could create a single entity that was as interesting, if not *more* interesting, than Liesl, Friedrich, Kurt, and Gretl. Unfortunately, their efforts didn't pan out. Their attempts to establish a folk band, a rock band, a jazz trio, a theater troupe, a traveling circus, a street-corner puppet team, and a think tank all failed miserably. So in 2003, they went back to doing what they do best: Being supporting players in a Vampire dramedy, which meant moving back to Austria, taking up residence in Salzburg, and engaging in the kind of wacky, bloody hijinks that will make *My Favorite Fangs* a darling of readers, critics, and Vampire book clubs alike.

And Maria? Well, when Maria wasn't blowing the Captain von Trapp's, er, mind, she was blowing her tenor saxophone. And blowing. And blowing some more. In 1963, she had gained enough "confidence in me" to track down her old spiritual advisor, John Coltrane; the following year, the two of them took to the studio and recorded an album called *Coltrane and von Trapp Swing the Classics,* a collection of jazzed-up Austrian folk songs that sold exactly seventy-eight copies. Despite the unimpressive sales of that and the fifteen follow-up records— not to mention the 1974 passing of her beloved Georg from complications due to (surprise, surprise) cirrhosis—today, the former Governess is a happy, cat suit–wearing Vampire. Unless she's really, really hungry—an event that only comes about once or twice a decade—she doesn't want to murder you, or maim you, or torture you. She just wants to sit you down, cook you a tasty meal, play you a couple tunes on her tenor, and tell you a few war stories.

Why? Because Maria von Trapp loves you most of all.

# READER'S GUIDE

## Chapter 1

- If you were the lone male Zombie in an Abbey filled with female Zombies, would you take Viagara, Cialis, or Levitra? Can male Zombies get erectile dysfunction? Can male Zombies get erections? Oh, really? Is that right? Well how the hell do you know *that*? Are you some sort of Zombie fetishist or something? You're nasty.
- According to both Maria and Mother Zombie, killing and/or eating children is a worthwhile endeavor. Taking that into consideration, would you rather hire a Vampire or a Zombie to be your babysitter?
- It's clear that Maria must be punished for her transgressions, but it's also clear that Maria enjoys being punished. How would you punish her? How do you like being punished? Because if you beg us just right, we'll dish out

punishment in the manner with which you desire. Oh yes, we will.

## Chapter 2

- Who would make for a better afterlife bandleader: John Coltrane, Miles Davis, or Kenny G.? As of this writing, Kenny G. isn't dead; that being the case, how would you kill him?
- How would you describe the stench of vomit that originated from the stomach of a horny female Vampire? How would you describe the stench of vomit that originated from the stomach of a mortal male alcoholic? How would you describe the stench of vomit that originated from the stomach of a non-gender-specific alcoholic Vampire?
- Why do composers from Broadway's golden era have such atrocious grammar? Is it worth sacrificing syntax for pentameter?
- If your youngest child is a pretentious know-it-all snot, how would you get her to cease said snottiness? Is duct tape the best way to quiet a child?
- Throughout the chapter, Friedrich experiences several erections. Approximately how many erections do you experience when in the presence of an attractive Vampire?

## Chapter 3

- Could Rolfe be viewed a metaphor for the Christian right? Are his tattoos stupid and lame? Does he have a stupid and lame trendoid haircut? Is he like that big fat poser friend of yours who claims that he was into Death Cab for Cutie before they blew up and everybody else in the world started liking then? You know, the guy who always says crap about random indie bands like, "Their first record on their own label that cost them six dollars to make was way better than the overproduced piece of tripe that the suits at the major label made them put out." Do you like Death Cab? How about Bon Iver? Isn't he kind of overrated? By the time this book goes into its tenth printing, will anybody even know who Bon Iver is? Shit, they probably won't even know who he is when this book goes into its *second* printing. I mean, look at Ray LaMontagne, who Justin Vernon pretty much ripped off. Ray's been around for a few years, and the best he can do is fill up a mid-sized club. A piece of advice to Justin: Make sure you sock some money away.
- Why are Friedrich's bed sheets always stiff and crusty?

## Chapter 4

- Would you have an affair with your best friend's fiancée? Would you have an affair with your best friend's fiancée if she were a Succubus? Would you have an affair with your best friend's fiancée if she were a Vampire? Would you have an affair with your best friend's fiancée if she were the daughter of a Succubus and a Vampire, and had six-and-a-half sets of boobs?

- According to a recent study at the Bauhaus University in Weimar, goosestepping is the world's fifth most efficient form of cardio exercise. How would you incorporate it into your workout plan?

- Do you have confidence in you? If you don't, what's your problem? Get over it.

- If you were starting a basketball team, who would you choose to be your point guard, Maria or the Baroness? Do Vampires have good outside jumpers? Would you allow a Succubus in an NBA locker room?

## Chapter 5

- If you wanted to destroy Austria, what kind of puppet show would you put on? Could a single Muppet take down an entire country? If yes, would it be Kermit, Fozzie, Scooter, or Beaker?

- If you were forced to sit through Kurt and Gretl's endless rendition of *Dracula,* how would you pass the time? Would you pull out your iPhone and play a few rounds of Angry Birds? What's your favorite Angry Bird? The author's favorite is the black one that turns into a bomb, with the white one who lays eggs a close second. The little blue one that splits into three littler blue ones is pretty lame.

- Why is this chapter shorter than the rest? Shouldn't the author have been more meticulous in organizing the book? And shouldn't have chapter nine been better? For that matter, shouldn't the author put away all that loose change he always dumps on the shelf by the front door? Seriously, what a disorganized slob.

## Chapter 6

- In this day and age, why are there so few professional glockenspiel players? What's the difference between a glockenspiel, a xylophone, and a vibraphone? Everybody refers to vibraphones as vibes, and the author likes vibes, but the author especially likes good vibes, and his favorite way to get good vibes is via a certain green leafy plant that shall remain nameless, which begs the question, where can the author get some bomb-ass chronic?
- If the D-minor Dorian scale is the saddest of all scales, what's the happiest? Can scales have emotions? Why do fish have scales? Do fish have emotions? Do fish have emoticons? What's your favorite emoticon? The author is partial to :-$
- How do you spell *flibbertijibbet*?

## Chapter 7

- This chapter doesn't merit any discussion questions. Please discuss.

## Chapter 8

- Would you pledge your life to Zombie Law? What's your definition of Zombie Law? What's the Supreme Court's definition of Zombie Law? How many of the Supreme Court Justices are Zombies? Why are there more Republican Zombies than Democratic Zombies? What smells worse, a Zombie or a Fox News personality? Who smells worse, Bill O'Reilly or Glenn Beck?
- If you were a middle aged widower with a drinking problem and a houseful of bratty kids who you were utterly unable to control, would you marry a Vampire, a Succubus, a Zombie, an Ogre, a Bigfoot, a Sea Monster, or Courtney Love?

## Chapter 9

- Women: Would you wear a cat suit to your wedding? Men: Would you wear a codpiece to your wedding? Women: Would you wear a baseball uniform to your wedding? Men: Would you wear a tutu to your wedding? Women:

How would you react if your soon-to-be husband wore a codpiece and a tutu to your wedding?

- Why, earlier on, were we asked to discuss the question, "Shouldn't have chapter nine been better?" Why is chapter five hating on chapter nine? If those chapters have a beef, shouldn't it be settled before the author gets to work on the *My Favorite Fangs* sequel, *The Sound of Sucking*? Think about it: If this inter-chapter bitching goes on and on and on, it could become one of those Tupac/Biggie deals, and who has time for that kind of bullshit?

## Chapter 10

- Which chapter merits less discussion, this one, or chapter seven? Discuss.

## Chapter 11

- If a Zombie shuffles out of Salzburg at 4:16 A.M., moving at a speed of .2107 kph, and it wants to get to Rome by sunset two days hence, what's the square root of 9,185?
- What's the Untersberg? (Wait, don't answer that. It's already been asked and answered, like, ten times. The author is driving everybody nuts with his running jokes. Mark Twain, he ain't.)
- Would you end a sentence with "ain't"?

- How much blood could a bloodchuck chuck if a bloodchuck could chuck blood?
- What's your favorite thing? And if you say kittens, or raindrops, or kettles, or snowflakes, or white dresses, or ponies, or brown paper packages, you're a stinking liar.